Praise for *Tagg...*

"*Tagged for Death* is skillfully render... and depiction of military life. Best... gent, resourceful, and appealing p... know better. Hopefully, we will have that opportunity very soon!"

Lynne Maxwell, *Mystery Scene Magazine*

"A terrific find! Engaging and entertaining, this clever cozy is a treasure—charmingly crafted and full of surprises."

Hank Phillippi Ryan, Agatha-, Anthony- and
Mary Higgins Clark-award-winning author

"Like the treasures Sarah Winston finds at the garage sales she loves, this book is a gem."

Barbara Ross, Agatha-nominated author of the Maine
Clambake Mysteries

"It was masterfully done. *Tagged for Death* is a winning debut that will have you turning pages until you reach the final one. I'm already looking forward to Sarah's next bargain with death."

Mark Baker, Carstairs Considers

Praise for *The Longest Yard Sale*

"I love a complex plot and *The Longest Yard Sale* fills the bill with mysterious fires, a missing painting, thefts from a thrift shop and, of course, murder. Add an intriguing cast of victims, potential villains and sidekicks, and interesting setting, and two eligible men for the sleuth to choose between and you have a sure winner even before you get to the last page and find yourself laughing out loud."

Kaitlyn Dunnett, author of *The Scottie Barked at Midnight*/
Kathy Lynn Emerson, author of *Murder in the Merchant's Hall*

"Readers will have a blast following Sarah Winston on her next adventure as she hunts for bargains and bad guys. Sherry Harris's latest is as delightful as the best garage sale find!"

Liz Mugavero, Agatha-nominated author of the
Pawsitively Organic Mysteries

"Sherry Harris is a gifted storyteller, with plenty of twists and adventures for her smart and stubborn protagonist."

Beth Kanell, Kingdom Books

"Once again Sherry Harris entwines small-town life with that of the nearby Air Force base, yard sales with romance, art theft with murder. The story is a bargain, and a priceless one!"

Edith Maxwell, Agatha-nominated author of the
Local Foods mystery series

Also by Sherry Harris

Agatha-Nominated Best First Novel
TAGGED FOR DEATH

and

THE LONGEST YARD SALE

ALL
MURDERS
FINAL!

Sherry Harris

KENSINGTON PUBLISHING CORP.
http://www.kensingtonbooks.com

KENSINGTON BOOKS are published by

Kensington Publishing Corp.
119 West 40th Street
New York, NY 10018

All Kensington Titles, Imprints, and Distributed Lines are available at special quantity discounts for bulk purchases for sales promotions, premiums, fund-raising, and educational or institutional use. Special book excerpts or customized printings can also be created to fit specific needs. For details, write or phone the office of the Kensington special sales manager: Kensington Publishing Corp., 119 West 40th Street, New York, NY 10018, attn: Special Sales Department, Phone: 1-800-221-2647.

Kensington and the K logo Reg. U.S. Pat & TM Off.

ISBN-13: 978-1-61773-021-4
ISBN-10: 1-61773-021-1
First Kensington Mass Market Edition: May 2016

eISBN-13: 978-1-61773-122-1
eISBN-10: 1-61773-022-X
First Kensington Electronic Edition: May 2016

10 9 8 7 6 5 4 3 2 1

Printed in the United States of America

To Bob,
the best thing that ever happened to me,
and that's no joke!

Acknowledgments

Thank you mom for reading mysteries to me when I was first learning to read. Because of that, a lifelong passion was born.

My deepest thanks go to my agent, John Talbot, and to my Kensington editor, Gary Goldstein, for trusting me with this series.

So many people advised me while I was writing this book! Elizabeth Harris helped me with my fictional PopIt app. Amanda Gruwell introduced me to the world of virtual yard sales and their conflicts. Ashley Harris (no relation, but a fabulous neighbor) answered so many questions (*so many*!) on how to run a virtual yard sale. Ashley also got me into a virtual admin site so I could sit back and read the admins' fascinating stories. They ranged from trivial complaints to actual death threats.

I am grateful to Officer Chris of the Fairfax County Police Department for taking me on an incredible ride along. When I asked him if he wanted me to name a character after him, he said, "Just call him Officer Awesome." So I did.

E. B. Davis, thank you so much for taking the time to read this on such short notice and for reading it so quickly. Your comments were invaluable. Also, thank you for the great interviews you do on the *Writers Who Kill* blog.

Clare Boggs, who would have thought when we took that creative writing class together all those years ago that you'd be my friend and keen-eyed beta reader? Your input makes my stories so much better.

Barb Goffman, superhero, friend . . . oh, and independent editor, I've told you more than once that this book should probably say "by Sherry Harris and Barb Goffman." You went above and beyond your duties as an editor by letting me question you incessantly, by punching up everything, from personalities to dialogue, and by helping me with plot holes larger than the black holes in space. Thank you, thank you, thank you. Barb reads an early version so any errors are all on me.

Mary Titone, beta reader, friend, and publicist, I am so glad to be your hobby. Thank you so much for making me get out there, for pushing me to do more book signings, and for cheering me on in so many ways.

To those of you who have read my books, come to my signings, invited me to be on your blogs, and supported me in so many different ways, thank you.

I'm so fortunate to be a member of two incredible chapters of Sisters in Crime—the Chessie Chapter here in Virginia and the New England Chapter in, well, New England.

My fellow Wicked Cozy Authors and Wicked Accomplices, what a fabulous bunch of women, authors, and friends you are! Jessie Crockett, Julie

Hennrikus (aka Julianne Holmes), Edith Maxwell, Liz Mugavero, and Barbara Ross, I treasure each of you for your uniqueness and for putting up with me. Sheila Connolly, Kim Gray, and Jane Haertel (aka Susannah Hardy), I've learned so much from each of you, on and off the blog.

Bob, you always said that someday you'd carry my books around for me. Someday finally arrived. Thanks for being my biggest cheerleader and for somehow working into almost every conversation you have with anyone that your wife is an author. (I'm sure that desk clerk, guy on the elevator, and woman waiting to cross the street worry about your sanity, but at least they have a bookmark.)

Chapter 1

I didn't expect to start my Saturday with a cup of Dunkin's coffee and a dead body. The coffee, yes, but the cup now lay at my feet, and a stream of coffee was melting the packed snow as I stared at Margaret More's lifeless face. She sat in her car in her driveway, the long and winding kind, where her car wasn't visible from the street. A vintage table-cloth, white with bright spring flowers, was stuffed in her mouth. It had looked like such a nice table-cloth online last night. Of course, then, it wasn't a murder weapon.

It was the tablecloth I'd wanted to buy from her yesterday on my virtual garage sale site. But now I wanted to flee from it and the sight of Margaret's dead body. I slipped and slid in my haste to return to my old Suburban. I yanked open the door and grabbed my purse. I did my usual "Where the heck's my phone? This purse isn't that big" search before spotting it in the cup holder. Finally, I dialed 911.

"I have to report a death," I said after dispatch answered. "It's Margaret. Margaret More."

The female dispatcher gasped. "It can't be."

"It looks like she was murdered." My voice sounded amazingly calm and didn't reflect my growing panic or the churning in my stomach as the reality of what I'd just seen set in. I heard what sounded like a muffled sob and some fumbling.

"Hello? Are you there?" I asked when nothing else happened.

"Where's your emergency?" This time the dispatcher was male. He sounded efficient and professional. I gave him the address.

"I copy that," he said. "But if this is some kind of sick joke, you should know there are laws against calling in false information."

"It's not. But I get it. Who would kill Margaret More?"

"No one. That's who." This dispatcher now sounded almost as choked up as the first one. He managed to run through the normal list of questions: "Are you safe?" "Are you injured?" "Is anyone else there with you?" After I answered all his questions, he hung up. I stared at my phone for a minute. So much for professional.

My phone chimed. It was a reminder that the Congregational church in Ellington was having a rummage sale today to raise money for organ repairs. I deleted the reminder as I made my way back up to Margaret. Somehow leaving her alone didn't seem right. Not to mention after my brief conversation with dispatch, I was starting to doubt my own story.

This time I walked carefully, trying to step only in the spots where I'd slipped and slid as I'd hurried to get to my phone. I studied the snow around me. It was only about an inch deep—February had been unusually mild this year. There was a mishmash of footprints around Margaret's car. Some poor sap would be taking casts of all of them.

I braced myself and looked back in the car. Margaret's thick silver hair hung in a neat bob around her face. Her age-spotted hands lay in her lap. Two giant diamond rings, one on each hand, sparkled in the sunlight. Part of me hoped I'd been wrong and had called the police for nothing. But Margaret was definitely dead. And unless she'd calmly stuffed the tablecloth in her mouth and sat there, waiting to die, I was right that she'd been murdered. I tried to open the driver's car door, but it was locked.

"Oh, Margaret, you'll be missed by so many." Margaret traced her roots back to the *Mayflower*, and her family was one of the first families to settle in Massachusetts. She was the president of the Ellington Historical Society and had a large extended family in the area.

I studied the interior of the car, something I knew police officers did when they pulled someone over. I'd picked up a fair bit of police know-how from my ex-husband, CJ, first while he served for over twenty years in the air force security forces and now as the chief of police of Ellington, the small town we lived in.

A traffic stop could easily change to something

more if drugs, money, or weapons were in sight. And that happened far more frequently than most people realized. But Margaret's car was neat as a pin. A black pocketbook sat on the front passenger seat. *Pocketbook! Good grief.* I was starting to use the native lingo. Nothing else seemed out of place. It didn't look like she'd been robbed, given the rings on her fingers and her purse sitting next to her.

My phone chimed again. I pulled it out and glanced down. I'd received a photo through PopIt, a popular picture-sharing app that lots of teens and twenty somethings used. I was far older than this app's typical user, but Lindsay, a former teenage neighbor from nearby Fitch Air Force Base, had gotten me hooked. I'd been using it to post items I wanted to sell on my virtual garage sale site, as well as to direct business to the site. It was also a fun way to stay in touch, and Lindsay always sent funny photos. Right now I could use a smile. I pressed the button to view the picture.

I could barely take in what I saw before the screen went blank. The photo was a shot of me standing by Margaret's car, looking in the window. Someone else was here.

Chapter 2

I whipped around, dropping my phone in the snow. I scanned the heavily wooded area across the broad lawn. Nothing moved, but there was a thick stand of trees and evergreens to hide behind. Now I realized how quiet it was up here, how alone I was. Why didn't I hear any sirens yet? Ellington wasn't that big. I strained, listening for any noise that might indicate someone's presence. Branches creaked as they rubbed together in the early morning wind. The silence, the isolation pressed in on me. Not wanting to turn my back or glance away from the woods for too long, I squatted and felt around in the snow until I found my phone. I scooped it up, wondering if I should call 911 again.

Sirens began wailing in the distance, I hoped coming here to help me. I flinched as a hawk burst from the woods. Its wings flapped loudly as it took off, while snow showered down from the vibrating branch it had just left. Was it the sirens that had startled him or the person who lurked out there, snapping photos of me? Was he or she watching now, enjoying my fear? I shook myself. I glanced at Margaret's house. Maybe the photographer was in there, or by now he or she could have circled around back to sneak up on me.

I looked back and forth between the house and the woods. I even managed a quick glance behind me. *Come on, cops. Drive faster.*

A few agonizing minutes later an ambulance roared up the driveway. Even though I'd told the dispatcher Margaret was definitely dead, I was grateful the EMTs had arrived. Grateful and safe. Next, a couple of squad cars showed up. Scott Pellner climbed out of the first one. He rubbed his hands and blew on them as he walked toward me. Until that moment I hadn't even noticed the cold. A terrible cold, like an ice storm, raged inside me. I hurried toward him, past my car and the ambulance. I slid again on the ice. He grabbed my arms to keep me upright.

"Is it really Margaret?" Pellner asked. He released me once I was steady.

"Yes." I pointed to the woods. "Someone's out there."

Pellner put a hand on his gun as he scanned the area I pointed to. "How do you know?"

"Have you heard of PopIt?" I asked him. The way this particular app worked, the picture had to be sent right when it was taken. And once you looked at it, unlike with other apps, it disappeared forever.

"It's all our daughter talks about. But what's that have to do with anything?"

I remembered Pellner had a high school–aged daughter. Explaining what had happened would be a lot easier. "I got a picture through the app while I was waiting for the police to arrive."

"And?" Pellner's brow wrinkled.

"It was a picture of me. Looking in the car, at Margaret."

Pellner scanned the line of woods again, eyes squinted. "Could you tell where it was taken from?"

"I'm not sure." I pointed to a spot in the woods. "Probably there. See the tallest pine, with the branch that hangs down funny?" I looked at Pellner, and he nodded. "A hawk flew from a tree right over in that area by the pine. Like it was startled. Maybe by the picture taker." I paused, thinking about the photo. "I guess it's possible it was taken from the house. But I don't think the angle was right."

While we'd been talking, more officials had arrived. Some looked at us curiously as they hurried up to Margaret's car.

"Stay here," Pellner said.

I watched as he joined a group of people now gathered near the front of the ambulance and started talking. They all turned and looked at me, and then Pellner motioned for me to join them. I hustled up the drive.

"Can we look at your phone?" Pellner asked, putting out his hand for it.

I handed him my phone. "I don't think it will help. That's the thing about PopIt. It doesn't save any of the information."

"That's why all parents hate it. And the police."
Pellner took the phone and passed it off to a woman
I didn't know. "Do you remember the user name?"

I scrunched my forehead up. "I was so startled by
the picture, I don't remember seeing the user
name."

"Show us where you were standing in the picture."

"You want me to go back up by Margaret's car?"

"No. Do a demo by my squad car."

Everyone followed me to Pellner's car. I stood by
the driver's-side window and bent over a little bit.
"This is about right," I said.

"What did you do after you saw the PopIt?" Pellner asked.

"I turned to see if anyone was watching me, but I
didn't see anyone."

The woman with my phone handed it back to
Pellner with a shake of her head. Pellner passed it
back to me. Two officers set off on a circuitous
route toward the woods.

"Are you okay?" Pellner asked.

My head did a little circle thing when I tried to
nod and shake it at the same time. Physically, I was
okay, emotionally I was questionable.

"Go sit in my car and warm up," Pellner said. "I'll
be there in a minute."

"Front or back?" I asked. At least I'd quickly have
some idea where I stood on the suspect list.

"Front."

Whew. "Can I just sit in mine?" Another test question tossed like a puck onto the ice in hopes that
Pellner would take a swing at it.

"No."

Rats. That meant Pellner considered my car to be part of the crime scene. Maybe he'd search it, seeking out a stash of vintage tablecloths used for murderous deeds. And the possibility of finding vintage tablecloths in the back wasn't that far-fetched. I often bought and sold them at the garage sales I loved to attend and organize.

I dutifully climbed into the squad car and wondered how long it would be before CJ showed up. He probably wouldn't be happy to find me here. I bit my lip. CJ could think whatever he wanted. We were divorced, and I didn't answer to him anymore. I turned the vents so the heat blasted me, and settled in for what I hoped would be a short wait. I stared at my phone, wondering if another photo would come in. I jerked upright sometime later, when the driver's-side door swung open and Pellner eased in.

"Did you fall asleep?" Pellner asked. His dimples stood out even when he didn't smile, but they didn't really soften his stern face.

I blinked at him. "I guess I did." Another strike against me. There was a saying in law enforcement that only the guilty slept. "I was up late last night, working on my garage sale site." I craned my head around. "Where's CJ?"

"Out of town."

The last time I'd talked to CJ was four weeks ago, when I'd called to ask him a question about our taxes. After he answered my question, I'd asked how he was doing. His answer had been all business. Arrest rates had gone up, but so had the number of petty crimes, there'd been an uptick in car thefts, the department basketball team was having a good season, a good cop was retiring, and he'd had to hire someone new. After his curt answer and his lack of interest in my life, I'd hoped this was the last piece of untangling our lives after our divorce just over a year ago. At least that was what I'd told myself. But now I wondered where CJ was. I knew Pellner well enough to know that asking for details and getting an answer was about as likely as an eighty-degree day in February in New England.

"Did they find anything out in the woods?" I asked.

"A few cigarette butts."

"Someone was out there smoking while they were snapping pictures of me?" I felt cold all over again.

"We don't know when someone smoked out there, but they bagged them just in case. How do you know Margaret?"

"Everyone in Ellington knows Margaret." The local joke was you couldn't go out of the house without running into someone related to Margaret. She was beloved. And apparently behated by someone.

Pellner twirled his hand. "Give me the details."

"I met her at the first Spouses' Club event I went to. You know, the club on base for the wives and husbands of the air force members stationed on base?"

Pellner nodded, so I continued. "It was three years ago, right after CJ and I were stationed at Fitch. She was an honorary member."

"So you were friends?"

"Friendly. It's not like we hung out."

"What are you doing here?" His dimple looked serious. He wasn't asking lightly.

Then I remembered my argument with Margaret last night on my virtual garage sale site. Oh, boy, that wasn't going to look good when it came out. I could delete the thread, but when the police started questioning people, it was sure to be reported. It would look even worse if the thread was missing. And I wasn't computer savvy enough to really, really make it go away. But that was not what Pellner had asked, so I wouldn't bring it up yet.

"Sarah?"

"I'm setting up a February Blues garage sale on Fitch. There's also going to be a silent auction to raise scholarship money. Margaret agreed to donate some items. I was here to pick them up."

Pellner then walked me pretty much step-by-step through my morning, up to his arrival. I left out the details of my showering and makeup routine but did mention deciding to wear my favorite aqua sweater. If that wasn't enough detail for him, so be it.

"I had an online argument with Margaret last night about the vintage tablecloth that's stuffed down her throat." I felt like smacking my forehead.

Why had I blurted that out? The image of Margaret and the tablecloth made me shudder. And by the surprised look on Pellner's face, my bluntness shocked him. But CJ had been in law enforcement the whole of our nineteen-year marriage. I'd observed his ability to detach himself from a situation all those years, and now it helped me to keep from cracking up.

Pellner pinched the bridge of his nose with his thumb and index finger. "How did you happen to want to buy something from her?"

"She's a member of my Ellington virtual garage sale site."

"Did she sell a lot of things?"

"Lately, she had been. She called me a few weeks ago and asked how the whole thing worked. I talked her through it, and she immediately started posting items."

"Did she tell you why?"

"I assumed because it was fun or because she had that thrifty Yankee side so many people do in this area." I was sure the saying "Waste not, want not" originated here.

"But she was loaded," Pellner said.

"I never thought about it. Some of the richest people I know here wear ratty clothes, clip coupons, and shop at garage sales."

"Quirky New England types," Pellner said.

I paused as I thought about one of my conversations with Margaret. "She once told me she couldn't take it with her, so she might as well sell some of the things she'd collected." How different that comment seemed now that she was dead.

"From the look of things, she tried her best to take the tablecloth with her."

I shook my head. "Really, Pellner?"

He shrugged. Pellner turned down the heat, so the air was more like a light summer breeze than hell's furnace blasting through the vents. "My wife talks about your garage sale site. She loves it."

Good thing I had brought up the argument, because it would have come out sooner than I'd have guessed.

"But I've heard grumblings about your virtual garage sale."

"Grumblings?" I wondered what that was about. There'd been the odd bit of drama here and there, but not as much as I'd seen on some sites.

Pellner sighed. "Just tell me about the argument."

"Shouldn't we just wait to go over all this when the state troopers arrive?" In small town Massachusetts the district attorney could ask the state police to take over a murder investigation. And with someone as high profile as Margaret involved, I was positive that would happen.

"The Triple A with guns will show up soon enough. Humor me. I know you didn't kill Margaret, but they won't." He pointed toward Margaret's car. People bustled around it.

Triple A with guns? I knew small town police departments preferred to do their own investigations, and they did, in a behind-the-scenes way, but that statement took agency rivalry to a whole new level.

"As you were saying, you had an argument of some sort with Margaret last night." Pellner twirled his hand again, a "Get on with it" motion.

"Last night Margaret posted a picture of the tablecloth on the site. I wanted to buy it, and we agreed on a price." I whipped out my phone. "I can show you the whole conversation."

"Do it," Pellner said.

"Margaret posted the picture of the tablecloth and the price at ten last night." I handed him my phone. "It's in great shape, and I liked the cheery pattern, so I told her I'd buy it for her price."

"What's that?" Pellner pointed at a comment under mine.

"Someone else wanted to buy it, too." I left it at that.

Pellner scrolled through the comments under mine. I wished he hadn't. "Who's Frieda Chida? Her comments don't sound very happy."

"It's not Chida, like China. It's pronounced Chee-duh."

"Her name is Frieda Chida?" Although, with his local accent, it came out like Frieder Chider. Pellner rolled his eyes at the rhyme.

"Yep. She's a member of the group. She saw the tablecloth and wanted it, too. But I saw it first and offered to buy it immediately."

"But Frieda offered to pay more money. Almost double what you did."

"It's an etiquette thing in the world of virtual garage sales. The buyer usually sells to the first person who offers to buy it, if they can agree upon a price."

Pellner pointed to the screen. "She's accusing you of getting advanced notice on things because you're the administrator of the site."

"We all get notices at the same time. Although I could set it up so I saw things first." And I might in the future—it was one of the few perks of being an administrator. "I just happened to be on the site when Margaret posted the picture."

Pellner continued to scroll through the conversation. But I knew what he was reading. Margaret said sorry to me and told Frieda she could have it. I told Margaret that wasn't fair or right, as we'd already agreed on her price. We'd even agreed that I would stop by at nine this morning to pick it up. I also told Frieda it was rude to jump in after arrangements had been made. She told me to suck it up and put my big girl panties on. I was so mad at both of them, I threatened to ban them from the site. Margaret said she could sell to whomever she wanted to. Then I realized she was right. Sometimes in the heat of the moment, when I really wanted something, I lost perspective. It was just a tablecloth, for crying out loud, and I had several similar ones at home. I apologized to both and made arrangements to come get the things for the silent auction.

"How do I get ahold of Frieda?"

"I don't know. I could send her a message through the group."

"You don't know her?"

"Not personally, but to be a member of the group, she has to know someone else in the group. That's why these kinds of sites are different than other bigger sites. Someone has to add you to the group. And virtual garage sale sites are more localized. I run the one in Ellington, but Bedford, Concord, and Lexington have them, too. It makes it safer to do business."

"Not so safe for Margaret."

Oh, no. If Pellner thought Margaret's death had something to do with my site, others might too.

Chapter 3

On our drive to the police station, where the staties would interview me, I called a lawyer, Vincenzo DiNapoli. He'd gotten Mike "the Big Cheese" Titone off racketeering charges, kept his own son out of jail, and helped my best friend, Carol Carson, last fall, when she'd been accused of murder.

"What'd you go and do that for?" Pellner asked when I hung up.

"Because a wise man once told me never to talk to the police without a lawyer. I should have called Vincenzo before talking to you." Especially before I mentioned the online argument.

Pellner glanced upward, as if sending up a silent prayer. "Since you called Vincenzo, I'm guessing it was Angelo DiNapoli who gave you that bit of advice."

"It was." Angelo and his wife, Rosalie, were two of my favorite people in Ellington. They owned DiNapoli's Roast Beef and Pizza and were almost substitute parents, since my family lived out in California. "They'll be so shocked when they hear that Margaret's dead. That she was murdered." I shivered, the ice storm back inside me.

"Everyone will be," Pellner said.

The rest of the morning was a blur. The state police arrived and were impatient when they found I wouldn't say a word until my lawyer showed up. It took Vincenzo a long time to arrive, and then he basically wouldn't let me say more than I already had. Under his watchful eye, I signed the statement certifying that what I had told Pellner was true.

"When can I get my car back?" I asked Pellner as Vincenzo and I followed him to the lobby.

"When they're done with it," he said. "I'll see what I can do."

"I'll drop you home," Vincenzo said, whisking me out before I could say anything else.

Vincenzo's driver held open the back door of the car for us to climb in. I thanked him as I scooted across the luxurious leather seat to make room for Vincenzo. He took up a lot of space in the back of the car. Part of it was his physical presence—barrel chest, long legs, big head, with slicked-back dark hair. Large hands adorned with a ruby-studded pinkie ring. The other part was a mixture of charisma and confidence.

"What a nice way to travel. My Suburban is ten years old, and I need it to last a lot longer." I ran my hand across the leather.

"It's comfortable, yes," Vincenzo said. "But it's also quite handy. I can work if I don't have to drive, and with the traffic in the Boston area, I get a lot done."

I would like to have a driver but didn't ever see that happening. Since my divorce I'd started a business organizing garage sales for people, but garage sales and snow weren't a good mix. I'd had to get creative, which was why I'd started my online garage sale site last October. I'd attracted some advertisers and sold my own stuff on the site, in addition to selling things for others and taking a commission. Last fall the town had hired me to run New England's Largest Yard Sale. I had tucked some of that money into savings, where I'd also put the money from our divorce settlement. CJ had insisted I take half our savings when we divorced, as well as half his retirement pay and alimony. If Margaret's murder was linked to my site I could be in big trouble.

The car glided to a stop in front of my apartment building—an old frame house with a large covered porch. The house had been divided into four units. I lived on the upper right side. The upper left side had been empty since last spring.

"Call me if you hear anything from the police," Vincenzo said as I slid out.

"Thank you."

As the car pulled away, my stomach rumbled, but it wasn't hunger for once, which was a good thing, since without a car, it would be a long, cold walk in the snow to pick up groceries.

My apartment was on the west side of the town

common. A thin layer of snow covered the lawn and made the beautiful old Congregational church on the south end look like the cover for a fancy coffee table book—*Winter Scenes of New England*. A corner of the common had been flooded to make an ice skating rink. A couple of families were out there, laughing and falling. It was the way a bright, sunny day should be—not shadowed by a murder.

I headed over to Carol's shop, Paint and Wine, on the north side of the common, just down the block from DiNapoli's. I wanted to talk to Carol. I'd known her for almost twenty years, and could rely on her to listen and be discreet. But as I walked toward the shop, a large group of laughing women went in, so I knew she'd be tied up for a couple of hours. Carol taught people how to create a painting in a couple of hours and made it a lot of fun in the process. I toyed with the idea of going to DiNapoli's, but the smell of food might make me nauseous. And I wasn't ready to be in the middle of the hub of gossip in Ellington.

As I walked back home, a few snowflakes started to fly. *Great. More snow.* While the ski resorts and the winter sports fans would be happy, I'd enjoyed the almost snowless winter. When I got home, my stomach rumbled again. Maybe it was hunger. I made a fluffer-nutter sandwich, which consisted of a thick layer of Marshmallow Fluff, invented in Massachusetts—I accepted no imitators—and a layer of peanut butter on white bread. Not the healthiest lunch, but a Massachusetts staple and the official state sandwich. It was completely satisfying after an awful morning.

I wrapped myself in a blanket and sat on the couch, which, like most of my possessions, was a find at a garage sale. I rubbed my feet on the worn Oriental rug that covered the wide-planked wood floors, which I'd painted white. My apartment was usually my safe haven, but Margaret's murder had me on edge. I grabbed my computer and opened it to my virtual garage sale site. There was nothing there about Margaret's murder, and I didn't want to be the one to break the news. At least not yet. I posted a couple of gentle reminders about always listing an item's price, condition, and location of pickup. People so often ignored my rules.

I decided to dive into the growing number of private messages about the site, hoping to be distracted. People in the group were always complaining about this item or that person. Someone who hadn't picked up at the arranged time, someone who thought a seller had picked another person to sell to, even though they had posted "interested" under the item. The only message that really concerned me was one about a ppu—a porch pickup. The seller had left the item on their porch for the buyer. When they had returned home, the item was gone, but the payment hadn't been left. They had made several attempts to contact the person but hadn't heard back. I banned the offender from the site and wrote a note telling the seller what I'd done. There wasn't much else I could do. If the banned person made payment, they'd be allowed back on and given one more chance. I'd learned quickly that you couldn't put up with nonsense from people, or things spiraled out of control.

I closed my computer and snuggled into my blanket. Big flakes drifted by the window. The sight of Margaret sitting in her car danced before my eyes. I wanted to push the whole thing aside. But I might as well face it now, instead of letting the reality of Margaret's death fester in some dark spot in my heart. Someone must have staged her body, because no one would sit calmly, with their hands in their lap, while someone else shoved a tablecloth down their throat.

It might mean she was killed somewhere else and moved. But I hadn't seen anything unusual that might indicate she'd been dragged from one place to another or deeper footprints, caused by extra weight if someone had carried her. Maybe the killer had surprised her from behind, killed her in some other way, and then stuffed the tablecloth down her throat after the fact. The police wouldn't know the cause of death yet. Not that they'd be running to me with it when they did know.

I'd have to research the old-fashioned way. I reopened my computer and Googled Margaret. Not surprisingly, a bunch of stuff came up. Honorary chair of this, president of that, her work to save the home where Thoreau was born in Concord, her position on the board of Orchard House, the home of the Alcott family in Concord. She had had her finger in a plethora of pies.

I moved on to searching for information about

her personal life. She had nine siblings, most of whom had stayed within a five-mile radius of Ellington, but a couple had moved to Boston. *Gasp!* The fifteen-mile move to Boston was, by Massachusetts's standards, the equivalent of moving to the moon. People stayed put here. Roots ran deep. I made notes of their names for further research, but from what I could tell, they looked to be a successful, productive bunch. All of them had their own large families. It could take days to sort them all out. One of her sons was an Ellington selectmen, a member of the executive body that ran the town, and was engaged to our sometimes prickly town manager.

I gave up on that and went back to my garage sale site. I'd promised Pellner I'd message Frieda Chida. He might have already tracked her down, but I was curious as to what she might know. Wording the note was a bit awkward. How did you tell someone, "The police want to talk with you," without telling them why? But my worries were for naught. She'd already messaged me. It read: Thanks for siccing the police on me.

Yeesh. Thank you, Ellington police, I thought.

Then the message said: They wouldn't tell me it was you, but I know it has to be. Who else would have known?

Oops, not the EPD's fault. Well, anyone who had read the post last night would know we were both interested in Margaret's vintage tablecloth. I should have deleted it last night, per the rules of the site, which stated that as soon as an item was sold, the post had to be deleted. That way the site wasn't clogged with old posts. Actually Margaret, as the seller, should have deleted it. But last night I'd been so mad, I'd slammed the cover of my laptop closed without following my own rules.

Now how to respond to Frieda's remark? I could deny it. The police had told me not to say anything. I could fess up or just point out that others had seen the post too. Or I could not answer at all. But my curiosity got the better of me. I wondered how much she knew.

So I sent a quick note. **Really?**

That seemed noncommittal enough. I didn't know how long I'd have to wait, but I'd barely hit SEND when I heard back.

No, she wrote. **I'm making the whole thing up.** Sarcasm almost dripped off her reply. **They asked me all sorts of questions about how I knew Margaret and how well. I told them I'd cleaned for the woman for years, until last spring, when she fired me. Besides, it's not like you can live in Ellington and not know about Margaret and her family. It's annoying. You'd think they were royalty, the way people fawn over them.**

Whoa. Frieda worked for Margaret and was fired? I wondered what the police thought about that.

I made sure the police knew how mad you were last night, when Margaret sold me the tablecloth.

Gee, thanks. I wrote back: **She shouldn't have said I could have it and then changed her mind.**

> You have too many damn rules. It should go to
> the highest bidder.

I shook my head. I didn't want to rehash our argument.

Another message popped up. I wanted the damn tablecloth. I just remodeled my kitchen, and it's the perfect finishing touch. I wonder how long I'll have to wait to get it now.

The twelfth of never. Apparently, the police hadn't told her the tablecloth was the murder weapon, or so it seemed to me. I have no idea.

> My grandma had one like that in her kitchen
> when I was little. She went to heaven's pearly
> gates way too young. My mom got rid of
> everything. Said it was junk. So I can't wait
> to get my hands on it.

If she'd told me all of this last night, I'd have lost more gracefully. And I wished she'd arranged for an early morning pickup. Then she would be the one who found Margaret, and I'd be here, doing something other than seeing Margaret's cold, dead body over and over in my mind.

I waited to see if she'd type more. When she didn't, I clicked on her profile picture. She had bleached blond hair, with dark roots and purple ends. Wrinkles framed her eyes, as did her thick black eyeliner. I clicked through her photos. She lived in a modest ranch, if anyone could call any home modest in this high-priced area, where the cheapest homes were almost four hundred thousand dollars. There were pictures of her with some twentysomethings, but none with a man. She didn't have anything marked on her relationship status. Most of her posts had to do with games she played and pictures of puppies. Nothing else to learn about her there.

Every time my phone chimed, I cringed. But no further pictures came in. I berated myself for not remembering the user name of whoever had sent the picture. It wouldn't be much to go on, but it might help. I closed my eyes more than once and tried to do some deep breathing, but nothing would pop the user name back into my consciousness.

As the afternoon wore on, I checked the local online news several times, but the story of Margaret's death hadn't broken yet. I was amazed that the police had somehow managed to keep it quiet for this long. I worried about Margaret's family, about how shocking the news of her death would be. I was so antsy, I couldn't stand myself. Staying busy seemed to be my best option.

Chapter 4

I grabbed my coat and a couple of sturdy tote bags. I'd go hit the last thirty minutes of the rummage sale at the Congregational church. Walking across the town common to the church, I wondered if anything good would be left. Sometimes going late meant losing out on the best stuff. Other times I'd managed to negotiate rock-bottom prices on great items as sellers packed up their things.

Across the common I spotted a woman and a well-dressed man loading bags of stuff into the trunk of a car. Hennessy Hamilton. I wouldn't have known it was her from this distance, but the doors on her car had large bright pink *H*s painted on them to promote her consignment shop, Hennessy's Heaven. I knew that underneath the large *H*, her slogan, "Where all your shopping dreams come true," was painted on the car. You'd have to be dead to miss it. I winced as I thought of Margaret.

There were still a lot of cars parked around the common and people going in and out of the church.

Drat. That didn't bode well for my bargain hunting. I trotted down the steps to the church basement and hung my coat on a hook in the hallway outside the fellowship hall, where the sale was being held. I kept the totes with me. At this kind of sale, where everything was paid for at the end, it was easier to set my finds in the totes than try to juggle an armful of things or depend on people having plastic bags available to put stuff in. At bigger events, like outdoor flea markets or sales at convention centers, I took a collapsible wire cart with wheels.

As I entered the fellowship hall and looked at the people milling about, I wondered if the news of Margaret's death was out. At the first table I had my answer. A woman was crying and blowing her nose. "They should have canceled the sale. It's not right being here when poor Margaret is dead," she said to a woman standing next to her.

"She wasn't even a member of our church," the woman replied.

"But she was a member of our community. A godsend for this town." She choked back a sob. "What will we do now?"

The woman next to her rolled her eyes and moved away.

I spotted a blue and white porcelain lamp a couple of tables down and strolled over to it. "How much?" I asked the woman behind the table. She'd started packing away a few of her things.

"It's broken," she said, looking around. "Have to be honest at a church sale."

I turned the lamp over but didn't see any cracks or chips in the porcelain.

"No," the woman said. "It doesn't turn on any-more."

Ah, so it just needed new wiring, an easy fix. Any hardware store carried socket kits, and I probably had one at home. I was pretty sure the base was from the forties, and once I fixed it, the lamp would be worth at least thirty dollars. A sticker on it said TEN DOLLARS. "Since it's broken, would you take three?" Was this lying in a church? Would a bolt of lightning strike me dead? Was it wrong to be here after finding Margaret this morning? Since nothing happened, I decided I was okay.

"I guess so, but why would you want it if it's broken?" She shook her head, clearly thinking I was an odd duck. She marked the price down on the sticker. "Terrible news about Margaret More, isn't it?"

I nodded my agreement, not trusting myself to say anything, and placed the lamp in one of my totes.

I bartered with a man over a set of salt and pepper shakers—vintage Mr. and Mrs. Claus. I'd found them at the bottom of a box full of old dish towels—not old in a good, antique way, but old as in worn and stained. It paid to dig through boxes. I'd turned up a lot of treasures over the years by doing just that. The man wanted twelve dollars for the shakers but agreed to five. I moved around the sale listening to people's reactions to Margaret's death. I bought a blue cobalt glass vase thick with dust. An unframed watercolor of a cabin in the snow was my last purchase. I'd fix it all up and sell it at the February Blues garage sale on base.

As I paid for my purchases and thought about the conversations I'd overheard, I realized about 85 percent of the people felt terrible about Margaret dying, another 10 percent seemed ambivalent, and the last 5 percent appeared almost happy. I wondered about those people.

My apartment had a slanted ceiling, so it was high on one side and sloped to a four-foot wall on the other. A small door in the wall allowed access to a good-size place to store things. My phone rang as I started to stash my purchases away in the storage space. CJ.

"I heard you had a rough day," CJ said. His low voice rumbled over the line like a lightning bolt into my heart. We might be divorced, but when he spoke to me with such a caring tone, it was easy to forget everything that had happened between us.

"I've had better, but compared to Margaret's day, I'm fine. Is there an official cause of death?" I sat down on one of the two chairs at my small kitchen table and started tracing the pattern of the flowers on the vintage tablecloth with my finger. It wasn't that different than the one stuffed in Margaret's mouth, the one I had wanted so much last night. Sometimes I was an idiot.

CJ sighed. "You know I couldn't tell you if there

was. You have to wait and find out like every other resident of Ellington."

"A girl can hope," I answered.

"Did you remember anything else about the photo that was sent to you?"

My heart dropped a little. This was an official call, not a personal one. A small town police chief doing his job. "I don't remember anything else. Where are you?"

"At a conference for chiefs of small police departments." He paused. "In Monterey."

Monterey? I'd grown up in Pacific Grove, a small town next to Monterey. When I was eighteen, my mother had warned me to stay away from the military men at the Defense Language Institute, just up the hill from our house. So, of course, I'd headed right up there. I'd bowled CJ over, literally, as I hustled out of a building I wasn't supposed to be in. The security guys had been hot on my heels as I exited, right into CJ's arms. He'd even lied to the MAs—the masters-at-arms, or navy police—saying that I was waiting for him and that he was late. The memory made me smile.

"I had dinner with your folks last night."

My folks? That wiped the smile off my face. I loved my parents, but since the fall they'd increased their pressure on me to move home. I'd spent Christmas with them, and much of the holiday had been them probing into why I was staying in Ellington. I loved it here, although the warm weather and the stunning coastal scenery of Pacific Grove tempted me.

But I didn't want to go back as a failure. If anything,

Monterey was more expensive than this area, and there was little possibility of finding a place I could afford on my own. I'd checked the classifieds there after CJ and I first split. It had helped to make my decision to live here easier. Plus, my parents hated garage sales, because they thought if you didn't want something, you should give it away. Which was fine and dandy if you had lots of money, but many people needed the money, and I liked to help them make it.

"Are you there?" CJ asked.

"Yes. I'm just . . . surprised." Surprised didn't begin to describe my feelings. My mother had been dead set against us getting married so young. My father hadn't been happy about the idea either, but at least he hadn't vocalized those feelings and instead had bent over backward to welcome CJ to the family. Even after CJ and I were married for nineteen years, my mother had continued to be a bit reserved with him. At least she'd managed not to say "I told you so" to me over Christmas. I wondered if she'd said it to CJ. I was flummoxed that she'd invited him over for dinner, now that we were divorced. Maybe she was trying to get him to tell me to move back to California.

"How did it go?" I asked, not sure I actually wanted to know the answer.

"No blood was shed, if that's what you're worried about."

"I wasn't too worried about bloodshed with my pacifist parents." "Aging hippies" was a better way to describe them. Me marrying a military man went pretty much against everything I'd been raised to believe. But over time, as CJ won them over, they'd mellowed a bit. "But they are opinionated, to say the least, and the fact that you hurt their only daughter . . ."

"They asked where we stood."

"What did you tell them?" I wasn't sure I wanted to know this, either.

"That they'd have to ask you."

Ask me? The last couple of times I'd reached out to him, he'd been all business. It sure felt like he'd reached a decision all on his own, even if I hadn't. Not that I'd blame him if he was tired of waiting around for me to figure my life out. I heard a woman in the background call to CJ.

"I've got to go," he said.

"When will you be back?" But CJ had already hung up.

Thinking of CJ with another woman upset me more than I wanted to admit. I crawled back through the small door to the storage space to finish putting my purchases away. A box in back of the things I'd accumulated for the February Blues sale caught my attention. I dragged it out from under the eaves and realized this unopened box was one from when CJ and I split up. So much for not thinking about CJ. I pulled off the packing tape and found a box full of CJ's sports stuff. A baseball bat, a basketball, and an old pair of cleats, apparently nothing he valued or things he thought were lost. I took out the baseball bat, hefting it in my hand. I went to my bedroom and stuck it under my bed as I thought about the photo of me standing by Margaret's car. The photo must have freaked me out a little more than I cared to admit.

I fixed another fluffernutter for dinner, realizing a diet of fluffernutters would get old quickly, but I still didn't have my car back. At six, I flipped on the news, and the story of Margaret's death was covered even by the Boston stations. Her family had a compound on Nantucket, but they'd called Ellington home for many generations. *Philanthropy* and *industry* seemed to be the main words used to describe the family. After getting my fill of Margaret's family history, I flipped on the Celtics game. During the commercials I approved posts for the garage sale site. If I'd known how much time the site would take up, I wasn't sure I would have started it. The admin of the Concord site had warned me and hadn't been overstating the amount of work.

At halftime there was a knock on my door. I hoped it was Stella Wild, my friend and landlady, who lived in the apartment below me, so I could vent about finding Margaret. I yanked open the door. Seth Anderson stood there.

Chapter 5

In his black cashmere overcoat, gloves in hand, he looked every bit Massachusetts's Most Eligible Bachelor, which he'd been named by a magazine two years running. I hadn't seen him in person in several months. I'd seen pictures in the newspaper—lots of pictures. Him at this gala or that charity event, always with some dazzling-looking model type on his arm, but never the same one twice in a row. He was a darling of the society pages, and every one of those pictures sparked a jealous twinge in me, as much as I'd like to deny they did. Here I was, dressed in sweats, a Celtics T-shirt, and pink, fuzzy slippers. At least I still had a bit of makeup on.

"I know I'm breaking the 'You don't want to see me' rule, but I thought finding Margaret dead and a trip to the police station allowed for relaxing the rule."

Seth was the district attorney for our county and thus would know when any major crimes occurred. He smelled heavenly—fresh air and soap.

I'd forgotten how deliciously tempting he was, even with his dark hair mussed, like he'd run his hands through it a hundred times recently. I was happier to see him than I wanted to admit to myself. We'd met in a bar last winter, and I was still embarrassed that I'd slept with him that first night. I hadn't seen him again until last April, and after that we'd dated on and off until last October.

"I take it by your silence that you want me to go."

"Yes," I said as I shook my head no. *Damn*. My subconscious was totally betraying me. I sighed. "Come in." I managed not to say, "Please, please, please come in and hold me and take me and never, ever let me go." Instead, I demurely stepped back so he could enter. But I wondered if the amused grin on his face meant he read every thought as it flicked through my mind.

He slipped out of his coat and laid it on the arm of the couch.

"Would you like a glass of Cabernet?" I asked. I definitely needed one.

"Sure. That would be great." He took off his red silk tie and loosened the top couple of buttons of his pristine blue shirt. His dark gray suit must have been custom made, because it fit him so perfectly.

Seth settled on my couch like he belonged there. I fled to the kitchen. Well, it was more of a shuffle in my fuzzy slippers. I gave myself a good talking to as I opened the bottle of wine and poured two glasses. *Do not get too close. Be friendly. Polite. Maintain a proper decorum, as much as one can when wearing sweats, a T-shirt, and pink fuzzy slippers.* I took a deep breath, gave my shoulder-length hair a toss, and shuffled back into the living room.

Trying to look composed in fuzzy slippers wasn't all that easy. As I handed Seth his wine, I stepped on the back of one slipper, lost my balance, and tossed the wine all over Seth's shirt.

"Oh, no. I'm so sorry." Heat flamed my face. "Give me your shirt and I'll rinse it out."

Seth stood and laughed. "It's fine. It's just a shirt."

"Hand it over."

Seth unbuttoned his shirt, and I braced myself for the sight of his bare chest. Fortunately, he had a white T-shirt on, but it was also soaked with wine. He yanked it off over his head. I held my hand out for both, trying not to stare at his chest. *Eyes up.*

"Do you have a towel?" he asked.

"Yes." I kicked off my traitorous fuzzy slippers and dashed off to get one. I returned and watched as he carefully blotted up as much of the excess wine on his blue shirt as he could.

"Do you have any club soda?" he asked.

"Yes. Give me the shirts and I'll rinse them."

"Just point me to where it is, and I'll take care of it."

He followed me into the kitchen, which seemed smaller than normal, considering his proximity and bare chest. I opened the fridge and pointed. "There's the club soda." I hustled out of the kitchen and grabbed a couple of hangers from my bedroom.

"Here," I said, when I returned to the kitchen and handed him the hangers. "We can hang your shirts from the shower rod so they can dry." After Seth put the shirts on the hangers, I took them to the bathroom. I couldn't sit out there with him half naked. I only had so much willpower when it came to Seth. So I went back into my bedroom and scrounged around in my dresser until I found the biggest T-shirt I owned.

Seth sat on the couch and I tossed him the T-shirt. God help me, if I didn't watch him pull that thing on. It hugged his chest and flat abs, but this was much better than bare. I hustled back into the kitchen and fanned myself with a dish towel. I needed to turn down the thermostat. After pouring him another glass of wine, I went back into the living room. I meant to sit in my grandmother's rocker by the window, but Seth grabbed my wrist and pulled me down next to him. I'd like to say I shot off the couch. Instead, I stayed, took a drink of my wine, and smiled when I felt Seth's lips brush across my hair. I fit next to him so well. But that made me think of CJ and the promise I'd made to myself to keep my distance from both of them until I could figure out—with a clear head—what I wanted. Or whom. I put a little space between us. I felt more than heard Seth's sigh of resignation.

"I'm sorry you found Margaret," Seth said. "Are you okay?"

I found my head circling in a yes-no motion. I propped my feet up on the old trunk I used as a coffee table, grateful I'd given myself a pedicure a few days ago. "It was horrible finding her."

"Tell me about the picture."

I quickly told him all I remembered. Which was what I'd told the police and the state troopers. "You must have read my statement."

"I did, but I wanted to hear it from you."

"So you could tell if I was guilty?"

"No. So I could see how I could help you." He studied me for a minute. "As a friend."

I gave a little snort. *Friend.* Funny. I didn't feel like ripping the shirt off and jumping into the lap of any of my other friends.

"And I know CJ's out of town."

Apparently, everyone had that bit of information. "So you thought I needed protecting. I'm not some fragile damsel in distress." *Yes, yes, I am. Please don't buy my bravado and leave me.*

"No. Like I said, I thought you might need a friend."

That took the wind out of my sails.

We talked and finished the bottle of wine. I woke at three, sprawled across Seth's chest, his arms wrapped around me. He snored gently. I slipped out of his arms, got a blanket from my room, and put it around him. Part of me wanted to snuggle under it with him, but I couldn't see that leading to any place good, or maybe I saw it leading to someplace very good that I needed to avoid. So I crawled in my own bed and slept better than I would have thought possible given my day.

* * *

At 9:30 a.m. I scurried to the bathroom because I needed to freshen up before facing Seth. Seth's shirt and T-shirt were no longer hanging from my shower rod. I peeked around the corner into the living room. The blanket was neatly folded on the couch, and a piece of paper lay on top of it, but my T-shirt was nowhere to be seen. The piece of paper was a note from Seth: *Let me know if you need anything. Call me if anything else happens.* He'd underlined the word *anything* twice. I crumpled the paper and threw it in the trash. Needed, wanted, I could barely tell the two apart anymore, which was why last October I'd told both him and CJ that I needed a break. But now that I'd seen Seth and knew I still had feelings for him—lots of messy, wonderful, scary feelings—I realized I needed to see CJ again and soon.

Pellner called and told me I could pick up my car at the station, which was a good thing because I had a meeting on base this morning. I bundled up, hoping that Stella was home and could give me a ride. If she wasn't, I'd make the walk. Even though the sun was shining and some of the snow was melting, it was cold out, according to the weather app on my phone. I trotted down the stairs and knocked on Stella's door. She answered, also bundled up and looking like she was leaving for the day. Her cat, Tux, meowed behind her. He was black, with a white chest. I'd found him a collar that looked like a bow tie in the front. He was the George Clooney of the cat world.

"It's okay, boy. I'll be back," Stella said as she started to close her door. I waved at Tux, but I wasn't sure he appreciated the gesture. Stella taught voice at Berklee College of Music. We were about the same age and height, but she had exotic Mediterranean looks, with olive skin and deep green eyes, while I had dark blond hair and blue eyes.

"Where are you off to this morning?" I asked.

"I'm meeting the family for Sunday brunch in Boston. Then giving some private lessons this afternoon. You?"

"I need a ride to the police station."

"The police station?" Stella's voice sounded concerned, with a hint of amusement.

"I'll explain on the way."

Stella murmured sympathetically while she drove and I told her the story. It didn't take long to reach the station.

After thanking Stella, I trotted up the steps and entered the lobby. It was a square space with a couple of chairs, two doors, which I knew were locked and which you had to be buzzed through, and a bulletproof glass window with a small opening for speaking through. No desk in the lobby with a gossipy receptionist sitting there who might fill me in on what was going on with Margaret. Or even a stoic Yankee receptionist who might walk off to get something, allowing someone like me to snoop.

No, this lobby was snoop proof. Darn the Ellington police and their modern ways. I walked up to the window. The desk on the other side was empty. "Hello," I called, putting my lips near the vent-like thing embedded in the window. I hoped it amplified my voice so someone would hear me. After a few moments a woman with puffy red eyes showed up. Her name tag read MORE. I wondered if she was the dispatcher who couldn't talk to me yesterday morning and how she was related to Margaret.

"I came to pick up the keys for my Suburban. Officer Pellner said I could pick it up."

The woman gave a short nod and disappeared from my view. She returned a few minutes later and slid the keys through a contraption like you see at the movie theater. "The car's round the side of the building."

She turned away before I could even say thank you.

It was 10:30 a.m. by the time I stood in the community center on Fitch Air Force Base, the site of the February Blues garage sale. I handed Laura Nicklas, my good friend and the base commander's wife, one of the two cups of Dunkin' Donuts coffee I'd swung by and picked up on the way over here. Mine was almost gone, because I'd needed the jolt of caffeine this morning. I dropped my purse in a corner to keep it out of the way.

Laura took a drink. "Yum. Just what I needed. Thanks." Laura stood about two inches taller than my five-six and looked a lot like Halle Berry. She'd actually gotten into arguments with people who insisted she was indeed Halle. As if she wouldn't know she was a rich and famous movie star. Laura had sponsored me on base, which allowed me access after I went to the visitors center, filled out a form, and got a pass to display on the dashboard of my Suburban.

The security forces were sticklers for procedure,

even with people like me, who used to live on base. Usually, the pass they gave me was only good for a few hours, but with the work leading up to the February Blues garage sale, Laura had gotten me a thirty-day pass. Woo-hoo! Now I wouldn't have to go to the visitors' center and fill out a form every time I came to base to help with the sale. By showing the pass and my driver's license to the security guard at the gate, I'd be able to sail right through. It would feel like the old days—just over a year ago—when CJ and I were still married and I had a dependent's ID that allowed me on base.

I looked around the room. My status on base might have changed, but the carpet here hadn't. It was still old and stained, and the crystal chandeliers seemed to be at odds with our purpose, but we were able to use the room for free, so neither of those things really mattered.

"Why are we doing the sale on a Friday? Aren't they usually on Saturdays, when more people are off work?" Laura asked. One of the many duties Laura had as the base commander's wife was running the base thrift shop, so she was savvy about sales.

"That would usually make sense, but more people are on base during the week because of all the people who commute to work here, so I thought Friday would be better." I hoped my theory was right. "More people means more sales."

"Okay. You're the expert. Where do we start?" Laura asked. "I don't have much time, because I have to go to mass."

"Let's go to the storeroom and measure what size

tables are available. Then we can start laying out a floor plan for the room."

"I hate that creepy storeroom. I always think I'm going to find a dead body in there."

I winced, thinking about Margaret.

"What? What do you know?" Laura asked. We started walking across the room, which was about the size of an elementary school gymnasium. "Do you know something about Margaret More? Did CJ tell you something juicy?"

"CJ didn't tell me anything."

"But . . . I know you have a *but*." And that was why Laura always knew what was going on around base. She was observant, she asked the right questions, or she could stare you down like you were a teenager fibbing about where you'd been.

"I found her."

"No." Laura's mouth dropped open so far, I was pretty sure her jaw hit her toes. "How'd you happen to be the one who found her?"

"I went to pick up the stuff she was donating for the silent auction."

"Where'd you find her? How'd she look?"

The image of Margaret there in her car, looking so peaceful, floated through my mind. I shuddered. "I can't believe you asked me that."

"Sorry. I watch too many of the *CSI* shows. It's fascinating. Are you okay?"

"As okay as anyone can be after finding someone you know dead."

"How'd it happen? They didn't say anything on the news last night."

"I can't say." I finished my coffee to keep myself from adding anything else and tossed the cup in a trash bin.

Laura didn't press me. "Fine. I get it. This is going to sound shallow, but she promised us a Cartier watch to auction off. No way we'll be able to come up with another one."

"How well did you know her?" I asked.

"I saw her at a lot of events. You know, charity balls, silent auctions, military functions." Since Laura's husband was the wing commander for Fitch, they got invited to a lot of functions. "I've been to tea at her house a number of times."

"Did she go with someone to the events? I read her husband has been dead for five years."

Laura stopped in front of the storeroom door and sorted through a set of keys. "There was one man I saw her with a few times."

"Mess dress or tux?" Mess dress was what the air force called the uniform that was formal wear. CJ had worn his mess dress to our wedding and had looked oh, so very handsome.

"Tux."

"So not military."

"Probably not."

"What did he look like?"

"A bit younger than her. Nice looking, but nothing that really made him stand out in a crowd."

"Do you remember his name?"

"No. What is this? An inquisition?"

"Sorry. I blame it on CJ's influence."

"Maybe you should go into law enforcement."

"No thanks. I'd never make it through the academy. I can barely do one pull-up. And garage sales are a lot less scary. So did Margaret and the man seem like a couple?"

Laura pursed her lips. "Not really. But the last time I saw them, they had some sort of argument. He stormed off, and Margaret's face was bright red. A couple of her friends rushed over to her, and they all disappeared for a while."

"When was that?"

"A couple of weeks ago."

"Interesting." Maybe it was interesting enough that I needed to tell someone at the Ellington Police Department.

Laura unlocked the storeroom and threw open the door. The space was dimly lit and musty smelling. We could barely see into the dark corners.

I pointed to the round tables stacked to the left. "Those won't work. They're too hard to stand behind and sell from."

"How about the rectangular ones?" Laura gestured toward the right.

"Yes. Those look perfect." I whipped a tiny tape measure out of my pocket, measured the tables, and jotted the dimensions in the note section of my phone.

"Ladies."

Laura and I jumped, screamed, and turned almost simultaneously.

Chapter 6

James stood there, holding his beret. Because of military regulations, he had to take his beret off inside and wear it when he was outside.

"Whoa. Sorry. I didn't mean to scare you." James was a cop for the security forces on base. He always introduced himself as "James, not Jim," so most people called him Not Jim. I stuck with James because I knew he liked it better. But I'd noticed the few times I'd seen him since he returned from his deployment last October that people were calling him James instead of his jokey nickname. He'd returned a harder man than he'd been when he left last spring. It worried me.

"I saw the door open, and then I saw Sarah's Suburban, so I thought I'd stop and say hi."

"Don't sneak up on people," Laura said, patting her chest.

"I didn't mean to, ma'am. I apologize." James's light brown eyes had a few wrinkles around them. I'd like to think they were laugh lines, but I wondered if they were stress lines instead. His dark brown hair was longer than a lot of military guys wore theirs, just barely within regulations.

"It's okay. You don't have to go all 'ma'am' on me," Laura said.

But really he did, not because of who Laura was, but because of her husband's position and superior rank. I used to get the same treatment, but since CJ was out and we were divorced, I could just be Sarah.

Laura glanced at her phone. "I have to run. Can you finish measuring the space and lock up, Sarah?"

"Sure."

She held up her coffee cup. "Thanks for the coffee. I'm sorry to desert you. I owe you one."

"No you don't," I said to Laura's back. I hated it when I did something for someone and they said "I owe you." I did it because I wanted to, not so someone would owe me something.

I turned to James. He was a bit older than most of his peers, because he had enlisted at twenty-seven, instead of right out of high school, like so many kids did. James and I got along well, and for a while last spring I'd thought he had a crush on me. When CJ had still been active duty and we'd lived on base, James had always swung by when CJ was deployed or TDY, off on temporary duty, to see if I needed anything. "How are you?" I asked.

"I was worried about you. I heard you found Margaret More yesterday."

The base had memorandums of agreements with

the local police departments of the surrounding towns, which meant they helped each other with crimes. But I guessed that bit of information didn't come over official channels, since Ellington wouldn't need base law enforcement for Margaret's case.

"How did you hear?"

James shrugged. "The old gossip mill. You know Fitch. It's like a small town. Word gets around."

It didn't look like James had anything else to say on that subject, and I didn't want to push him. The pre-deployment James I might have, but this James just wasn't as easygoing.

"Have you heard if there's an official cause of death?" he asked.

"Not yet. You probably know as much about that as I do. Maybe more."

We stared at each other for a moment. It felt like something needed to be said, but since I didn't know what, I snapped back to my purpose for being here. "I've got to measure the room so I can start making a map of how many tables I can cram in here for the garage sale."

"Do you want some help?" James asked. That was the pre-deployment James I knew and loved, the one who was warm and helpful.

"Sure. If you have time, it will go a lot faster."

I trotted over to where I'd dropped my purse, and pulled out my industrial-sized tape measure. With James holding one end of the tape measure, we finished up quickly. I added the dimensions to the notes on my phone.

"James to the rescue again," I said when we finished.

James didn't smile at my quip. In fact, he didn't smile as much as he used to. It made me sad.

We locked the place up and exchanged an awkward hug. "Thanks for your help," I told him.

James waited until I was in my car and pulling out of the lot before he took off in his patrol car.

I walked into the lobby of the EPD and approached the window. Two trips in one morning. This time a man sat there. "I need to speak to someone," I said.

"Who?"

"I'm not sure." Maybe I should ask for Pellner. He was better than someone I didn't know very well or one of the state police officers, if they were still around. I drummed my fingers against my leg.

"What's it concerning?"

"Margaret More's death."

"Sarah?"

I turned and CJ stood there. My heart did that push-pull thing it did every time I saw him. One part wanted me to fling myself into his arms, the ones that had cocooned me many times during our marriage. The other, more logical side of me knew it wouldn't be fair to either of us if I did that. I'd left him because I believed he'd cheated on me. He'd let me go without a fight. So here we were, eyeing each other. I wondered if he felt all the same things I did.

I forced a smile. "You're back." *Brilliant, Sarah. State the obvious.*

CJ nodded but didn't return my smile. "I took a red-eye. Why are you here?"

"I need to report something."

"Okay. Come on back."

I trotted down the hall after CJ, his back sturdy, almost rigid. He still walked like he was in the military and might need to throw a salute anytime. He turned into an interview room on the right, instead of taking me farther down the hall to his office.

"Have a seat."

I perched on the edge of the uncomfortable, serviceable chair.

"I'll get someone to take your report."

"CJ, I'd rather—" But he left the room and closed the door before I got the words "tell you" out.

"Okay, then," I said to the mirrored wall. Maybe I should have called Vincenzo. If the state police came in, I'd clam up, call, and wait for him. I just wanted to help, but I didn't want that help to be misconstrued by someone who didn't know me.

Pellner strolled in and straddled the chair opposite me. "What's up?"

Whew. After a rocky start to our relationship last spring, I now felt pretty comfortable with Pellner. Even though I was violating Angelo's "Don't talk to the police without a lawyer" policy, I filled Pellner in on what Laura had told me. He stood when I was finished.

"I'll make sure someone looks into this," he said. With that worry off my shoulders, I trotted down the steps of the police station. My phoned chimed, and I whipped it out. A picture of me in my red winter coat on the steps of the police station popped up. **You look good in red** was printed at the bottom. I jerked my head up and scanned the area. People were going in and out of the library to my right and the town hall to my left. Some kids were out in front of the high school. Maybe Lindsay was one of them. I waved over in that direction, and someone waved back. I crossed my eyes, stuck out my tongue, snapped a selfie, and sent it off to Lindsay.

I let myself into my apartment, happy that Pellner had taken me seriously, but CJ's behavior puzzled me. Although mine probably puzzled him too. I sat on the couch with my computer and found dozens of messages from different people on my garage sale site. I couldn't believe the number of them since yesterday. I took a deep breath and started scrolling through them. Thankfully, the majority of them were just from people who needed things approved so their posts would show up. Those I took care of quickly. I needed to do a better job of staying on top of this.

The next batch of messages was complaints about a cleaning woman, Juanita Smith, who I'd let advertise on my small business Tuesdays. Tuesday was the slowest day for posts, so I allowed people who sold everything from protein shakes to skin-care products to post about their businesses. But I didn't vouch for their businesses. I told the people who complained that they had to contact the cleaning lady. If my small business Tuesdays ended up being a problem, I'd quit doing them.

I made a sandwich and went back through old posts, deleting things that were really old or didn't follow the posted rules. My phone rang. It was CJ.

"I'm sorry I was so short at the station. I had a million things going on."

"It's fine." I could be short myself.

"Are you free for dinner tonight?"

I almost dropped my phone.

"Sarah, are you there?"

"Yes."

"Yes, you're there or yes to dinner?"

"Yes to both."

Chapter 7

"Are you excited?" Carol asked a few hours later. She sat, with her long legs in a yoga-like pose, on a wooden chest I'd converted into a laundry hamper, watching me get ready for my dinner with CJ. We'd met twenty years ago in Monterey, California, when I was only eighteen and was dating CJ. Carol had already married her husband, Brad. They had been stationed in Monterey, as had CJ.

I'd sent her a text earlier, telling her I was going out to dinner with CJ. She'd come over for moral support. Over a glass of wine, we'd hashed out my finding Margaret. Carol empathized because she'd found a man murdered in her shop last fall.

I leaned over the pedestal sink in my bathroom to apply light gray eye shadow. If I took two steps back, my legs would bump my beloved claw-foot tub. "Sort of," I said. "Maybe more nervous than excited."

"Why nervous?"

"Seth spent the night here last night." I didn't look at her when I said it.

Carol almost fell off the hamper. "You slept with Seth *last night,* and now you're having dinner with CJ?"

"That sounds really bad, but it wasn't like that. Seth came over to check on me. He heard I found Margaret and was worried about me."

"And you said, 'Come on in and stay over'?"

"*No.* We were waiting for his shirt to dry and fell asleep. On the couch."

"I don't even think I want to know why his shirt had to dry." But she said it with an impish grin that highlighted her cheekbones and put a sparkle, which I hadn't seen much lately, in her eyes.

I gave up all pretense of trying to do my makeup. "I tripped over my fuzzy pink slipper and tossed wine all over him. His clothes are expensive, so I wanted to rip off his shirt. I mean rinse off his shirt."

Carol snorted. "Rip off is more likely. Are the buttons still intact?"

I couldn't help but laugh. "Yes. We fell asleep on the couch. I woke up around three and went to bed. Alone. When I woke up, he was gone. Nothing happened."

"Does he look as hot with his shirt off as I think he does?"

"Yes. I almost drooled." I put the light gray eye shadow away and searched my makeup bag for a darker shade.

"But you have feelings for him."

I blended some darker gray eye shadow on the

outer corners of my eyelids, going for a smoky look. "I do. He's fun to be around, smart, caring."

"Hot. Don't forget that."

I thought about him standing there without his shirt and laughed. "You'd have to be dead to forget that." That made me think about Margaret and the man Laura had seen her arguing with. I hoped CJ found out who it was and would tell me.

"So you don't feel at all awkward about seeing CJ tonight after what?" Carol looked at her watch. "Having been with Seth just fourteen hours ago or so?"

"Yes. But being with Seth made me feel like I needed to spend some time with CJ. So when he called, it seemed like the best thing to do." I hoped to heck I was right. "Can we change the subject? I need a steady hand to get my eyeliner on right."

Carol looked like she wanted to say something else. "How's the garage sale site going?"

"Okay."

"I thought you loved it."

"It's been great up until recently. It's just the past few weeks. There's been a couple of fights in the comments section about the quality of merchandise being sold."

"That doesn't sound so bad." Carol shifted on the hamper.

"I know. Mostly, I stay out of it, unless I get a lot of complaints in my messages." I lined my upper lid with eyeliner and leaned back to see how it looked. "I've had to ban more people from the site lately."

"Oh, that's not good. How come?"

"It runs the gamut from people repeatedly not following the posted rules to people not meeting for exchanges to people not leaving payments and taking items, anyway." I didn't add that sometimes I got ugly messages when I banned a person. I swiped on my mascara and turned to Carol. "How do I look?"

Carol took in the red wrap sweater, the black pencil skirt, the black tights, and the knee-high boots. "Stunning, Sarah. As pretty as the day we met."

"Yeah, right."

"You could adjust the sweater to show a bit more cleavage." Carol stood and demonstrated.

I looked in the mirror. A bit of my lacy black bra showed. "That's a little too much for me." I adjusted the sweater back to a more modest position.

"You are certainly going all out for your dinner with CJ. He's going to be blown away."

"I hope so." Even though I'd been the one to put the moratorium on seeing each other in place, I wanted him to know what he was missing. "He's been really distant the last couple of times we talked."

"You did tell CJ to leave you alone. Did you expect him to be happy about it?"

"No. But I didn't expect him to act like a block of ice, either. Is he seeing someone? Do you know?"

"Do you want to know?"

I studied myself in the mirror, found a brush, and stroked it through my hair. "Yes."

"He stopped by a few nights ago with a redhead."

"Pale and freckly?"

"Pale and gorgeous."

Hmmm, maybe I should wear my sweater the way Carol suggested. Stop it, I told myself. "And?"

"They weren't there very long. She was *very* flirty. Even with Brad." Carol slid off the hamper. "Brad said I was shooting death rays at both of them."

"It's probably why they didn't stay long."

"Probably. I miss how we all used to be. We had so much fun."

Memories flitted through my mind: volleyball on the beach in Monterey, cable car rides in San Francisco, ski weekends at Tahoe. "It was fun. But life changes."

"It does. Have fun tonight."

Fun. Dinner had been anything but. CJ had picked me up and taken me to our favorite Italian restaurant in Bedford, the town adjoining Ellington to the east. It had seemed like half of the restaurant was filled with people from Ellington and the other half from the base.

"Thanks for the information about Margaret fighting with a man at a party," CJ had said when the waiter set our entrées in front of us.

"Did you find out who it was?"

"Sir. Sarah."

Before I even looked up from my shrimp verdicchio, CJ leaped up. "Not Jim. How are you, man?"

I did look up in time to see the small tightening around James's eyes before he smiled. It was a very fake smile. CJ stuck out his hand, and they shook.

"You don't have to call me sir anymore. I'm a civilian now," CJ said.

James gave a short nod before looking over at me. "How's the pasta?"

"It's good. Are you here with someone? Do you want to join us?" Even though originally I'd wanted to spend time alone with CJ, right now having someone around seemed like a better plan.

"I came to pick up a take-out order. Shrimp verdicchio." James smiled at me. His smile was a real one this time. "You two, have a good evening."

That was the story of our evening. So many people stopped by, we were barely able to talk. There were couples we knew from base, a group we'd once been part of, staff from DiNapoli's—they'd better hope Angelo didn't hear about this, unless he'd sent them to check out the competition—and even Stella, who was there on a date. Most seemed surprised to see us together, some darted looks back and forth between us, and some stayed at their tables, watching and whispering. Evenings like this made me think I should move into Boston, where you had some degree of anonymity.

Finally, when things calmed down, we talked about the weather and a rash of car thefts in Ellington, we complimented the Chianti we'd ordered, and we concentrated on our pasta. My shrimp verdicchio had succulent shrimp, black olives, artichoke hearts, and sundried tomatoes in a wine-butter sauce over a bed of spaghetti. CJ powered through his lasagna and meatballs. I was surprised when CJ agreed to share a tiramisu with me, because at this point it was abundantly clear that he wasn't interested in sharing any other part of my life.

I wondered why we were here as I took a first bite of the tiramisu.

"I wanted to talk to you about your virtual garage sale." CJ fiddled with his fork but didn't dig into the tiramisu. I almost spit mine out. That was the last thing I had expected this dinner to be about.

"Okay," I said. "What do you want to know?"

"It's what *you* need to know. They're dangerous."

I took a small bite of the tiramisu. Either to give myself a moment to think or to keep from stabbing my fork into CJ's hand. I swallowed. "We haven't had any problems." At least any problems that were worth notifying the police about. "They're designed so people know the members in the group."

"How many people are in your group?"

"Three thousand." I'd been amazed by how quickly the group had grown.

"And you know every single one of them?"

I tightened my hand around the fork and decided to set it down. I clasped my hands together. "Not personally. But each person is recommended by someone else that's in the group. I check out their profiles to make sure they're a real person before adding them."

"It's very naive to think someone can't fake a profile."

"I get that. But if there's a problem with someone, I ban them from the group." How odd that CJ would bring this up now, after I'd been a bit worried about the complaints about the cleaning lady.

"It's not the only issue. I've heard that people go to a stranger's house to pick up and drop stuff off. It seems . . . foolish."

Now I wished I'd driven over here myself, because I'd be excusing myself and leaving, minus the excusing part. "I encourage people to meet at a neutral place, like Dunkin' Donuts. That isn't practical if you're selling a couch. I ask people not to go to someone's house alone. And not to be home alone when someone comes to pick something up during any transaction."

"Look at the things that have happened to people on national sites."

"That's why this is safer. It's smaller groups of people who have some connection. A lot of police departments are letting people use their lobbies to make exchanges. Maybe you should consider that."

"I'll look into it."

"Have you heard something specific about my site?"

"No. But it's my responsibility as chief to make sure the townsfolk are safe."

"Noted. Do you also always take the townsfolk out to dinner to do so?"

CJ didn't answer.

I stood and tossed some cash down on the table to cover my share of the bill. "Please take me home."

Chapter 8

When I woke Monday morning, I felt like I'd spent half the night thinking about Margaret and the other half about the picture of me looking into her car. If the picture taker was the murderer, I might be lucky to be alive, if not well that was just plain creepy. No matter how many times I turned it over in my head, nothing made the situation okay.

On the ride home last night CJ had told me they found the man Margaret had been arguing with at the party Laura had attended. It was one of Margaret's brothers, although he wouldn't say which one, and the argument didn't seem to have anything to do with Margaret's death. After that he hadn't answered any of my other questions about the investigation. The rest of the drive home last night had been chillier than the weather, and our good-byes had had a finality to them, which had left me shaken.

I made myself a strong cup of coffee, read the newspaper, and watched the morning news. None of that provided me any insights into what had happened to Margaret or why. CJ had been quoted as saying it was an ongoing investigation. Since I didn't have anything scheduled until this afternoon when Juanita Smith was picking up Pez dispensers I'd sold through the garage sale site for a client, I decided to start fixing and pricing some of the things I planned to sell at the February Blues garage sale. After New England's Largest Yard Sale was such a success, Laura had asked me to run the base event. I planned to have my own table, and since last fall I had been squirreling away stuff I bought, like the things from the church rummage sale Saturday, or items I found on the curb.

Maybe while I worked a next move would come to me to find out new information on Margaret. I pulled out a box of dishes, a small end table, the lamp from yesterday, and a box of assorted stuff. I'd start with these things. I might as well make the lamp repair first. I grabbed a three-way socket kit from under the kitchen sink and after some fiddling had the lamp working again. The blue and white porcelain lamp would look great in my bedroom, but I resisted the urge to put it in there.

The end table needed a good dusting and some screws tightened. When I finished with it, I set it by my couch. It fit perfectly. That wasn't good, because now I'd have to decide if I wanted to keep it for myself or sell it, like I'd originally planned. The sale wasn't until a week from Friday, so I didn't have to decide right now. I turned to the box of dishes, which I'd found on someone's curb. They looked like they were from the fifties, with their atomic-themed starburst pattern. I turned one of the plates over. The mark indicated they were hand painted in France, and then there were some words written in French. I wondered if they were worth anything. You never knew what goodies people just threw away. I'd have to look online for more information about them before I priced them.

I filled the kitchen sink with warm, sudsy water and started washing the dishes. I'd promised myself when CJ and I divorced, and I moved from a large house on Fitch to this small apartment, that I'd have a "something in, something out" policy. I set the clean dishes on a towel on the counter. After I dried them, I peeked into my already overcrowded cupboards. Maybe with a little rearranging . . . I shook my head and managed to put them back in the box, instead of in my cupboard.

Fixing and pricing took longer than I'd thought it would, but at 3:15 p.m. I was waiting impatiently for Juanita Smith, the cleaning lady I'd gotten complaints about, to show up. The impatience seemed to be more because of my mood after my evening with CJ and that I hadn't come up with any further ideas about Margaret's death.

Juanita was coming to buy a box full of Pez dispensers I'd listed for a new client on the garage sale site. Last week the client had contacted me, saying she'd decided to sell her collection of Pez dispensers. Most of them had been lumped together in one lot, but we'd kept out a few that had a bit more value. Juanita had snapped them all up. I'd been surprised by the number of people who were interested, and I'd realized I should have sold them in smaller lots, which would have meant more money for my client and me.

The wind gusted hard enough to rattle the windows. But other than that, the house was quiet. The apartment next to mine was empty. Stella was teaching, and the Callahans, who lived across from Stella, were in Florida for the winter. I guessed CJ's lecture had spooked me a bit, because after I'd gotten home last night, I'd tried to change the Pez exchange meeting place to Dunkin' Donuts. But since I hadn't heard from the woman, I waited for her here. The box of Pez sat next to the door. CJ's baseball bat now leaned against the wall on the other side of the door, just in case, not that I planned on letting her in.

I put on some music and scrubbed the claw-foot tub while I waited. If she didn't show up, I'd give her one warning. If she did it again to me or any other member, I'd ban her from the site. Sometimes I felt more like a kindergarten teacher trying to control a class full of rowdies than the admin of a Web site. The tub sparkled by the time I finally heard a knock on the door.

I opened the door and smiled at the woman standing in front of me. She had large dark eyes and a bit of an overbite. Her brown hair was pulled back in a ponytail. Before I had a chance to say a word, she was shoved into me. I stumbled back. A man in a black ski mask, sunglasses covering his eyes, shoved her again. She fell. Her head smacked against my hardwood floor. She didn't move.

I grabbed the baseball bat. The man wrenched it from my hands and tossed it aside. He pulled another mask out of his coat pocket and yanked it over my head. Backward, so I couldn't see a thing. He spun me around and propelled me across the apartment. His hand settled between my shoulder blades and he pushed me hard. I staggered forward until my head rammed into a wall. A door slammed behind me.

Chapter 9

I snatched the ski mask off and realized I was in my bathroom. Alone. Only a thin line of light showed under the door. Three giant steps got me across the bathroom. I found the light switch and flipped it on. Instead of trying to get out, I dragged the chest I used as a laundry basket across the door. I slid to the floor and braced my back against the chest. I snatched my phone out of my pocket, then dialed 911.

When I heard CJ yell my name ten minutes later, I thanked the 911 dispatcher and hung up. "In here," I called. "Give me a minute."

CJ tried to open the door, but he was stopped cold by the chest.

"Just a minute. I blocked myself in."

"Good move, Sarah," he said through the door.

I shoved the chest. It was hard to move, unlike in my panic, when it had slid so easily. After some pushing, I inched it out of the way. CJ threw the door open. He looked me up and down before reaching over and pulling me into his arms. I latched on, burying my head in his chest. His heart pounded, like he'd run all the way over here from the station.

"Did you catch him?" I asked.

I felt CJ shake his head. "He was gone."

"What about Juanita? Is she okay?"

"The EMTs are with her."

"Hey, Chuck? Whoa. Sorry, ah, Chief," Pellner said at the door of the bathroom.

Pellner seemed to be CJ's go-to guy at the station. CJ pulled away from me. I wanted to reach out and grab him back. I braced myself on the sink instead.

"It's no problem, Pellner."

Yep, no problem here. Even though I hated it when people called CJ Chuck. Charles James Hooker would never be Chuck to me.

"What did you need?" CJ asked Pellner.

"The EMTs want to know if Sarah needs them," he said.

They both turned and looked at me.

"We'd better have them take you to Leahy to look at that bump on your forehead," CJ said.

I whipped around and looked in the mirror. A small red bump rose over my right eye, probably from when I'd rammed the wall. "It's fine. I'm not going to the hospital."

"You might have a concussion or internal bleeding." CJ planted his hands on his hips.

I touched the bump gingerly. A pain seared through my head that made my eyes water.

"You winced," CJ said.

"I'll just have the EMTs take a quick look before they leave."

I pushed by CJ and went into the living room. A few officers stood around, chatting in low tones. Juanita sat on my couch, with EMTs on either side of her. She looked pale but otherwise okay. It seemed she, too, was refusing to go to the hospital.

"I'm so sorry," I told Juanita.

"I'm the one who's sorry," she said. "I don't know where he came from. Like thin air. I didn't hear him on the stairs behind me."

CJ held up a hand to stop her from talking. He grasped my arm and led me toward my bedroom. I smiled at Juanita as I left the living room. Her brown eyes looked tired and sad.

"What? Why'd you bring me in here?" I asked when we reached my bedroom. "I want to talk to Juanita."

"We need to take her statement. Check her out."

"You think she had something to do with this?" I shook my head and winced again. It felt like a spring thunderstorm had taken over my brain. "She was attacked, too." I replayed the assault over in my mind. It made me shiver. I wanted to pull the throw off my bed and wrap it around me, but I didn't want to look like a victim.

CJ picked up the throw and settled it around my shoulders, as if he'd read my mind or maybe it was the shivering. "I'll be right back." He returned with one of the two female EMTs. "Check her out," CJ said. "Talk her into a quick trip to the hospital." He stepped out of the room.

"CJ, wait."

Instead of answering me, he closed the door. The man could be completely frustrating.

The EMT sat down next to me, and she started a concussion examination. She talked in a calm, soothing voice as she ran through questions and checked me out. She told me what to watch for. "You don't have signs of a concussion, but you really should go to your doctor. Your blood pressure is slightly elevated."

"I'm fine. My blood pressure probably has more to do with my ex than anything else." I flicked my head toward the door and regretted it as another bolt shot around in my head.

As the EMT was leaving the room, CJ and Pellner walked in.

"Pellner will take your official statement," CJ told me. "We can do it here or down at the station, wherever you feel more comfortable."

"Here, please," I said.

CJ left the room and closed the door behind him again.

While my bedroom wasn't that big, it wasn't uncomfortable. I gestured toward the only chair. Pellner eyed it.

"It's sturdier than it looks," I said.

I had found it on the side of the road last fall and had re-covered the seat with a delicate blue-and-white toile fabric that complemented my blue-and-white comforter. Airy white curtains hung at the single window, which overlooked the town common and the tall white Congregational church. The bare branches of the trees waved frantically in the wind, and the sounds of the church bells seemed more like clangs than rings today.

"You don't want me to hear what Juanita's saying, do you?" I asked. "Do you think one of us is lying?"

Pellner sat on the chair and pulled out a note-book. I perched on the end of the bed.

"How do you know Juanita?" Pellner ran a hand through his military-short dark hair.

It was obvious Pellner wasn't going to answer any of my questions, so I gave up. "She's a member of the virtual garage sale site I run."

"So you don't know her personally?"

"I do now."

Pellner frowned at me. "Walk me through what happened, starting with why she was here today."

I scooted back on the bed and leaned back against the headboard, not wanting to admit how much my head hurt or how scared I felt. I briefly described the sale of the Pez.

"Do you have a description of your attacker?"

"He wore a ski mask and sunglasses. So none of his face showed. Maybe a black turtleneck and jeans. Gloves on his hands. It was all a blur."

CJ opened the door. "Juanita left. You two can come back out."

Pellner looked relieved. I dropped the throw. I slipped on a black cardigan as we walked back out into the living room.

My front door was open, and Juanita stood on

the landing, talking to one of the officers. She was tiny, maybe five-two, but she looked strong.

Juanita gestured back toward the box of Pez, which had been knocked over at some point. Pez dispensers were scattered across the floor. "I guess I can't take these right now?" she asked.

The officer shook his head.

"Okay," she said. She mouthed, "I'm sorry," to me and left.

"So the sale was all arranged," Pellner said. "What happened when she showed up?" Pellner jerked his head toward where Juanita had just been.

"I opened the door. Juanita stood there. I wasn't going to let her in," I said. I glanced at CJ as I said this, my voice a bit more defensive than I meant it to be. I gestured to the box the Pez had been in by the door. "I left the box right by the door so I could just hand it to her. The guy forced his way in, knocking Juanita out in the process." I emphasized the word *knocking* a little more than normal. But I had to admit that doubts about Juanita's innocence in this whole episode had already crept into my brain. I tried to remember who'd recommended Juanita join the group. Nothing came to me. I'd have to see if I could track the information down on the virtual garage sale site later.

"Did he have a baseball bat with him?" Pellner asked. He pointed to the bat on the floor over by my grandmother's oak rocking chair.

I felt my face warm. "No. I stuck it behind the door for protection."

CJ looked at the wooden bat. "Is that my bat?"

I nodded. "I just found it in a box in the storage space under the eaves." After our divorce last year I'd kept thinking we'd finally sorted out who had whose stuff. But then something like the baseball bat would turn up and have to be returned.

I filled them in on the rest of what I knew. Pellner took notes. CJ listened to the whole thing, careful to stay in the middle of the room so he didn't whack his head on the slanted part of the ceiling. I kept waiting for CJ to lecture me or tell me, "I told you so." He didn't. But he had to be thinking it.

I looked at CJ. "Maybe you should check the apartment next door. It's still empty, as far as I know. Maybe the guy hid in there and popped out when Juanita showed up. But why would he do that?"

CJ and Pellner exchanged glances but didn't answer.

"Pellner, will you go check it out?" CJ asked.

Pellner disappeared through my front door.

"You need to see if anything is missing," CJ said to me.

I looked around the living room. Nothing seemed to be out of place, but everything seemed a bit messier than normal.

Pellner came back in. "It's locked. But the lock is flimsy. Wouldn't take much to open it."

I wondered if he had.

I went into the kitchen with CJ and Pellner, a space where three was definitely a crowd. My computer wasn't on the small kitchen table and the vintage tablecloth was askew. "My computer's gone. Please tell me someone moved it."

"No one moved it," CJ said.

I wanted to stomp my foot or kick something or someone, like the jerk who'd taken my computer. I needed it for work. I could use my phone for lots of it, but it was easier to use the computer. Plus, I had files I kept of people who had complained or broken the rules. And I had tons of pictures stored on it. I wondered when I'd last backed the thing up. Maybe everything was accessible instead of gone.

"Is there anything on it that someone would want it for?" CJ asked.

"Nothing I can think of. It's more the inconvenience and expense of replacing it if you guys don't find it."

"Your renters' insurance should cover it," Pellner said.

My nonexistent renters' insurance. But I didn't want to admit that in front of CJ. "The deductible is probably more than the computer." I walked into my bedroom, CJ and Pellner in tow. I picked up my purse and looked through it. "My credit cards are all here. I don't think I had any cash, or at least not much. Why wouldn't he grab my credit cards?"

"I don't know. You keep saying 'he.' Are you sure it was a man?"

I thought for a minute, going back over what had happened. "I just assumed it was, but I don't know that for sure." I opened the top drawer of my dresser.

The small amount of cash I kept there was missing. There was an empty space in the back corner of the drawer and it left an empty place in my heart. "I had about forty dollars in cash in the drawer. It's gone."

"Anything else, Sarah?" CJ asked.

I looked him in the eye. "My wedding ring."

Chapter 10

Pellner looked back and forth between CJ and me then left the room in a hurry. Maybe the fact that my wedding ring was gone was a sign my relationship with CJ was over. CJ was only here because I was one of the townsfolk he had to protect. I moved to follow Pellner into the living room.

"Sarah, wait," CJ said. "I'm sorry."

"Because I'm one of the townsfolk or because of us?" I asked. The two steps separating us had never felt farther.

"Chief?" Pellner called from the living room.

CJ glanced toward the door and then back at me before he walked out of the room.

I pulled my cardigan tighter around me and followed him.

"Can you find someplace to go for a couple of hours?" CJ asked me. "This is still a crime scene."

"You've got to be kidding me," I said. "Where should I go?" I thought about Seth, but he was probably at work. Why did I think of Seth before friends like Carol or Laura?

"You can come to my place." Stella stood in the doorway. Her dark green eyes stood out against her paler than usual olive skin. "And then you can explain what's going on."

"I'll explain now, because they"—I cocked my thumb at CJ and Pellner—"want to go through the empty apartment."

"Yes, with your permission, Stella, we'd like to take a look around," Pellner said.

Pellner and Stella had known each other since high school. They'd even dated at one point, but Stella hadn't wanted to settle down as Mrs. Scott Pellner and had pursued an opera career instead. Her own demons had eventually chased her back here to Ellington.

"Can I at least grab my purse?" I asked CJ after Stella led Pellner over to the empty unit.

CJ nodded and followed me into my bedroom. I was beginning to feel like a suspect. CJ leaned against the doorjamb, arms folded, watching me. He didn't move when I picked up my purse. Now for the lecture. I waited. But instead of a lecture, he reached out and trailed a finger down my cheek.

"I'm sorry," he said. Then he turned and left.

Sorry for what? I wondered.

I ended up going to the doctor. The bump on the head and the headache scared me enough that I let Stella drive me over. Living alone made me wonder what would happen if I keeled over in the middle of the night. How long would it be before anyone noticed I was missing? One thorough exam, a few hours, and a scan or two later, I walked out with a clean bill of health. Then we went to a big-box store, and I bought a new computer.

An hour later Stella and I sat on her couch, each with a glass of wine, and with the remnants of a big salad Stella had thrown together on the coffee table.

"Did Pellner find anything interesting in the empty apartment?" I asked.

"Not unless you find dust bunnies interesting. I need to find a new tenant."

"So it didn't look like anyone had been in there?"

"I guess not. Wouldn't you have heard someone? Not that I don't love this place, but the walls aren't that well insulated."

"I had the music up, and I might have been singing . . . just a little." We grinned at each other. Stella liked to drag me to karaoke with her at an Irish pub and restaurant called Gillganins. But my voice, while usually on key, was no match to hers. My smile changed to a frown.

"What?" Stella asked.

"I wonder if the attack today had anything to do with Margaret's death."

"Why would you think that?"

I shrugged. "I don't really have a reason. Just a thought." I stood and stretched. "I'm tired. I think I'll head up to bed."

"I'll walk you up," Stella said.

When we got upstairs we decided to go through

the empty apartment just to double-check. All the windows were locked, and no one leaped out of the closets at us. Stella helped me clean up my apartment, too. We put all the Pez dispensers back in the box and cleaned off the fingerprint powder.

"Do you want me to stay?" Stella asked.

"No, but thanks. I'll be fine." I think I even sounded like it might be true.

Tuesday afternoon I trudged up the stairs after another meeting with Laura about the February Blues garage sale. She'd asked about the bump on my head, which now was little enough that it was more like a pimple than a bump. But my head still ached. The thought of stretching out on my couch kept me moving up the stairs. I was almost to the top when a man came out of the apartment next to mine, dressed in jeans, a leather jacket, sunglasses, and a Red Sox baseball cap. I opened my mouth to scream and turned to run.

"Hey, you must be Sarah," he said. "Stella told me all about you."

I clamped my mouth closed but went down two steps, in case I needed to bolt.

He put his hands up like he was surrendering, but I still didn't trust him. "I take it Stella didn't tell you I'd be staying here a few days. She said she'd send you a text."

I slipped my phone out of my pocket. I did have a text from Stella. Mike Titone's moving in for a few days. I'd heard that name before. She'd sent a picture.

I looked from the picture to the guy and back again. It seemed to be the same guy. I snapped my head up. Mike Titone was the name of the Mob guy Vincenzo had represented, but that guy lived in Boston. Maybe it was a common name in this area. Below the front door banged open. Two guys started carrying a couple of large suitcases up the stairs.

"Excuse us, lady," the one closest to me said.

Now my only choice was to go up the stairs. I edged as far away from Mike as I could and fished in my purse for the keys to my apartment without taking my eyes off him or the movers. My hand finally landed on them, so I quickly unlocked my door and slipped in.

"Nice ta meet cha," Mike called as I shut the door.

I dropped my purse on the trunk. I Googled Mike Titone, and a huge list of articles popped up. Vincenzo represented Mike "the Big Cheese" Titone when he'd been charged with racketeering. Mike got off on all counts and went back to running his cheese shop in Boston's North End and doing whatever else he did out of said shop. What in the world was he doing here, and for just a few days? I could hear furniture being moved around through my thin walls and a bit of swearing as someone occasionally bumped something against the wall.

I dialed Stella and paced as the phone rang.

"You let a mobster move in next door to me," I said when Stella answered.

"What are you talking about?"

"Mike 'the Big Cheese' Titone. Vincenzo got him off racketeering charges."

"Hmmm. I'm sure he's fine. Vincenzo asked me to do him a favor and let Mike move in for a few days. That's what we do here. Help each other out."

I was all for being a good neighbor, but this carried it a bit too far. "I Googled him. It says he killed a man with a hundred-pound provolone. That if you're on his bad side, he leaves a slice of cheese on your doorstep as a warning."

"Don't believe everything you Google. Besides, it will be nice to have someone around after what happened to you yesterday."

"It's your building," I said and hung up. I felt a bit bad, because Stella and I hadn't had a cross word since we became friends last spring. Having someone around might be nice, but I wasn't sure this was the someone I wanted it to be.

A knock on the door interrupted my thoughts. I answered, and Mike stood there, holding a large cellophane-wrapped gift basket full of cheese and wine. Two big, burly guys stood behind him. He thrust the basket into my arms.

"This is for any inconvenience the presence of me and my family might cause," he said.

I felt a little color drain from my face when he said *family*.

Mike laughed. "Not that kind of family. These are my two brothers. They'll be around a lot."

Then I noticed the resemblance, the full heads of dark hair; the startling blue eyes, all the same shade; the variations of the same build, broad shoulders, thick chests, and long legs. The tallest brother, who stood in the back, obviously lifted weights more than the other two, as his neck muscles bulged and his black T-shirt strained around his biceps. He had a thick dark mustache that made me think of Tom Selleck.

"Thank you," I finally managed to say. "It wasn't necessary." I wondered if accepting a basket meant I owed them something. "Let me know if you need anything."

"Will do," Mike said. "I stuck my card in the basket with my cell phone number on the back. Call if we get too noisy. These two"—he jerked his head toward his brothers—"can be rambunctious."

The biggest brother winked at me as they turned almost in unison to go.

I took the basket into the kitchen and set it on my small kitchen table. The vintage tablecloth on my table made me think of Margaret More. I unwrapped the cellophane and put the ten blocks of various cheeses in my almost empty refrigerator. I took the Brie back out and set it on the counter. The basket was full of crackers, olives, dry salami, and a couple bottles of wine. I'd have a feast tonight. I called Stella back and asked her to come up and share the feast.

Stella showed up at seven. I heard her talking to someone in the hall and popped my head out the door. The biggest of the three brothers sat on a folding chair outside the door, working on the *Boston Globe* crossword. I waved and pulled Stella into the apartment.

"What the heck is going on with them?" I asked her, jerking my head toward the other apartment.

"I don't even get a glass of wine first?" she asked.

"Ugh. Sorry. I'm not sure what's wrong with me. I'm sorry I hung up on you."

"You've had a stressful few days."

"It's no excuse."

Stella followed me into the kitchen. I opened a bottle of wine, and she poured while I arranged part of the contents of the basket along with plates on a tray. We carried it all out to my living room and put it on the trunk before settling on the couch. We filled our plates.

"This Brie is amazing," I said. "But I'm still a little surprised that the Big Cheese is my neighbor."

"Vincenzo called me up yesterday and asked if a friend of his could stay in my empty apartment."

"He didn't say why or who?"

"Not at first, but I wore him down. I knew he wouldn't stash someone unsafe in our building."

"I sense a *but* somewhere in what you aren't saying."

"After we talked earlier, I called Vincenzo to ask him what was up." Stella put some Gouda on a cracker and stuffed it in her mouth.

"Either you're really hungry or I'm not going to like what you have to say." I popped an olive stuffed with blue cheese in my mouth and waited for Stella to continue as I chewed.

"Someone tried to kill Mike two days ago."

I almost choked on the olive. "And it's safe for him to be here?" I asked once I'd managed to swallow.

"They've taken precautions. Mike and his two

brothers booked tickets to Miami. Their sister lives there. They went to the airport and then slipped back out."

"They could have been followed out here."

"They weren't. None of them brought their normal cell phones. One of their other brothers is driving down to Miami with the phones and will turn them on once he gets down there."

"Living in Ellington is certainly different than I imagined."

Stella laughed. "Ain't that the truth."

"How'd someone try to kill him?"

"I guess Mike goes jogging at the same park every day, at the same time."

"That doesn't sound smart."

"He didn't have any reason to think someone had it in for him."

This whole conversation seemed unreal. I couldn't believe we were sitting here, talking about a mobster who had almost been killed.

"He runs around some heated track. There was an ultimate Frisbee game going on. He paid no attention, because they're always out there playing."

"Ultimate Frisbee in February?"

Stella shrugged. "Someone threw a disk edged with razor blades at him. But he bent to tie his shoe just then, and it embedded in a tree, right where his head would have been."

"Oh, good heavens. It doesn't even sound believable. Are you sure he didn't make the whole thing up?"

"According to Vincenzo, Mike doesn't like to leave the North End unless he has to."

"Why hasn't it been in the papers? Trust me, I looked him up today."

"He didn't report it. The disk was removed, and the players are being looked into. Although it could have been some other random person at the track. It's a popular place."

We ate in silence for a while.

"How was your date the other night?" I asked.

Stella blushed. "He's coming over in an hour."

"A second date? I thought you had a strict policy against that recently." Stella and man troubles seemed to go hand in hand. "Are you going to tell him about your new tenant?"

"Not if I don't have to. Vincenzo and Mike assured me this was just for a couple of days."

"Good luck with that," I said.

We moved on to other topics as we ate and drank the wine. I walked Stella to the door. I peeked around the corner. The big brother had moved on to reading *The Pillars of the Earth* by Ken Follett. He looked up and winked. I blushed and hustled back into my apartment. In the past few days I had found Margaret dead, had been attacked in my own home, and now I had mobsters hiding out next door. My life seemed like it had turned into some crazy sitcom, and I only hoped I'd be the one with the last laugh.

Chapter 11

After spending Wednesday morning with a potential spring garage sale client, I walked over to DiNapoli's for a late lunch. It had warmed back into the forties, and the snow had all melted. I'd slept amazingly well, considering the guys next door, or maybe because of them. Margaret's wake was tonight, and I wanted to hear the scuttlebutt before the big event. Rosalie stood behind the counter, which took up half the room. Behind her was the open kitchen. I could see Angelo cooking chicken on a broad grill. To my right was a mismatched assortment of tables and chairs. Most were full. All of it could be seen from the kitchen, not because Angelo wanted people to admire his skills as a chef—which were incredible—but so he could see and hear what was going on.

Rosalie studied me with her warm brown eyes. "You need to have the special today."

I looked at the handwritten board but didn't see anything listed as a special.

"We don't have a special," Angelo yelled from the back without turning around. I didn't know how he'd even heard what Rosalie said.

"It's Sarah, Angelo."

Angelo whipped around, put his fingers to his lips, and kissed them.

Rosalie handed me a Coke. "Your special will be out in a few minutes." I took my drink and turned.

The woman behind me said, "I'll have the special, too. What is it exactly?"

"I'm sorry, but we just ran out. Maybe next time. But the Greek salad with pita is excellent or the eggplant Parm sandwich."

I suppressed a laugh and wondered what my special would be. But I assumed that whatever it was, it would be delicious. I sat down at the only empty table. I'd waited until 1:30 p.m. to eat because I was hoping the lunch crowd would have cleared out and Rosalie and Angelo would have time to talk. Rosalie brought over a large bowl of mussels in a garlicky broth, with a big basket of French bread for dipping. Since no one was waiting to order, she sat down with me.

I dug a mussel from its shell and dragged it through the broth. It was tender with just a bit of tang from the garlic. "What have you heard about Margaret? Any word about who might have done this?" I asked after I swallowed.

Rosalie shook her head, her brown hair fluffing around her face. "I haven't heard much talk at all."

"Why?" I hadn't expected to hear that.

"We've been in Cambridge almost nonstop. Angelo's uncle Stefano's been sick. I just haven't had time to catch up on the news."

"I'm sorry to hear that." I'd met Stefano last fall, when Carol was a murder suspect. "Who's been keeping the restaurant open?"

"Angelo's doing most of the cooking in advance. Lois and Ryan have been pitching in with everything else. They're a godsend." Lois and Ryan were two longtime employees.

"Are you going to the wake tonight?" I asked, dipping bread in the broth.

"Yes. Angelo and I are closing early. Do you want to come with us?"

"That would be wonderful. I'll walk back over. What time?"

"We'll close at seven." Someone walked in, so Rosalie patted my hand and went back to work.

I ate the rest of my meal and chatted with Lois and Ryan. Maybe I'd find something out tonight. The wake would surely be packed with people ready to talk about Margaret and how they knew her. If small towns had saints, Margaret would be the saint of Ellington.

At seven I walked over to DiNapoli's, dressed in my favorite black boots and a black, long-sleeved dress that fell just above the knee. Black tights helped keep my legs somewhat warm on my walk over, and my red coat added a splash of color. The DiNapolis were waiting inside, drinking a glass of wine. They offered me one, and we settled at one of the tables.

"So do you think the whole town will turn out?" I asked.

"More like half the state," Angelo said. He ran a hand over the top of his balding head. A fringe of graying hair clung to the sides and the back. But he was still a handsome man, and I could see why Rosalie had fallen for him.

"Really? Why?" I asked.

"She came from a moneyed family with a compound on Nantucket," Rosalie said.

"I read that online. So I guess she knows lots of people," I mused.

"Martha's Vineyard wasn't good enough for the Mores," Angelo said.

I looked back and forth between them. I'd been to Martha's Vineyard once, for a long weekend with CJ before the divorce. "What's the difference?"

Angelo leaned forward. "There's a saying that the millionaires live on the Vineyard, but the billionaires live on Nantucket. She acted like she was of the billionaire type."

"She wasn't?" I asked.

"She had plenty of money," Rosalie said. She patted Angelo's arm. "You shouldn't speak ill of the dead."

"How'd the family end up out here, then?" I asked.

"It's more about why," Angelo said. "Here they get to rule the roost. On Nantucket they were wealthy among the wealthy."

"It seems like from the price and the size of houses, there's lots of wealth around here, too," I said.

Angelo opened his mouth, but Rosalie jumped in. "There's plenty of money here. But look at the time. We need to go."

Angelo managed to find a parking spot in the crowded lot of the funeral home when someone pulled out. The line for the viewing wended its way around the lobby before getting to the actual room where Margaret rested. I hoped it was a closed casket, but I could tell when we inched into the room that it wasn't. Voices were low, as were the lights, and people shuffled by in an orderly manner. Occasionally, some dignitary or other was escorted past the line and right up front. All of them would cross themselves, then turn to the long line of family members to shake hands and commiserate.

I recognized one senator and the mayor of Boston, but not the others. I could see some of the local town officials chafing as they had to wait with the rest of us. My heart pounded a little as we approached the casket. But Margaret looked way better than she had the last time I'd seen her in the car. Really, she looked like she could jump up at any minute and start organizing some event.

I started down the receiving line, following Rosalie and Angelo, who knew everyone. I shook hands and murmured my condolences until one woman pulled me into a big hug. She clasped me to her and whispered in my ear, "You have your nerve showing up here." Then she released me and turned to the next person. It happened so quickly, I wondered if I'd heard her correctly as I continued down the line.

A guy about my age stood at the end of the line. "Join us at Gillganins. We'll continue to celebrate Margaret's life there."

Some people milled around, chatting, but Angelo was ready to leave. A few minutes later I sank into the black leather seat of the DiNapoli's Escalade.

"Are you okay, Sarah?" Rosalie asked after we'd driven a couple of blocks down Great Road.

"Something odd happened. A woman hugged me, but she said I had my nerve showing up there."

Angelo and Rosalie exchanged a glance so quickly, I almost missed it.

"I wouldn't worry about it. People get emotional at these things," Angelo said.

I might have bought it if it hadn't been for the glance. I wondered what they knew that I didn't. "Are you two going to Gillganins?"

"We have to get up early to open the restaurant. What about you?" Angelo asked.

"I'm not sure."

The DiNapolis dropped me off at my apartment. I waved good-bye and noticed that Stella's car was gone. Maybe she was at the wake. Even if she wasn't, if I wanted to find out more about Margaret and who might have killed her, this was my opportunity. I also wanted to talk to the woman who had said I had my nerve showing up at the viewing. What could that have been about?

Chapter 12

The parking lot at Gillganins was jammed. I didn't see Stella's car, but that didn't mean it wasn't there. I parked off to the side, near a Dumpster. As I walked into Gillganins, my phone chimed. It was a picture of my backside. The message said, **Sexy boots!** I didn't bother to turn to see who was behind me. I ran as fast as my sexy boots would take me. It was dark, and amazingly quiet out here. I trotted into the bar and ran into Kathy Brasheler, who was coming out. Her husband was retired air force, and they lived in Bedford.

"Are you okay?" she asked. She looked over my shoulder. "Did something scare you?"

"Fine. Just cold. How are you?" I asked. I jammed my hands into my coat pockets so she wouldn't see them shaking.

She said, "Good, except for a headache from the noise in there." She pointed back toward the bar.

It sounded like an Irish jig was playing. Hands clapped in time, and there was raucous laughter. "If I didn't have to volunteer tomorrow, I'd stay."

"Are you still volunteering at Orchard House?" Louisa May Alcott wrote *Little Women* and many other books while living there.

"I am." We heard another burst of laughter. "You'd think everyone thought Margaret could still do them a favor. Or maybe they're relieved because they don't owe her one." Before I could ask her what she meant by that, a car horn tooted behind me. "There's my husband. Have fun."

After hanging my coat up on a rack, I plunged into the crowd, edged around a group of people, and then made my way to the bar. It was five deep, but I managed to wiggle my way through and land right in front of a bartender.

"I'll have a gin and tonic, extra lime," I said.

"Add her to my tab." *Seth*. I turned, and he was right beside me, one elbow leaning on the bar, a cosmo set in front of him. His comment to the bartender was an exact repeat of the first words he'd said to me the night we met. I couldn't believe he remembered them and that he had that same cocky grin.

"It's an open bar," the bartender said.

"It's not necessary. I can pay for my own drinks," I told the bartender, saying the first words I'd ever spoken to Seth. I smiled in spite of myself and the scare I'd just had.

The bartender shook his head. "It's an *open bar*. No money required." He made my gin and tonic and handed it to me. I took a healthy swig.

"What is someone like you doing alone in a place like this?" Seth asked. He managed to look sincere as he spoke, but a little gleam in his eye gave him away.

I turned to face him. His white dress shirt, open at the collar, strained across his muscular chest and forearms. It made me think of the other night, when I'd seen him without his shirt. Warmth spread through me. It wasn't because of the gin, but because Seth had remembered our conversation from the night we met. It didn't seem like something most men would do. Then again, Seth was no ordinary guy.

"Really? That's the best you can do?" I asked him. "That's your opening line?" I was amazed I remembered our conversation so clearly. But it had been a monumental evening for me, the first time I'd been out alone after CJ and I separated. Seth had been there celebrating his appointment to fill in for the ailing district attorney.

"You got something better?" he asked.

"Of course," I said, repeating our first conversation, too.

"So let's hear it."

"What?" I took another sip of my drink to hide my smile.

"Your line. You said you had something better. I

want to hear it." He grinned again, which highlighted his sturdy jaw.

"What are you doing for Patriots' Day?" We smiled at each other. My heart felt like it was melting. CJ had been so distant lately, and Seth so lovely. *Why have I been having such a hard time deciding who I want to have a relationship with?* The choice seemed more obvious every minute.

Seth leaned in close. His spicy aftershave wafted off his warm skin. I breathed it in, thinking once again that every man in America should be mandated to wear this stuff. "You think that's a better line?" he asked.

I smiled. "And you shouldn't make assumptions that I'm alone. My friends might be in the back." I waved a hand toward a corner of the bar.

Seth glanced over his shoulder. A bunch of pimpled adolescents were playing video games. The first time it had been bikers playing pool. "You're going with those guys are your friends?"

"They could be." At this point on the first night we'd met, his buddies had come and pulled him away from me, but tonight would be different.

"Seth," a pouty voice said. I turned to see a tall, slender woman dressed in a fitted black suit standing next to us. "Did you get my cosmo?"

That explained Seth's drink. I should have realized it wasn't for him. My melting heart shored up a bit. Of course he wasn't alone. Why would he be? And here I had thought my choice seemed so clear.

Seth handed her the drink, and she linked her arm through his. "This is Nichole More. Margaret's granddaughter."

I said hello and realized I'd seen her in pictures with Seth over the past few months. I tried to remember what the society page had said about her. I think she was a lawyer, too, but unlike Seth, she was a defense attorney. They must have some interesting discussions. Her suit looked expensive, her hair glistened even in the dim light, and she stood about two inches taller than Seth. She looked like a model, even though I knew she wasn't one.

"You'll have to excuse us," Nichole said to me. "Seth, my mom is insisting she needs to ask you something." She tugged on his arm. Good heavens. Would he buy such a blatant made-up line?

"Okay," he said.

Yup, I guess he would.

As he moved past, he whispered, "I'll be back. Wait for me."

I wasn't the waiting kind of girl anymore, so as soon as they left, I took off in the other direction, trying to ignore the jealous thoughts darting around my head. I hoped to find the woman who'd told me I had my nerve attending the viewing, so I could ask someone who she was. But she was nowhere to be found. I chatted with a few people as I moved around the increasingly tipsy crowd. But there were a lot of people I didn't recognize, and they all looked wealthy. I headed for the door. Just before I opened it, a hand grabbed mine. *Seth.*

Chapter 13

"I want you to meet my parents," he said.

"Your parents are here?" I looked over my shoulder, like they might be right behind me. "Why?"

"My family and the Mores go way back. So will you meet them?"

I felt unsure. I was no model or lawyer, the kind of woman Seth usually seemed to be with, but I needed to snap out of that kind of thinking. I ran my own business, and I looked pretty good tonight. Someone out there thought my boots were sexy. *Ugh*. Why had I thought of that? I straightened my shoulders, told myself it would be okay.

"Okay," I finally said.

Seth took my hand and guided me through the crowd. I gripped his hand like he was a towrope and I was a rookie skier going back up a hill. He gave my hand a squeeze, which made me feel a little better. Seth stopped by two couples and waited until one of the women turned. She looked like a taller, more stylish version of Queen Elizabeth. I resisted the urge to curtsy.

"Seth, darling, Nichole was just looking for you." She glanced at me, our two linked hands, and then gave me a thorough once-over. I was thankful that I'd worn my vintage 1970s Diane Von Furstenberg wrap dress, a yard sale find, and a simple necklace I'd made from some old pearl earrings. Hopefully, my black boots weren't too scuffed.

"Sarah, my parents, Aldrich and Paige," Seth said.

Seth's mom gave me a cold, limp hand to shake. She had on the largest single-carat diamond I'd ever seen in real life. No wonder her handshake was limp: holding that thing up had to be exhausting. His dad enveloped me in his arms. He smelled of scotch and cigars.

"We're so glad to meet you, after hearing so much about you," he said.

They'd heard about me? I wondered if that was true or if Aldrich said that to all of Seth's friends. I glanced at Seth, but his face gave away nothing.

"You must come to our cottage in Nantucket when the weather warms up," Aldrich added.

I almost choked. I confess that I'd looked up their "cottage" on Google Earth. It was a sprawling complex of buildings on a piece of land that jutted out into the ocean.

"Mustn't she, dear?" he said to his wife.

"Of course. That would be lovely." But she said it through clamped teeth. I wasn't sure if that was just her way or if she was biting back a response. "But as I was saying, Seth," Paige went on, "Nichole is looking for you. We've invited her to the family dinner on Sunday." She glanced at me sideways, with a glimmer of triumph in her look. It was apparent that she was on team Nichole.

"You should come, too, Sarah," Seth's father's voice boomed out, much to the chagrin of his wife.

"That's lovely, but I already have plans," I said. Reading a good book was a plan, wasn't it?

Seth turned to me. "Any chance you could change your plans? We'll be at our place in Beacon Hill."

"Nonsense, Seth," his mother said. "Sarah doesn't look like the kind of girl who'd break plans when she's gotten a better offer."

"*Mom*, that was rude," Seth said. "I'm sorry, Sarah."

"Oh, me too, dear. That came out all wrong." Seth's mom smiled, but it was the least sincere smile I'd ever seen.

"It was lovely meeting you both." I managed to get out. A better offer, my . . . Okay, it was a better offer, but how did she know? I turned and steamed toward the door, grabbed my coat off the rack, and slipped into the dark, cold air before I said something I shouldn't.

"Sarah, wait," Seth called out.

I stopped by my Suburban, surprised to be here, without even wondering if the photo taker was lurking. Seth caught up with me, pressed me up against the side of the SUV, and kissed me well and thoroughly. I kissed him back. My anger and resistance were all shot to hell by his lips. He rested his head against mine, his hand holding the back of my neck.

"I'm sorry. She's not always like that. It's just she and Nichole's mother have been plotting to marry us off since we were toddlers."

"What does that have to do with her not being nice to me?"

"Nichole moved back here over Christmas, and my mom's hopes were renewed. Even though I've told her multiple times that Nichole isn't for me."

He looped his arms around my coat and pulled me to him again. After another thorough kissing, he said, "I remember so well the night I met you."

I smiled at him. "Me too." That he remembered that night so clearly stunned me.

"Let's re-create the rest of that night. Come home with me."

It had been a long time, a really long time. And it had been a long, terrible week, and I liked him so much.

"Please?" he asked.

"Okay," I said. "I'll follow you home."

"You won't change your mind?"

"No. You can follow me, if you don't trust me."

Seth laughed but then turned serious. "I trust you, Sarah. But I want you to trust me."

The sun was shining when I pulled into my parking space beside my apartment Thursday morning. I trotted up the steps and was heading up to my apartment when my phone chimed. I shook my head. Seth had sent me three photos of himself with sad faces as I drove home. I waved at a big guy sitting on a small folding chair outside of Mike's apartment as I pulled up the picture. It was of me walking into the apartment building and was rimmed with a black heart. **Same outfit as last night** was written across it.

Chapter 14

I must have gasped, because the big guy stood. "Everything okay, miss? Mike said to keep an eye on you."

I looked at him but didn't really see him. "I'm fine. Thanks." I didn't know if having a mobster keeping an eye on me was a good thing or not. I unlocked my apartment door and ran to the window that looked out over the town common. No one was out there lurking with a camera. No one stood there with a phone pointing this way. I saw Mike running around the town common with a brother on either side of him. He looked up and waved. Maybe he'd seen something.

I ran back out not even bothering to lock my door, yet alone close it. I figured the big guy would make sure no one went in. I bounded down the steps, burst out the door, and jogged after Mike as fast as I could in my boots. "Mike, guys, wait a minute," I yelled.

They turned and jogged back over to me.

"Did you see anyone out here taking a picture of me?"

"Naw," Mike said. "But when we're back behind the church, we can't see nothin'."

"You got a problem we can help you with?" the taller brother asked.

"No. Thanks." I was pretty sure I didn't need their kind of help.

I took my time showering, blow-drying my hair, and putting on my makeup. As much as I didn't want to admit it, I knew I had a stalker. It all added up: the picture of me at Margaret's house, the creepy comments about my outfits, and the photo today. Thinking about it made me want to take another shower. I knew I should tell the police about the photo from this morning and probably about the other ones, too.

Explaining this morning's photo meant admitting I'd spent the night with Seth. And I didn't want CJ to know. I puzzled over that for a few minutes. On the one hand, it was because I wouldn't want to know if CJ had slept with someone, but on the other, I knew I felt slightly guilty about doing it. I was an adult, but I didn't want to hurt Seth or myself or CJ. I'd jumped the gun with Seth. Again. Why was it so easy to say yes to him and so hard to say no?

I shook my head. With Mike next door to me and his brothers sitting out in the hall, I didn't have to worry about being attacked in my home. I'd be extra cautious when I was out and about. The person who had taken the photo of me at Margaret's house either was the killer—gulp, I hoped I was wrong about that—or knew who the killer was, which wasn't a much better option but was a little more comforting than the first. So if I figured that out, I would know who the stalker was and could end this.

I wondered if the stalker had any connection to my virtual garage sale site. I grabbed my computer and opened the site. For once everything seemed to be in order, although I had a few messages to go through.

The first one complained about people advertising their businesses on the site. The person reminded me that this was a buy-sell site and not a job site. Frankly, if someone wanted to mention his or her business, as long as it was legal and was advertised on a Tuesday, I didn't care. I didn't allow people to sell animals or guns or breast milk, but if someone sold beauty products or jewelry, it was fine by me. I wrote a quick response, reiterating the site's policy.

The next few messages were all variations on the same theme—the person thought he or she should have gotten something someone else did. I knew how they felt, given that I'd lost out on the vintage tablecloth in what I'd thought was a breach of virtual garage sale etiquette. Why had Margaret sold it to Frieda instead of to me? It wasn't like she'd needed the extra money. It was probably one of those things that I'd never have an answer to. I wrote back to everyone, explaining that it was ultimately up to the seller to decide whom to sell to. I wasn't going to be the "sales" police. I didn't have time for that, nor would it be fun.

A woman who was downsizing wrote a lovely note, letting me know how helpful the site had been. She was on a fixed income, and the money from her sales would be a huge help in her life. The next message was a virtual Valentine, a pink heart with the words *You're the best, Sarah* written inside. For a moment my skin prickled, but then I realized this was from someone who was happy with the site. Finally, a little appreciation. Every once in a while someone would send me a nice note, but two in one day was almost a miracle. I wrote thank-you notes before dealing with the rest of the messages.

I finished up with the garage sale site but still didn't have a clue as to who could be stalking me. I decided to go over to DiNapoli's for lunch. The more information I had about Margaret, the better chance of finding her killer, which in turn might lead me to my stalker. It was kind of like using one of those reverse phone book sites and going at the information backward. Maybe I could worm some information out of Rosalie and Angelo about that glance they'd exchanged last night.

I threw on a light winter jacket and left my apartment. I stopped on the front porch and scanned the common and the sidewalk. There were skaters at the rink, a group of people walked around the perimeter of the common, and a couple of men headed into the church. No one was paying any undue attention to me.

When I walked into DiNapoli's, the place was packed, and I had to wait in line to order. I hoped I could snag a table. Lois was taking orders, instead of Rosalie. Her black hair was in a low bun, and she wore a black T-shirt and slacks, as did most of the employees. Rosalie was back by the grill, talking to Angelo. From all the hand waving going on between them, it didn't look like they were happy.

"What's going on with them?" I asked Lois when it was my turn to order.

She tucked a strand of long black hair that had escaped her bun behind her ear and glanced back at them. "They've been at it all morning. The rest of us have just tried to stay out of their way. Not easy to do in this place."

"Why's it so crowded today?" I asked.

Lois's pale face looked exasperated. "Angelo put an ad in the base paper offering ten percent off on Thursday lunches for military. Not only did the military show up in force, but half the surrounding area somehow found out and claims to have served."

"What's good today?"

"Angelo would tell you, 'Everything.' Try the eggplant Parm sandwich."

"As good as that sounds, I'd better have a salad." I patted my stomach. "An iced tea, too, please."

"Sarah Winston, you and your virtual garage sale are ruining my business."

I turned at the voice, which grated more than the metal grater the DiNapolis used for shredding cheese. I knew before I turned that it belonged to Hennessy Hamilton, owner of the consignment store on the west side of Ellington.

Hennessy stood near the door, in a luxurious camel-hair coat that made her broad shoulders look broader. A hint of an expensive-looking red dress peeked out from under the coat. Her long legs were clad in black tights. She stepped forward in spike-heeled black shoes and jabbed a red-lacquered nail in my direction. "People would rather shop online than get the quality merchandise available at my store." She looked at the people sitting at the crowded tables as if she wanted them to applaud. The crowd in the restaurant was a mix of locals and military. Her beautiful silver bob swung as she held her hands out beseechingly.

I'd heard Hennessy used to be an actress and had even had some minor success on Broadway. With this performance I wondered why she'd given up acting. The customers eating swung their heads toward me. I wished I had a script, but I'd already had enough drama for the day.

I looked up at her and held my ground. I spouted a line I'd read over and over when I worked for a financial planning company years ago, during one of CJ and my assignments. "Past performance is no guarantee of future success."

"What does that mean?" Hennessy asked.

A few people nodded, but most returned to their food.

"Just because you were successful doesn't mean you'll always be."

"So you think it's okay to just steal business from me?" Hennessy asked.

"I really don't know what you are talking about."

"Margaret. I'm talking about Margaret." Hennessy humphed, grabbed her to-go order, slapped some money on the counter, and exited stage left in a performance worthy of Meryl Streep. As she left, I saw a glimpse of a red sole. Her shoes were Christian Louboutins. How hard up could she be if she could afford those? If that was the kind of merchandise she now had in her store, maybe I needed to go back. I hadn't been in a while.

"Any truth to that?" Lois asked me.

"I'm not sure what she's talking about. But business is always about the competition." *But why the heck did she bring up Margaret?*

"Let me get your order." Lois grabbed my salad and handed it to me.

"Thanks." I scooted over to a table that a group had just left, even though it hadn't been bused yet. I stacked some of the dishes to the side and tried to catch Rosalie's eye.

Ryan Jones came over and started loading the dishes into a big rubber tub. He had a round Irish face sprinkled with freckles and light hair that looked more red than blond. "That Hennessy," he said, shaking his head. "Trying to blame you for her problems. Last time I was over there, the place smelled musty and didn't look organized." Ryan had worked for the DiNapolis for years, although he was around my age. He not only bused tables but was also their all-around handyman, one of those guys who could fix anything.

"I thought the same thing. But if she's shopping in her own store, maybe things have picked back up."

"Naw. The quality has gone downhill faster than a skier in Vermont. I was there recently, looking for a gift for my girlfriend."

"She's a lucky girl, Ryan."

He turned a little red. "Thanks. I've done some work at Hennessy's shop. She's always blaming someone else for her problems. No matter what the problem is. So don't let her get to you."

Angelo came up behind Ryan and clapped a hand on his shoulder. "Let her eat."

"Sorry," Ryan said.

"No worries," I said. "I always enjoy talking to you." And I'd found out something interesting.

Angelo sat across from me. "Eat," he said and watched as I took a few bites.

I put my fork down, even though the salad was delicious, full of sweet tomatoes, kalamata olives, feta, and Angelo's secret dressing. "You ought to bottle this dressing, Angelo." That way I could have it anytime I wanted.

Angelo got a far-off look. "A lot of competition in the area, what with the Cape Cod brand, Newman's Own, and Ken's Foods just down the road in Marlborough."

"Can't you just picture a bottle with 'DiNapoli's' written across it and your picture?" I asked him.

"Rosalie's picture might sell more dressing than

my ugly mug." He looked at me in a way that made me think he had something on his mind.

"What's going on?" I asked. Angelo wasn't one to sit during the lunch rush.

"There's something I need to tell you. Rosalie doesn't think I should."

"You two were back there arguing about me?" I looked toward the kitchen to see Rosalie watching us with an anxious look on her face.

"Discussing. We were discussing you."

"I saw the look you two exchanged last night in the car. I came over to find out what it was about."

Angelo rubbed a hand over his face. "You know how some of the people in this town can be."

I nodded, even though I wasn't sure what he was getting at.

"And a lot of them are related to Margaret."

I nodded again, hoping he'd get to the point. When it came to Angelo, not getting to the point quickly was an anomaly. One of the things I loved about him was you always knew where you stood. He might be opinionated, but he had a big heart. "Who was the woman who told me I had my nerve being at the viewing?"

"One of Margaret's sisters. She has a 'kill the messenger' attitude." He said the last words fast and then leaned back.

I thought for a minute about what he'd said. "So because I found Margaret, I'm somehow in the wrong."

"Exactly, kid. And she's been sharing her opinion all over town."

I gasped, my appetite gone. "She thinks I killed her." Sometimes I didn't understand this close-knit town. "Thanks for telling me, Angelo." I looked over and smiled at Rosalie so she'd think I was okay. "I think I'll take the rest of this home with me." I waved at my salad. I realized town gossip would kill my business faster than anything. I knew I didn't kill Margaret, but now I was even more determined to find out who did.

Chapter 15

I pulled up in front of Orchard House around four, hoping Kathy Brasheler would be volunteering this afternoon. I wanted to ask her what she meant last night, when she'd mentioned people owing favors to Margaret. When I walked in, she was just getting ready to start a tour.

"Join us," she said, a smile on her heart-shaped face. "I'll have time to talk after."

I bought a ticket, even though I'd been through the house many times. It was one of my favorite places to take people who came to visit. The hardships the Alcott family had endured and the love between Louisa and her sisters always warmed my heart. The group was mostly retirees, but there were a couple of school-aged kids with a mom. First, we watched a short film in a room that had drawings on the wall done by May, Louisa's youngest sister. At one point in her life May, an accomplished artist, gave Daniel Chester French his first art lessons. He went on to sculpt *The Minute Man* statue in

Concord, which honored the men of the colonial militia who fought the British regulars at the Old North Bridge in the first battle of the Revolutionary War. But he was more famous for carving *Abraham Lincoln*, the statue in the Lincoln Memorial on the National Mall in Washington, D.C.

After the film was over, we roamed through the kitchen and then upstairs to the bedrooms. Louisa's room was my favorite. It was at the front of the house, and she must have had a fine view. There were several drawings on her bedroom walls, too— also done by May. But I loved her desk above all else. It was more of a horseshoe-shaped piece of wood attached around a beam than something I'd picture as a desk. But it was there that she wrote *Little Women*, and it seemed special to me.

We finished the tour in the parlor, where the Alcott sisters had put on plays and played the piano. Some lovely oil paintings by May hung on the walls. The group then exited through the front door, but I stayed behind with Kathy.

"What can I do you for?" Kathy asked when we sat on chairs in a staff office.

"I was curious what you meant about people owing Margaret favors."

Kathy fiddled with a pencil she'd picked up off a desk. "Do you know anything about Lyndon Johnson?"

"The president?" I asked. "Not really, other than he was sworn in after Kennedy was killed."

"He liked to do people favors—congressmen and senators. Then, when he wanted something done, he'd collect. He got a lot done while he was president."

"Margaret did the same?"

"Yep. I'm not saying it's a bad thing. She got a lot done. Towns need people like Margaret."

"But someone might not have liked owing her."

"Exactly."

I drove west on the 2A because I liked to drive through Concord. I loved the old colonial homes, some of which dated back to the 1600s. I looked longingly down the main street, but I didn't have the time or the money to go antiquing. Instead, I drove through the two rotaries, past the Colonial Inn, and headed back to Ellington. I realized it would be easy to swing by Hennessy's shop on my way home. Our earlier encounter had left a bad taste in my mouth. We were grown-ups, and businesswomen at that. We should be supporting each other, not arguing like middle school girls. Plus, after my talk with Kathy, I wondered if she was one of the people who had owed Margaret a favor. Hennessy didn't seem the type to want to owe anyone anything.

When I pulled into the parking lot, there was only one car, Hennessy's, parked in it. I straightened my shoulders and walked in the shop but stopped right inside the door. Ryan had been right; things did look run-down. The air was filled with a floral scent that had to be from some kind of air freshener. I wondered what odors it masked.

"You have your nerve showing up here," Hennessy said. She stood behind the counter, fingers posed on a laptop.

That's the second time I had heard that line in two days. I moved forward, anyway. "Look, I feel bad about the scene at DiNapoli's. We're both business-women. Maybe we can find a way to help each other."

Hennessy's mouth dropped open. "I'm not sure I want to help you after you snatched Margaret's business away from me."

"I have no idea what you're talking about."

"Really?" Her eyebrows popped up.

"Really. Margaret called me up one day and asked how the virtual garage sale worked. She had some things she wanted to sell. I went over and helped her set up an account. Showed her how the whole thing worked." Now that I thought about it, Margaret had told me as I left that she owed me one. I'd assured her that she didn't, that I was happy to help. Now I pictured her sitting at her desk with a ledger. One column was who she owed, and the other was who owed her. I was guessing that the second one was a much longer column. "Margaret didn't mention she'd talked to you."

"Well, she did. She was going to consign her things here. But I guess she decided she didn't want to pay me the thirty percent commission. I even went over and priced some things for her. She owed me." Hennessy looked down when she said the last bit, which made me wonder who owed whom and if there was any way to find out.

"I heard Margaret liked people to owe her."

"You said we could help each other. What did you have in mind?" Hennessy asked.

Okay, change of subject. That in itself was intriguing. "I could push business your way when people can't sell things on my site. They could bring them here. And I'll let you post items you want sold on my site."

Hennessy squinted her eyes. "You don't get a commission on the sales, right?"

"Only when a client hires me to sell stuff for them." Which wasn't as often as I wished.

"What's in it for you? Why help me?"

"You'll call me first if you get any size seven Christian Louboutin shoes in."

Hennessy laughed and put out her hand. We shook. "It's a deal," she said.

I stopped by Stella's when I got home. I could hear someone singing an aria from an opera. Stella taught private lessons in her apartment, but I knocked lightly on the door, anyway. The singing went on as Stella answered. The girl singing had her eyes closed, and her hands clasped to her heart. Her voice was pure and clear. I stood there, mesmerized. When she finished, she opened her eyes.

"Oh, I didn't know anyone was here," she said.

"This is Chelsea Pellner," Stella said. "Sarah knows your dad."

"You have a beautiful voice, Chelsea. Sorry to

interrupt. I was just wondering if you could come up later, Stella."

"Sure." She lowered her voice. "Anything urgent?"

"No. Just girl talk and a glass of wine."

"I'll be up at seven."

I trotted up the stairs and waved to the brother sitting outside Mike's door. I had to wonder if something else was going on, that Mike needed so much protection. But I'd been sleeping well ever since he moved in, so I wouldn't complain.

I opened my computer to check the site. I had a message from a woman who had items she wanted to get rid of and asked if I could help. I sent her a note about what I could do and how much I'd charge.

At seven Stella showed up. I heard her talking to whoever was sitting out in the hall, and opened the door before she could knock.

"That guy's hot," she said once we settled on the couch with our wine.

"He's one of Mike's brothers. With all the protection, I wonder if something's going on that they haven't mentioned."

"Not that I know of. So what'd you want to talk about that you didn't want to mention in front of Chelsea?" Stella was exceptional at reading people, until it came to men. Then she was a disaster.

"Hennessy Hamilton." I filled her in on what had happened at DiNapoli's and on my conversation with Hennessy at her store.

"That was nice of you to stop by and try to clear things up."

"I try to be an adult on Thursdays. But what's her story? What's with her name?"

"She was the sixth kid in a family that could barely afford one. Although there was always money for alcohol. At least according to my aunt Nancy."

Nancy Elder was not only Stella's aunt but also the town manager, the one who'd hired me to run New England's Largest Yard Sale last fall. Nancy had political aspirations beyond Ellington and, now that I thought about it, was dating one of Margaret's sons.

"Someone had given Hennessy's dad a bottle of cognac, and when it came to picking another name, her mom was too worn out to bother," Stella said.

"Wow. That's sad."

"But it explains a lot about who she is. Why she went into acting. She needed the attention, and that was the only way to get it."

"I asked her if she owed Margaret, but she changed the subject."

"Half the people in this town owed Margaret, or at least Margaret thought they did." Stella took a long drink of her wine. "Look, I'm glad you and Hennessy worked things out. But she's known around town for her grudges, and taking Margaret's business away from her seems grudge-worthy to me."

"She seemed fine when I left her. We shook hands."

"That's lovely. But I'm not sure you should trust her." Stella sipped her wine. "Any news about the robbery? Have they found your stuff or caught who did it?"

"Not that I know of." Surely, CJ would have let me know if they'd found any of my stuff.

"I saw you come in the building this morning . . . early and all dressed up but looking a bit, um, bedraggled."

"Did you see anyone else? Someone out on the common, taking pictures?"

Stella thought for a moment. "No. Why?"

I told Stella about the photos. "I think I have a stalker." It sounded a bit ridiculous when I said it out loud. I was hoping Stella would laugh, but she didn't. She frowned.

"Have you told CJ?"

"No."

"Anyone with the police?"

"No. Because if I do, I'm going to have to mention my being out all night. And I don't want to do that if I don't have to."

"Do you have any ideas who the stalker could be?"

I didn't want Stella to take this seriously. I wanted her to tell me I was nuts. "None. Who would stalk me? It's crazy."

"That's the problem. It *is* crazy."

Chapter 16

A few minutes after Stella left, my phone rang. It was Hennessy.

"So you come by my store, play all nice to me, and then you go out and slash all my tires."

"Someone slashed your tires?"

"Don't play all sweet and innocent. I can't believe I bought your whole 'Let's work together' spiel."

"Why would you think it was me? I didn't do it."

"Because you are the only person who came by the shop today. So it had to be you. I've already called the police."

Argh. That was the last thing I needed. "Where are you?"

"At my shop, waiting for a tow and the police."

"I'm coming over." I might as well get it straightened out while I could.

* * *

I got to Hennessy before the police or the tow truck. "I didn't do this, Hennessy." I could tell in the dim light filtering out of her store that the tires were flat. I got a heavy-duty flashlight out of my trunk and walked around the car. The tires on the side away from the store weren't just flat but also slashed almost to shreds. "I couldn't have done this when I was here. Someone would have seen me. And I've been home since I left here."

"So you could have come back."

"I didn't, and I have witnesses that can prove it." I guessed that was another advantage of having Mike living next door to me. Someone always knew when I was home. "Besides, it seems like it would take someone stronger than me and someone very angry to do this much damage."

A police car pulled up, and Pellner hopped out. "You're here?"

"Hennessy called me and told me about the tires. I didn't do it and thought it would save time to show up and hash this out now."

"Do you have any proof Sarah did this?" he asked Hennessy.

"She's the only one who was here today. She says she has an alibi. Like her friends would be reliable."

Hennessy's business had to be really slow if I was the only one who was there today. I wasn't sure I'd consider Mike and his brothers friends or if anyone would think they were reliable.

"Pellner, I couldn't have done this while I was here." I gestured to the road in front of the store. "Someone would have seen me." Although I realized now that very little traffic came by here—another problem for Hennessy's business. "And I have people who can account for where I was right up until Hennessy called and accused me of doing this."

Pellner walked around the car and kneeled down by the tires. "This is bad." He snapped some photos and then took our separate statements. "You have a tow truck coming?" he asked Hennessy.

"Yes. They should be here soon."

"I'll wait with her until it shows up," I said.

Both Pellner and Hennessy looked surprised.

"Great. I'll let you know if we find anything out," Pellner said. He took off with a little spin of his tires.

"I can give you a ride home after the tow truck comes."

A gust of wind kicked up. Hennessy brushed back her hair. "Why? Why would you be nice to me after I accused you of doing this?"

I didn't want to tell her it was because I felt sorry for her after Stella told me about her lousy upbringing. "I'm here, and you'll need a ride." Another gust of wind blasted us. "No one's going to want to come out on a night like this, anyway."

Hennessy climbed in my Suburban after the tow truck pulled out. She strapped in and twisted her body toward me. She looked older than she had when I saw her at DiNapoli's this morning. Her lipstick had worn off, and I noticed lines radiating out from her eyes. She told me where her house was.

"I did owe Margaret," she said as I pulled out.

I was so surprised, I couldn't think of anything to say.

"She paid for my acting classes and helped with my living expenses in New York."

"But that was a long time ago," I said.

"Not to Margaret. Once she helped you, she felt like you were hers for the duration."

I concentrated on the dark road, not because there was a lot of traffic, but because it was narrow and winding. Trees crowded either side, along with low stone walls.

"Margaret loved being known as a patron of the arts. I'm not the only one she helped."

I pulled up in front of her house. No lights were on.

"She arranged for Pellner's daughter to sing 'The Star-Spangled Banner' at a Celtics game last year."

"I saw her. On TV. It was a nationally televised game," I said. Which meant Pellner and his wife had owed Margaret.

"It got Chelsea attention from the big music schools. She'll have her pick." Hennessy's voice sounded bitter. "And since Margaret's dead, Chelsea and her family won't have to pay up."

Was Hennessy insinuating that Pellner had killed Margaret so he wouldn't owe her? Was that possible? He was the first cop to show up at the scene after I called 911, which had to mean he'd been in the area. And as nice as Pellner had been to me lately, I'd seen another side of him when I went snooping at his house once. He'd protect his family at all costs.

"I'll wait until you're in the house and have the lights on." Now it was my turn to change the subject.

Hennessy climbed out of the car but turned back. "You might want to ask your landlady about Margaret. She was up to her ears in it with Margaret. Way worse off than I was."

I stared after her, waiting until she got in the house. Stella had ties to Margaret?

Stella's lights were off and her car was gone when I got home. From the bottom of the stairs I smelled cigarette smoke and heard a burst of laughter. It wasn't that Stella had ever said we couldn't smoke in the building; it was just the first time anyone had since I'd moved in. I walked up and looked toward Mike's apartment just as his brother came out. A group of men who all looked like they came out of the movie *Goodfellas* sat around a poker table. Smoke hung over it like smog hung over Los Angeles. A man ducked back when he spotted me, and he looked an awful lot like Seth. Mike waved. For a guy who was supposedly out here to lay low, it seemed like he was having a lot of friends around. I waved back and unlocked the door to my apartment.

Before I went in, I craned my neck to see if that was Seth or just someone who looked like him. But Mike's brother quickly shut the door, so there was no chance to tell. I closed my door but left the lights off. I went to my window and scanned the street, looking for Seth's car, but I didn't see it.

What did it matter if he was there? It wasn't really any of my business.

I checked the garage sale site. Someone had sent me a message, asking if I needed another admin to help run the site. It was tempting. As the group grew, so did the amount of bickering and the volume of posts that had to be managed. And even though the rules were clearly stated in a static display right above where people posted what they had for sale, they continued to post too many pictures, which slowed the site, or they bumped their item up more often than once a week.

However, I'd heard horror stories about people adding admins they didn't know and the admins taking over the site, sometimes even blocking the person who had set it up. So I sent the person a thank-you and said I didn't need anyone right now. If I decided I did, it would be someone I knew well and could trust. Juanita had left a post, asking if I could deliver the Pez dispensers to her tomorrow morning at ten. Yeesh. I kept telling people not to arrange times publicly. I left her a reply that I'd send her a private message. Then I sent her a message, saying ten would be fine.

We'd been trying to meet for several days now, but she'd been working long hours running her cleaning business. I'd be glad to have them out of the house, but I wasn't going over there just to deliver the Pez. Juanita was a cleaning lady, and Margaret must have had one. I couldn't imagine Margaret down on her knees, scrubbing a floor. With any luck, Juanita either

would be her cleaning lady or would know who
was. How many cleaning people could there be in
Ellington?

I drove to Juanita's house to give her the Pez
dispensers. It was another sunny day, with no chance
of snow. If this weather kept up, people from Florida
would start retiring here. Although thirty-five was
considered balmy only in the winter up here. I
parked, grabbed the box of Pez, and rang her doorbell. She lived on one side of a duplex. She didn't
answer, so I set the Pez down and knocked hard.
The door swung open. Juanita was lying facedown
in the entry. Blood pooled next to her.

Chapter 17

I clapped my hand over my mouth and stumbled back. I grabbed my cell phone and called 911 as I ran to Juanita. She didn't look good. I tried not to touch anything, assuming this was a crime scene. I put my fingers to her neck and felt a weak pulse. "She's alive," I told the dispatcher. "Hurry."

I threw my coat over her to try to keep her warm. I didn't want to move her and make things worse, because I couldn't tell where the blood was coming from. "Come on, Juanita. It's going to be all right. Help is on the way." *What the heck is taking them so long?* "I can hear sirens. They'll be here any minute. Hang on." I didn't know if talking helped her, but it seemed to help me keep calm, so I kept it up until the ambulance arrived.

The EMTs went right to work, asking me a few questions, then talking over Juanita as they worked. They gently turned her to put her on a gurney. What looked like a silver serving fork stuck out of her stomach. Black dots appeared in my eyes, and I scrambled back outside. I leaned my head down to my knees until my vision cleared. Two squad cars arrived. A woman officer stayed with me, while Pellner ran into the house. They loaded Juanita into the ambulance and took off, lights flashing and sirens blaring. I hoped they weren't too late.

"We need to take your statement," Pellner said when he came back out.

I shook from the cold. I could see that my coat had been tossed aside in the hallway. Blood rimmed one side. Pellner slipped out of his jacket and handed it to me. I put it on, enjoying the warmth infused in the fabric from Pellner's body. Maybe I should invent a coat warmer. "You'll get cold," I said to Pellner.

"I'm fine. I have my vest on."

"Do you work every shift?" I asked. It seemed like I'd been giving him an awful lot of statements lately.

"Apparently, only the ones where you're in trouble. Which seems to be all of them lately. With five kids, I need all the overtime I can rack up. What happened?"

"I came to deliver the Pez dispensers." I pointed to the box, which was sitting to the side of the door. "I knocked on her door. It opened, and there she was." I gestured toward her house.

"You sure you didn't open the door?" the woman officer asked.

"Check it for prints. You wouldn't find mine."

"You might have been wearing gloves," the woman said.

We all looked at my bare hands. My gloves hung out of my coat pockets, visible to all in the hallway.

"Did you see anyone or hear anything?" Pellner asked.

I thought through the whole scene in my mind. "Nothing. No one."

"No cars took off?" the woman asked. "Or anyone walking away in a hurry?"

"I'm sorry. I didn't see anything."

I picked up my mail with jittery hands, owing partly to the cold, since I'd given Pellner his jacket back before we parted ways. I found a package and smiled a little bit as I carried it and the Pez back up to my apartment. It looked like it was the fourth in a series of packages from my "anonymous" admirer that had shown up over the past several months. I knew they were from CJ, but then I hesitated. At least I thought they were up until this moment. No way my stalker knew me well enough to send this stuff. No one else knew me that well.

The first gift had been a DVD of *The African Queen*, my favorite classic movie, with Humphrey Bogart and Katharine Hepburn. The second had been a box of chocolates from See's Candies, famous on the West Coast but not so much on the East. After that a red Coach purse. And now this little box. One of these days I'd bring it up to CJ, but for now I just wanted to enjoy the moment. It meant that for all his gruff behavior, some part of him still had feelings for me. And with the joy each gift brought me, it meant I had more feelings for him than I'd been able to admit to.

I was still so conflicted about both CJ and Seth. If it weren't for Margaret's death, I wouldn't have seen either of them until I'd been more ready. But now I was all over the place with both of them, literally when it came to Seth. I wished there was a search function for life like there was on my garage sale site. In search of a happy relationship, in search of a man who understood me, in search of the person who murdered Margaret More. It would make my life so much easier.

I sat on the couch and opened the box. It was a small cameo on a delicate gold chain. The background was a coral color, and the head was white. I flipped the cameo over, and engraved on the back was *My love*. My heart beat a little faster. But part of it was from conflict. I liked that CJ was trying to win me over, but like Seth, he was violating the no contact rule. Conflicted or not, I put the necklace on and went to the bathroom to admire it in the mirror. Stunning. And a lovely thing to receive after such a rotten day.

Around eight I heard voices in the hall, followed by a knock on my door. I was growing more and more fond of having Mike's crew out in the hall. I opened the door, and CJ stood there.

"So you have your own personal security now?" CJ sounded grumpy. "They asked who I was and what I wanted with you."

I leaned out and waved to one of Mike's brothers. "They're not out there for me. But it has been nice, especially after getting attacked in here."

"I don't like having those thugs around."

It made me think about Seth and whether he had been playing poker over there.

"Can I come in?" he asked.

"Sure." CJ looked serious. "What's up?"

"It's Juanita. She didn't make it."

I walked over to the couch and collapsed on it. "What happened?"

"The fork caused internal bleeding. It was just too late."

"Oh, no." I toyed with the cameo, trying not to think about all that blood. "I guess I'm not shocked. There was a lot of blood. Do you think it has anything to do with what happened here?"

"I don't know. It's why I came over."

"Is there any chance her death was a horrible accident? Like running with scissors, only in this case it was a fork?"

"We won't know for sure until there's an autopsy. Maybe not then."

"Did Juanita and Margaret know each other? Two murders so close together in a small town seems unusual."

CJ rubbed a hand across the stubble on his chin. "How long are those guys going to be next door?"

Ah, the nonanswer. I'd have to try to find out on my own. "I'm not sure. They told Stella for a few days." It had already been a few days, and that made me wonder if this arrangement was going to be something more permanent.

"Let me know if they leave." CJ stood. I walked him to the door and held it open for him. He looked down at me. "Nice cameo." He lifted it with a finger. "I know how much you like them."

"Thanks. It's very special to me."

He ran his finger across my cheek and down my jawline. We gazed at each other, and it seemed like we were trying to say a thousand things without saying a word.

"Hey, everything okay?" It was Mike's brother.

"I think so," CJ said as he left.

After a night of crazed dreams where a stalker chased Juanita as she tried to clean Margaret's house, I decided some research was in order. I started with Jaunita's cleaning business, because of the complaints. She'd run a special almost every week on the garage sale site. I checked, but she didn't have a Web site. So I went through my notifications in my business e-mail and found the last time she'd placed an ad. It was a week and a half ago. Several people had posted that they were interested in hiring her. I copied their names down and decided nine wasn't too early to make calls. If I nosed around, maybe I could find a connection between Juanita and Margaret or see if Juanita had been up to some kind of funny business. No one answered at the first three numbers I called. Apparently, some people actually had lives and went out to do things on Saturday mornings.

The fourth person answered.

"Hi. I wanted to ask you about Juanita's cleaning."

"How'd you get my number?" the woman asked.

Damn. "Juanita listed you as a reference. I hope that's okay."

"I guess. She did a great job. House looks better than it has in years, and she's a real sweet lady, too."

"Well, thanks. I'll give her a call." That was interesting. It seemed like some people loved her and some people complained about her. It was almost as if she had had two different sides to her.

"I've been trying to reach her all day. Some idiot broke in and made a mess."

If I were a dog, the ruff on the back of my neck would be standing straight up. "I'm sorry to hear that. Was anything taken?"

"Computers, TVs, a set of china, my dad's old camera. That's what hurt the most. I've got another call I need to take. If you talk to Juanita, tell her to give me a call."

I leaned back on the couch and wondered what to do next. I called the first three people again and left messages for them, hoping they'd call back before the news of Juanita's death hit the streets. One of them called back right away. They, too, were happy with Juanita, but I couldn't very well ask them if they'd been robbed or not. After we hung up, I searched the police incident reports online to see if there was anything listed that pertained to their house. I didn't find anything, but I hadn't asked when Juanita had cleaned, and I didn't feel comfortable calling back and asking now.

Maybe there wasn't a connection between the robbery and cleaning, anyway. Juanita hadn't cleaned my house; she'd just stopped by. She could be one of those people whom trouble followed. But sadly, even I didn't buy that theory. Something else was going on, and I had to figure it out. I glanced at the time. Margaret's funeral was in an hour, but I couldn't attend. I had an appointment with a woman in Bedford who wanted me to look at what she had to sell and help her price things. We'd decide while I was there if she wanted to sell her things on the garage sale site or do a garage sale in the spring. And as much as I wanted to go to the funeral, I wasn't in a position to turn away business. My suggestion that we reschedule had been met with silence. I'd have to have the DiNapolis fill me in.

Chapter 18

By the time I went over to DiNapoli's, it was nearly 8:30 p.m. and almost time for them to close. I'd been with my client for hours. Thank heavens I'd told her she had to pay me by the hour for pricing. The woman thought everything had value and was worth more than what I thought was possible to get. She wanted to sell old aluminum foil tins that had obviously been used, paper bags, and pencils that were down to the stub. I'd explained putting those things out would detract from all the good items she had, and she had some great things. But she'd heard a story about someone putting an old dirty sock up for sale on a site and someone else buying it. We'd agreed to disagree, and I'd priced everything she wanted me to.

Many people thought Angelo should stay open later than he did, but Angelo had opinions about restaurants and hours. He thought people should eat by nine, and if they didn't, they'd just have to lose out and eat somewhere else. His family was important to him, so when his kids were young, he made sure he was home in time to tell them good night. Even though his kids were grown and gone now, he continued to close the restaurant at the same time. I'd heard him say more than once that if you ate too late, the food didn't sit in your stomach right, and why people would eat a pizza at ten at night was beyond him. Personally, I thought pizza was good anytime.

Only a couple of tables still had people at them when I walked in. I knew that soon some not so subtle methods of getting people to leave would be employed. First, the lights would be dimmed, and then the cleaning staff would come out, and if that didn't get people out, Angelo would ask Rosalie in a loud yet innocent voice if everyone had gone, so they could leave. People put up with it because the food was good and the prices were reasonable.

Angelo turned from the grill with an exasperated look when he heard the door open. But his expression softened when he saw it was me.

"I'll just get something to go. I know you're about to close." I said it loudly enough that not only Angelo but also the other diners would hear me. Angelo winked at me.

Rosalie leaned over the counter. "Stay and eat with us. Go sit over at a table. If anyone asks, you're waiting for your to-go order."

I went over and sat, smiling at the people at the table closest to me as they gathered up their things and left. I'd secretly been hoping that I'd be invited to eat with Angelo and Rosalie. I wanted to hear all about Margaret's funeral. The other group left, too, and Rosalie switched the sign to CLOSED. The staff got busy cleaning. I talked to Ryan for a few minutes while he mopped and to Lois while she wiped down tables. I felt guilty for just sitting there, even though I'd had a long, hard day of work too.

A few minutes later Rosalie brought wine over in plastic kiddie cups, plates, and a basket of cheese bread. "Go ahead and start. We'll be over in a minute."

They sent the rest of the staff home—most with packets of food. Angelo didn't want anything to go to waste. The mozzarella dripped off the bread as I picked a piece up. Angelo carried over a steaming bowl of clams, and Rosalie followed with seafood over pasta in a fra diavolo sauce—a spicy tomato-garlic sauce.

"Expanding the menu?" I asked as they sat down. I'd never seen fra diavolo or clams on the menu before.

"Rosalie thinks we should."

"Ryan suggested we start catering events," Rosalie said.

Angelo shook his head. "I like things the way they are. Dig in. It's better hot."

I dug my fork into a large chunk of lobster and popped it in my mouth. I made a noise, almost a moan, which made Angelo look up, eyebrows raised. "It's delicious," I said. "The fra diavolo has just the right amount of spice. I hate it when it burns my tongue."

"That's why you should only eat here. You try this

over at Tony's in Billerica, all you're gonna get is a heavy hand with the hot stuff. This is a delicate blend to bring out all the flavors," Angelo said. But for all of Angelo's bravado, his cheeks pinked up, like he was pleased.

"How was Margaret's funeral?" I asked.

"We almost didn't get seats," Rosalie said.

"I would've found you a seat if I had had to ask the priest to give up his," Angelo said, patting Rosalie's hand.

Rosalie smiled at Angelo. "Some people didn't even make it into the church. They set up loud-speakers outside."

"I bet Margaret would have loved that," I said.

"An archbishop from Boston came, a couple of the lesser Kennedys, and of course, half the church was filled with her family." Angelo plopped a couple more clams on each of our plates. "The eulogies would have made you think she'd be up for saint-hood."

"Stella sang 'Ave Maria.' It filled the church. She has the voice of an angel," Rosalie said.

"And the past of the devil," Angelo said. "But her voice gave *me* goose bumps."

That reminded me I wanted to talk to Stella. With all that had been going on, I'd forgotten. I hadn't seen her since Hennessy told me Stella owed Margaret for something. I wanted to know what it was. "What else went on?"

"Lot of crying from the front of the church," Rosalie said.

"Or fake crying," Angelo said. "A lot of people stand to inherit money."

"What about the back of the church? Why weren't they crying?"

Rosalie and Angelo exchanged one of their looks. They might love me, but by Ellington standards, I was still an outsider.

"The front of the church was family. The back, friends or associates. She belonged to a lot of organizations," Rosalie said.

"And they don't have a reason to cry?" I asked.

"Let me put it this way. A lot of them are relieved they no longer owe Margaret a favor."

"That's the third time someone has mentioned Margaret and people owing her. What's going on? It sounds like she was in the Mob."

"She wasn't in the Mob. Not that I know anyone who is," Angelo said.

I wondered about that. Angelo spent a lot of time denying that his extended family's businesses had anything to do with the Mob. But Vincenzo certainly had dealings with the Mob as a lawyer. And their uncle, Stefano, had certainly seemed to want me to think he was a mobster when we met last fall.

"She liked power," Angelo said. "And she built a whole system of power by looking like she was helping people, until she got her hooks into them."

"It seems like a lot of people might resent that," I said.

"Yes and no," Rosalie said. "It wasn't fun to owe her, but she got things done. Things that helped not only Ellington but the surrounding communities."

"Rosalie's just being nice. It's one of her best qualities," Angelo said. "People resented Margaret. Plenty of people."

I walked home with a huge box of cookies, still a little shocked to hear about this other side of Margaret. Even though both Kathy and Hennessy had mentioned it, the DiNapolis' opinions gave it weight. Here I'd thought so highly of Margaret. Next thing I'd find out was that she was broke, not that I really believed that would happen.

The DiNapolis never let me leave empty handed—thus the cookies. I'd insisted on washing the dishes, since there weren't enough to put in the dishwasher, and on cleaning the kitchen while Rosalie and Angelo enjoyed the rest of their wine. For once they'd let me do it. Washing dishes was about all I could do in the kitchen. My lack of cooking skills was well known. Maybe one of these days I should ask Angelo to teach me to cook a simple dish.

I noticed Stella's car was home and her light was on. I figured she liked cookies, so I knocked on her door.

"No date tonight?" I asked when she opened it.

"Two dates with the last guy was enough. And don't ask."

"I have cookies from DiNapoli's." I held up the white box tied with string.

"Are there any of Rosalie's pistachio ones in there? Her cookies are the best." Stella held the door open. I followed her in. We plopped down on her couch, with the box of cookies between us. Stella found a pistachio cookie, and I snagged a chocolate one. As full as I was, there was always room for a cookie.

"I heard you sang at Margaret's service today."

Stella licked a crumb off her finger. "Yes. And now I'm free. Let's have a glass of cava to celebrate."

Stella grabbed a bottle from her fridge, uncorked it with a resounding pop, and poured the sparkling Spanish wine into two flutes.

"What do you mean, you're free?" I had a good idea, given what Hennessy had told me, but I wanted to hear what Stella had to say. "Until recently, I thought Margaret was just a nice old lady who liked to help people."

Stella laughed, but it wasn't the happy kind. "Without Margaret, I wouldn't have had a career in opera. My aunt Nancy took me to her house when I was in high school so Margaret could hear me sing. After that she paid for my private lessons and schooling." Stella snagged another cookie but just stared at it. "She's the one who made it possible for me to go to Europe. Provided the clothes, the luggage and, most importantly, the contacts. In return, I was expected to be an overnight sensation. I wasn't."

"But your voice is amazing."

"I did okay. Given time, I think I could have developed a great career."

"Margaret didn't realize that?"

"She wanted bragging rights and didn't want to wait for them. So when someone mentioned that a little amphetamine would keep me going longer so I could take more lessons, I tried it."

I sipped my cava. I knew Stella had eventually left Europe and had ended up in Los Angeles. Where she'd gotten in trouble for using.

"Margaret even paid for my lawyer and rehab." Stella sighed. "I tell people I came back because I missed being here. But in reality I came back because Margaret told me to, and I felt like I owed it to her."

"You didn't have to. What would it have mattered?"

"She knew about my aunt Nancy's political ambitions and said she'd squash them like a bug if I didn't do what she wanted. Or she could help her. I could take Margaret being mad at me, but not my family. So I came back."

"You don't have to stay here now. I don't want you to leave, but you could."

Stella looked around her apartment. "I'm happy here. I like my job. And now that I'm not at Margaret's beck and call, I can really enjoy it."

"What do you mean?"

"When she wanted someone to sing at something, she'd call me. Whether it was for a hundred people or two. When she called, I dropped everything and went. Sometimes she'd let me know in advance, but she also delighted in waiting until the last minute."

"I'm starting to feel very lucky that I didn't know her very well."

"You are. She expected miracles at the drop of a hat. If she'd told me I owed her one more time, I might have killed her myself."

"Don't go around saying that. Someone might believe you."

Stella flicked her hand in an "I don't care" motion. "She hated owing people, but she loved them owing her."

"I helped her set up her account for my garage sale site. She told me she owed me one, but I thought it was just an offhand comment at the time." I shuddered. "She doesn't sound like a very nice person. Any thoughts on who might have killed her?" I asked.

Stella munched on her cookie and sat without speaking for a minute. "No. People might say they wanted to, but I can't think of a soul who would actually do it. Now I'm really, truly free." Stella finished her cookie and held her glass up toward the sky. "Here's to you, Margaret. I sang one last time for you. May you rest in peace or burn in hell."

I trudged up the steps to my apartment. Stella wouldn't let me leave the cookies and didn't buy my "Opera singers are supposed to be fat" line. I thought about Margaret having her finger in the political world, which made me think of Seth. His family obviously knew Margaret. And I remembered hearing that eyebrows had been raised when Seth, at such a young age, was appointed to take over for the ailing former district attorney. And now hoped to be elected as the DA.

I didn't recognize the guy at the top of the steps, but I went over, anyway. "I have some cookies for Mike. Is he home?"

The guy stood and looked me over. "No one's supposed to be up here."

I glared up at him and pointed at my apartment. "I live right there." The guy raised an eyebrow, so I dug around in my purse and found my ID. "Here. Now, please get Mike." I said it loudly. "Or do you want to go through the cookie box, too?"

He reached for the box as the door whipped open, and one of Mike's brothers stood there.

"I have cookies for Mike, and I don't appreciate being questioned about being here."

"Sorry, He's new. Come on in."

Mike sat on a leather couch, watching the Celtics play on a ginormous-screen TV, which hadn't been here before Mike moved in. "Hey, Sarah. What's up?"

I stepped around the poker table. "I brought you some cookies." I handed him the box. "And I have two questions. Do you know Seth Anderson, and was he over here playing poker the other night?"

Mike flipped open the box and picked a cookie. "Of course I know who Seth Anderson is. A guy like me always knows the players in the area." He looked me in the eye. "But no, he wasn't over here. Why would he be?"

I left, knowing that Mike was a consummate liar. Not because of anything he'd said or done, but because I'd glanced at his brother, who had had a panicked expression on his face. If this whole mess were at a garage sale, I wouldn't buy it, because something stunk.

Chapter 19

I settled on the couch, flipped on the Celtics game, and called Seth.

"Sarah, come over." He sounded so happy to hear from me. I heard voices in the background. "I have people over watching the Celtics game."

Darn. I couldn't very well quiz him on his relationships with Margaret and Mike if he had a house full of guests.

"I can't. I had a long day with a client."

"How'd it go?"

"Good." Always Miss Upbeat all of a sudden, as I didn't want anyone to feel sorry for me.

"I'd get rid of everyone if I could." Seth's low, soft voice made me tingle, even though I had questions for him.

His friends cheered as one of the Celtics shot a three-pointer from half-court to finish the half.

"Seth, darling, what's taking you so long?" It was

Nichole talking in the background. I couldn't believe she called him "darling."

"I've got to go, Seth," I said.

"Wait. Why'd you call?"

"No particular reason." I hung up. I didn't want to give him a heads-up about Mike before we talked in person.

Sunday morning, after a long soak in the tub, two cups of coffee, and a failed attempt at the Sunday crossword puzzle, I read an article in the paper about Juanita's death. It was splashed all over the front page of the local paper. Two murders within a few days of each other in a small town like Ellington was unheard of. Although technically at this point Juanita's death was a suspicious death, and, boy, did I have my suspicions. But the article didn't tell me anything new.

To keep busy, I flopped on the couch, popped open the laptop, and worked on my garage sale site. One hundred notifications sat there, waiting for me. I took another drink of coffee and started sifting through them. Most of them were easy: a question about how to post something, someone wanting to add a friend to the site, a complaint about someone else bumping their posts up more frequently than the once a week that was allowed.

I breezed through most of them in a half hour. There were a couple of posts about Juanita. One person asked if anyone had heard from her, because she was supposed to clean her house yesterday. She had company coming and was very upset. Then there was another complaint and, finally, a post about Juanita's death, with a link to the story in the newspaper.

I sent a message to the person with the complaint, asking what kind of problems she'd had. I heard back right away. It wasn't a problem with Juanita's cleaning, which was fine, but she'd come home on two different occasions after Juanita had cleaned and left to find a door or a window unlocked. I asked if anything had been taken, but nothing had. It worried me, nonetheless. With Juanita dead, I guessed it didn't really matter if she'd been involved in something bad. It must have died with her.

I noticed that a nor'easter was expected to hit this evening, bringing with it our first significant snow of the year. Right now the sky was blue and cloudless. My phone rang, and I had mixed feelings when I saw it was Seth. But not so mixed that I ignored the call.

"You hung up pretty quickly last night," he said.

"You had company and were busy."

"Is this about Nichole? We're just friends. I didn't even invite her. She just showed up with other people I did invite."

"You don't owe me any explanations."

"But I want to. I want to mean that much to you." He always knew what to say to break down my resistance. And since I wanted to talk to him about more than one thing, it wasn't very hard.

"Seth—"

"Come to lunch with me."

"I have a lot to do." *Liar.* "Besides, don't you have a thing with your family today?"

"Mother got a better offer and ditched us. So I'm free, and you have to eat. If I know you, all you have in your house is Marshmallow Fluff, peanut butter, and bread."

"They're staples. Besides, there's a nor'easter headed this way."

"You are such a California girl. I'll have you home safe before the first flake falls. Please come to lunch."

"Okay." I really didn't want a fluffernutter, anyway.

I figured we'd go to Helen's, my favorite breakfast and lunch place in Concord, but Seth kept driving. "Where are we going?" I asked.

"The Wayside Inn in Sudbury."

"Longfellow's Wayside Inn?" I couldn't keep the excitement out of my voice. I'd always wanted to go, and it wasn't that far from Ellington. I'd just never made it.

"Yes, but it was around long before Longfellow wrote about it. It's the oldest continually run inn in the States. The road it sits on is one of the first mail routes in the country."

Seth took the back roads, and I was content to

watch the low stone walls roll by and to admire the colonial-style houses, which actually were from colonial times.

"When the inn first opened, the Howe family called it a 'house of entertainment,'" Seth said as he pulled into the parking lot of the inn.

"That sounds kind of naughty."

"Maybe it was."

As we got out of the car, Seth pointed to a window on the second floor of the red clapboard building. "That room's haunted."

Hairs prickled on the back of my neck when I looked at the window and saw a shadow pass it. I grabbed Seth's arm. "I think I just saw the ghost."

He looked up and laughed. "It looks like the cleaning woman is vacuuming. Are you afraid of ghosts?"

I squinted my eyes and was relieved to see it was a woman vacuuming. "Maybe. Just a little."

"If you plan to stay in New England, you're going to have to toughen up. We have a lot of ghosts and a lot of snow. You can't let either of them scare you."

"Any other tips?"

"You should date only lawyers named Seth." He linked his hand with mine and pointed at the window again. "This ghost story is tragic. Jerusha Howe, the daughter of one of the owners, fell in love with a guy from Britain. He pledged his love to her. But he had to return to England and promised he'd be back."

"He didn't show back up, did he? Scum."

"He might have died at sea or in a carriage accident, pining for her with his last breath."

I rolled my eyes. "Or had a wife and five kids back at home. What happened to Jerusha?"

"She never married but supposedly lived a happy life and died single."

"If she was so happy, why's she haunting the place?"

"She never gave up looking for her love."

We walked to the front door of the inn. As we entered, a greeter in colonial clothes told us he was dressed in garb from the Sudbury Company of Militia and Minute. We strolled down the hall, looking at the historic photographs, until we were seated in the Tap Room, at one of two tables in front of the fireplace. The room's post and beam framing only added to the romantic atmosphere. A girl could get carried away in a place like this. But I didn't plan to end up like Jerusha.

"How did you manage to get a table right in front of the fireplace?" I asked.

"I had a reservation."

A woman handed us two menus. "It must have been months ago if you snagged one of these tables," she said.

Seth smiled at me. "I called as soon as you said yes. Sometimes a guy gets lucky."

I studied my menu to avoid saying anything. I ordered the broiled Boston scrod, a traditional New England dish of baked cod with lots of butter and a crumb topping that originated at Parker's Restaurant at the Parker House in Boston. Seth ordered the Belgian Endive Scoops stuffed with lobster for us to share and a steak.

"This used to be called the Howe Tavern, but after Longfellow made it famous when he wrote *Tales of a Wayside Inn*, they changed the name to Longfellow's Wayside Inn in the late eighteen hundreds," Seth said.

"How do you know so much?"

"I love history, but it's also on the back of the menu."

I loved the history of the area, too, so this was another thing we had in common. Before our divorce, CJ had gone with me to a few historical sites, like the Old North Bridge in Concord, and to Salem. But he had just gone to please me, while I had breathed in the history and had felt it in my soul.

We ate our appetizer and started on our entrées before I brought up the subject of Margaret. "I've been hearing a lot about Margaret More."

"Don't tell me you've been listening to the stories about Margaret. She's almost an urban legend."

"Do you know Hennessy Hamilton?"

"No."

I was surprised, but then I remembered that Seth had grown up in Boston and Nantucket. As an adult, he'd lived in Lowell and Bedford. He wasn't as plugged into the Ellington people as I might have believed. And as far as I knew, Hennessy hadn't committed any crimes beyond being overly dramatic. I filled him in on what Hennessy had told me.

"Then I talked to Stella. She said Margaret pressured her to be a star and then, when things fell apart, to do Margaret's bidding."

"But maybe that was how Stella felt, instead of what Margaret thought. Stella might have felt guilty and thought she'd wasted Margaret's money. She could have just told her no."

"I guess she could have. But Stella said Margaret threatened to ruin her aunt's political ambitions. Do you know Nancy Elder?"

"Yes, and I have no doubt that Margaret liked to manipulate people. But I think some people just buy into it and others called her bluff. How long have you known Hennessy?"

"I don't really know Hennessy. I've shopped at her store some."

"And Stella?"

"She's been my landlady for just over a year. But we didn't really start getting to know each other until last April." I hadn't known Seth much longer than that, either.

Seth leaned back when I finished eating and asked the waiter for more coffee.

"How long had you known Margaret?" Seth asked.

"Several years, through the Spouses' Club. But not well."

"And what did you think of her before you started hearing all of this?"

"That she was a nice old lady with a lot of money who liked to help people." I thought Seth was working his lawyer voodoo on me. He had a point but I wasn't done yet. "I heard she helped you, too."

Seth took my hand. "She backed my appointment as DA, and you think I owe her. Her influence probably did help me get the appointment, and she was backing my campaign to get elected."

I thought about yelling, "Aha," but listened instead.

"To assume I got the job because of who my family is and who they know, and not because of my hard work, hurts. It's something I've had to deal with since I was appointed. But I think I've proved most of the naysayers wrong by doing a damn good job."

"I didn't think that. I'm sorry if it came off that way." I knew what long hours he worked, and maybe now I knew why.

"Margaret was a philanthropist. She had a lot of money and enjoyed helping people. If people looked at that as owing her, it's on them. She might have been a bit of a meddler, but so what?"

"So you didn't feel like you owed her?"

Seth shook his head. "When Nichole moved back, I occasionally took her to events if Margaret asked me. Margaret wanted to make sure that Nichole knew the right people."

"You're sure she didn't want you to be more than a go-between?"

"She might have, but I made it clear that wasn't my intention. To both of them. I was just trying to help an old friend. The only thing I owe Margaret is to make sure whoever killed her goes away for a very long time."

I sipped my coffee, thinking about all Seth had said.

"Are there any leads?" I asked.

"Nothing that I can talk about. Do you want to share a dessert?"

I hesitated before nodding. We'd fallen into the habit of sharing desserts before I'd put the relationship moratorium in place.

"You look reluctant."

"Dessert sharing is a big step in a relationship. It shows a level of trust and a willingness to be a part of someone's life." CJ and I had started to share a dessert the night I'd gone to dinner with him, and I hadn't even thought about it. When we were young, we'd skipped the dessert-sharing portion of our lives and gone right into sharing everything. But we'd been young and impulsive.

Seth stared at me. He had to think I was a nut. I'd slept with him the other night. Here I was, out to lunch with him and suddenly worrying about sharing a dessert. I felt a little nuts. I blamed it on lack of sleep.

"It's just dessert. A willingness to enjoy without overindulging. But I like your take on it. I want to be a part of your life, and I'm glad you trust me," Seth said.

"How does the deep-dish apple pie and ice cream sound?" I should have kept my mouth shut.

Chapter 20

When we finished, I stood and headed for the door of the inn, but Seth grabbed my hand and led me upstairs.

"Let's see if we can peek inside Jerusha's room," he said.

The door to the room was open, and the maid's cart sat outside, but she was nowhere to be seen. We walked in. The room had wood paneling and a low beamed ceiling. Seth's head almost touched one of the beams. CJ would have had to duck. People had written Jerusha notes and had tucked them into crevices around the beams in the ceiling.

I went over to the window. It looked out over the road, and I pictured Jerusha sitting there, waiting for her love to come back. It probably wasn't unlike how a military spouse felt when his or her loved one was deployed. Only Jerusha never moved beyond it. It made me wonder if I could ever truly move on from CJ or if I really wanted to.

Seth came up behind me and wrapped his arms around me. He pressed his lips to my neck, but instead of warmth, I felt cold, as if an icy hand had caressed my neck. I thought I smelled a faint whiff of flowery perfume. Seth stiffened.

"Let's get out of here," I said.

"Did you feel that?" he asked as we hurried down the steps.

"I did. Like a cold caress, but it probably was just a draft."

"Or Jerusha trying to tell us something."

"What would that be?"

"Don't wait on love?"

I wasn't sure if he was talking about him or me, but once we were back out in the bright sunlight, it didn't seem to matter.

A few snowflakes were falling when we pulled up in front of my apartment. Seth glanced up, not at my apartment but at Mike's.

It had been such a nice afternoon that I hadn't wanted to bring up Mike, but now I felt like I had to. "Were you playing poker with Mike Titone the other night?"

Seth looked down at his hands before turning to me. "Does it matter?"

"It looked like you ducked back so I wouldn't see you."

"I was smoking. I do it about once a year, but I didn't want you to see me."

I thought about the cigarette butts at Margaret's house.

"Lots of guys smoke on poker night. Is that so bad?" Seth asked.

I shook my head, but I wasn't quite sure I believed his story, and that made me uneasy. "He's in the Mob. I think that's what you didn't want me to see."

Seth tucked a strand of hair behind my ear. "No one knows that I play poker with him on occasion. If anyone saw me go in, they'd think I was going to see you."

"I don't even know what to say to that. I'm not sure which is worse, that you'd risk your career for a poker game or that you'd use me to do it." I opened the car door. "Thanks for lunch."

Seth snagged my hand. "Don't be mad. I have my reasons for playing with Mike."

"Let's hear them."

"I can't tell you."

How many times had I heard that over the years from CJ, while he was active duty in the air force? Part of me understood that some jobs required great amounts of discretion, clearances, and secrets. But another part of me was sick of it. Was there any such thing as an easy relationship?

"I stood outside your door that night after I left Mike's. It was late, so I didn't knock. I didn't want you to misinterpret my being at your door so late. Please understand."

I thought about Jerusha waiting for her love. Had she tried to tell me something? "Okay."

Seth pulled me into his arms, and we kissed until neither of us could catch a breath. I climbed out of the car and watched him drive off. Dark clouds had gathered to the southeast of the church steeple. It looked like a storm was coming.

I walked over to DiNapoli's Roast Beef and Pizza, knowing the state of my larder was right up there with Old Mother Hubbard's. I could buy a pizza, a salad, and some ziti, which would get me through the storm if things got really bad. Plus, maybe I could find a way to discreetly ask the DiNapolis about Seth and what was up between him and Mike. I yanked on the door, but it didn't budge. They were closed. I'd never seen DiNapoli's closed during the middle of the day. A little fissure of anxiety zipped through me. There was no note on the door. I hoped nothing had happened to Angelo or Rosalie. I whipped out my cell phone and tried to call Rosalie, but she didn't answer. I cupped my hands and peered in. Nothing stirred. Maybe Angelo had finally ruffled the wrong feathers and a health inspector had closed them down for a minor infraction. The second option seemed all too possible.

Angelo, whose name meant "messenger of God" in Italian, had a bit of a reputation in town for his opinions and temper. He regularly wrote letters to the editor, calling out anyone he felt was out of line on either side of the political fence. He reprimanded jaywalkers, and sometimes his priest came to him for advice. Angelo did it all out of the best place in his heart. He wanted people to be safe and happy. But not everyone saw it that way. Thankfully, there weren't any notices on the door indicating they'd been cited for a health infraction. Even the pickiest inspector would have a hard time finding fault at DiNapoli's. Although the fixtures were old and worn, the restaurant was always spotless.

I stood there, trying to figure out what to do. Maybe Carol would know why DiNapoli's was closed. She and Angelo weren't the closest of friends—even the term *friends* was stretching it—but there'd been a bit of a thaw in their relationship since the fall. I turned to go to Carol's but realized it was Sunday and she was closed. One of the ways I found things out was through the local grapevine, and with DiNapoli's closed, the grapevine might be broken.

Around six in the evening the snow was hurtling down. I turned on the news. As predicted, a nor'easter had formed off the coast to the south and was moving more quickly than expected. It was going to come through hard and fast tonight.

Rosalie called. "I need a favor," she said.

"Of course. Anything." They'd fed me and comforted me so many times, I was eager to repay them in some small way. "But are you and Angelo all right? Why's the restaurant closed?"

"We're fine, but Stefano took a turn for the worse."

"Oh, no. What's wrong?"

"He had a heart attack this afternoon. The family is all here in Cambridge, trying to figure out who'll run the family business while he recuperates."

"Real estate," I heard Angelo yell in the background. It made me smile. Angelo had repeatedly told me the family business was real estate. I hoped it was.

"Tell Stefano I hope he recovers quickly."

"I will. Could you move my car for me? I heard Ellington has a snow emergency going into effect. I left it parked up the street from DiNapoli's and rode over here with Angelo. I don't want it to get towed."

I glanced out the window. The flakes were small and moved sideways, obscuring my view of the Congregational church and the town common. As much as I wanted to help, I was reluctant to drive to Cambridge in this weather, even in my Suburban. But this was for Rosalie and Angelo. "I'll come get the keys."

"You don't have to do that. The keys are under the mat on the driver's side," Rosalie said. "It's a gray Honda Accord, four door."

I shook my head at the thought of leaving one's keys in the car. Normally, Ellington had relatively little crime, but still. "Okay. No worries. I'll move it. Let me know if there's anything else I can do."

I slipped on my heaviest coat, pulled a hat low over my ears, and wrapped a scarf around my face. I checked my pocket for gloves and trotted downstairs. I was about to walk out when Stella walked in.

"Where are you off to?" Stella asked.

I pulled my scarf down to talk. "Moving Rosalie's car for her. I'm going to park it in the Callahans' spot since they're gone, if that's okay with you."

"Sure. I could use a walk. I've been inside all day, judging a middle school singing contest," Stella said. "Let me dump this stuff in my apartment and go with you." She had a briefcase and a bag from the packy—a state-run package store, or liquor store—that looked like it held wine. "We can have a glass of wine when we get back. Come on in. I have to feed Tux, too."

Tux, Stella's adorable cat, loved me, and as soon as we walked in, he wound between my legs, purring. I bent down to pet him, and he rolled on his back for a tummy scratch.

"Oh, sorry," Stella said. "He has a sixth sense about people with allergies."

"It's fine," I said, straightening up. "I just need to wash my hands and not touch my eyes."

Two minutes later we headed out. We stepped onto the porch, and a gust of wind swirled snow around us like we were inside a snow tornado. It let up for a second, but another gust followed.

"You don't have to come," I yelled to Stella, my voice muffled by the snow and the scarf over my face. "I can move the car and be back in a few minutes."

I stepped off the porch onto the steps. The flakes had turned into pellets of snow that felt like they'd been shot out of a cannon. I readjusted my scarf and pulled my hood up over my hat, drawing the strings tighter, hoping to protect as much of my face as possible. If this were for anyone but Rosalie, I would have hightailed it back into the house. Even out here, I couldn't see the big Congregational church on the town common.

"I'll come," Stella shouted. "You shouldn't be out in this alone. It reminds me of that scene in *Little House on the Prairie* where they can't see the barn and have to follow a rope. This is wild."

I was grateful Stella was coming, not because I was worried about getting lost, but because a tiny part of me was afraid that even on a night like this, my stalker might be around. We linked arms and bent over, walking into the wind. It was pointless to try to talk, between the wind, the snow, and our multiple layers of clothes. Our footprints were obliterated as soon as we took our next step. I was grateful for the Sorel boots I'd bought off my virtual garage sale site. At least my feet were dry and warm.

Great Road was deserted, businesses closed. It looked like a ghost town set in the Arctic instead of suburbia outside of Boston. We could barely see the stoplight and crossed even though it was red. There was a time last spring when I would have waited even on a night like this, because anytime I did anything remotely out of line, some police officer was there to catch me. Fortunately, that nonsense had subsided.

The area behind the businesses was more residential and darker. I smelled smoke from multiple fireplaces as we trudged up the street. A fireplace, a good book, and a glass of wine. I could just picture the cozy scenario. I tugged on Stella's arm and pointed. The car was up ahead. We hurried the last bit and open the doors, then almost bashed heads over the console as we both lunged into the car. I wrenched the car door closed after a brief battle with the wind.

"The keys are supposed to be under the mat," I said. The car was neat and tidy, except for the little puddles dripping off our boots onto the floor mats.

Stella pointed a mittened hand. "They're in the ignition."

"Rosalie is too trusting." I fired up the engine, blasted the defrost, and turned on the rear window defroster. Fortunately, the snow hadn't started piling up on the car, because of the swirling wind.

I put the car in drive and cautiously pulled out. A few seconds later we passed another parked car. "Poor sap is going to get towed."

"Rosalie's lucky you were willing to move hers."

I took a right down a residential street. Lights glimmered dimly through the snow from the houses lining it. Another right and we were headed back to

Great Road. As I turned onto Great Road, the car died. I used its forward momentum to steer it to the side of the road.

The locks on the car clicked down.

"What the hell?" Stella asked.

Chapter 21

"Some sort of power failure?" I really didn't know anything about cars. At least we weren't in the middle of the street, with the visibility so poor. I tried to unlock the door manually, but the lock wouldn't release. The window wouldn't roll down, either. "What the heck?"

I fished in my pocket for my cell phone. The car shuddered in the wind. The radio blared on. The tune from the TV show *Cops* rang out—the one about bad boys. Then the radio cut off as quickly as it had started.

"That was freaky," Stella said. She fought the door lock, but all her yanking and tugging didn't help. Her breath came in harsh pants.

"Are you okay?" I asked her.

"We've gotta get out. It's like a horror movie."

We both looked over the backseat. But no one was hiding back there.

"It's fine." But now I felt uneasy, too. "It's just an electrical problem." I held up my cell. "It's working.

I'll call for help." I glanced in the rearview mirror and noticed blue lights flashing as they came toward us. "Look. It's the police. Help is on the way."

"What if they go by?" Stella latched onto my arm like it was a life preserver.

"Then I'll call someone."

But I didn't need to. Two patrol cars pulled up. One angled in front of us, and one behind us.

"See? They'll jump the car for us," I said.

An officer knocked on the window. One I didn't recognize. I'd thought I knew pretty much every man and woman on the force after last spring. He stood out there, his bulletproof vest over his uniform shirt, with no hat, coat, or gloves, like it was a balmy spring evening.

"I can't roll the window down," I shouted. "Something's wrong with the car."

He smiled as the snow danced around him. It was all too eerie.

I turned to Stella. "What's wrong with that guy? Maybe *this* is the horror part of the story."

Stella leaned forward and looked past me at him. "Well, if it is, at least he's cute. Not some shaved-head, metal-toothed freak."

I looked at him again. I guessed if you liked chiseled cheekbones, big brown eyes, and long eyelashes, the guy would qualify as cute.

"I need your license and registration," the officer yelled.

"The car isn't working." I spoke slow and loud, hoping he'd understand.

"Try it again," he said.

I did, and it came to life. Wow. Did he have magical powers? Smiling, I rolled down the window. "Thanks. I live close by. Would you mind following us, in case it happens again?" The great thing about small towns was the police usually were very helpful.

"I need to see your license and registration," he said again. This time he spoke slow and loud. A snowflake smacked his nose, and he swatted it away like it was a fly in the middle of summer. The officer from the other patrol car came up on Stella's side of the car. He shined a flashlight in the car, checking us and the backseat out.

I realized I'd left my license in my purse at home. This was supposed to be a quick trip. "I don't have it. I live right over there." I pointed across the snowy town common, not that you could see through the snow to our building.

The officer nodded. "What about the registration?"

I was lucky I didn't get some hard-nosed, power-hungry cop who'd write you up or take you in for not having a license with you. In fact, he seemed to be enjoying himself more than most police officers did when they helped someone. A little shiver of doubt went through me.

"Stella check the glove box for Rosalie's registration."

She popped the glove box open. I could see from here that it was empty. I opened the console, and it was empty, as well.

"The, uh, registration isn't in the glove box or console." Well, this was embarrassing. "This isn't my car."

"You don't say," he said.

The two officers exchanged grins.

"Please step out of the car and keep your hands where we can see them," he said.

"My ex is—"

The officer on my side held up a hand, cutting me off. "Don't care. Out of the car. Both of you."

I stepped out. My feet barely had hit the ground before I found myself twirled around, up against the car, and handcuffed.

I looked across the top of the car at Stella. She, too, was cuffed. Her big green eyes were bigger than usual.

I tried to look over my shoulder at the officer. "This is my friend's car. She asked me to move it for her. The keys were in the ignition."

"Unless your friend's name is the Boston Police Department, you just stole the bait car they loaned us."

"Bait car?"

"There's been an uptick in car thefts in Ellington. The chief wanted to squelch it as quickly as possible. Looks like it worked."

I would have thunked my forehead with my hand if I hadn't been cuffed. CJ had mentioned a problem with car thefts when we had dinner. "This is a huge mistake," I said.

"Tell it to the judge." The officer jerked on my handcuffs and hustled me over to his squad car.

Stella was led away by the other officer. The only good news in this whole mess was there was no one out to see it happen because of the storm.

The normal seven-minute drive to the station took twice that, as the storm unleashed on us. The car was silent except for the snow attacking it. The officer held the wheel lightly, like we were out for a Sunday drive, despite the occasional wind gusts pushing us around.

"What's your name?" I asked. "You must be new."

"Awesome."

I choked back a snort of laughter. "You're Officer Awesome?"

He shook his head. "Bossome. With a B. Officer Bossome. You seem pretty casual for a car thief. Lots of experience?"

"Tons," I said.

Chapter 22

Awesome clasped my arm tightly as he led me into the station. Stella and her officer were right behind us. A cheer went up from the officers and dispatchers in the squad room but quickly died down. The station was more crowded than usual. Pellner looked at me, astonished.

"You stole the bait car?" he asked. He sounded so disappointed. He had to know that this was some kind of wild mix-up and that I wasn't out looking for cars to go on a joyride in.

"I'm not going to answer that until my lawyer's present." It didn't seem like a good idea to say yes and then try to get someone to listen to my explanation of what had happened without Vincenzo by my side.

Pellner looked at Stella. "Do you want to explain?"

Stella shook her head no. Considering her past troubles with the law, she probably thought it was better to say nothing, too.

"Where's CJ?" I asked Pellner.

"He went home to grab some sleep. Uncuff them," Pellner told Awesome and the other officer.

"Are you sure?" Awesome asked.

"Yeah," Pellner said. "She's the chief's ex-wife. We know both of them."

I loosened the hood of my coat and unwrapped my scarf. The officer with Awesome did a double take when he recognized me.

"The chief's ex-wife is a criminal?" Awesome checked me out, assessing me with wise cop eyes, as he uncuffed me.

Stella and I both rubbed our wrists and shook out our arms as soon as we were free.

"Thanks, Officer Awesome," I said, perhaps in my own attempt to bait him.

Everyone around us laughed.

"Officer Awesome," someone said. "Good one."

I expected Awesome's ego to flare up. But he just joined in with the others, laughing.

"Everyone told me a small town force would be different, but I didn't realize we'd be joking around with the thieves we caught," Awesome said.

"Oh, for goodness' sakes," I said. "Just call Rosalie DiNapoli. She asked me to move her car. Said that it was a gray sedan and that the keys were in it. I didn't think there'd be more than one gray sedan with the keys in it on the street on a night like this."

"No one's going to believe that," Awesome said.

"It's true," Stella said. I swore she batted her lashes in the direction of Awesome and blushed a little. Even though she'd been dating a lot recently,

I hadn't seen her batting and blushing in a long time.

"I'll call her," Pellner said. "Crazy as it sounds, Awesome, it's probably true."

"She might be hard to get a hold of. She's with Angelo at a hospital in Cambridge."

Several people said, "Oh, no," and others shook their heads.

Someone said, "I wondered why there were closed today."

"It's not either of them. It's Angelo's uncle, Stefano."

Everyone looked relieved and then drifted back to their own desks as Pellner made the call. He left a message. "Just go sit over there, out of the way, until we hear back from her." He pointed to a couple of chairs by an unoccupied desk.

"Can someone move Rosalie's car so it doesn't get towed?" I asked, not moving from my spot.

"Sure," Pellner said. "We'll take care of it."

"Any word on what happened to Margaret?" I asked him.

His dimple deepened as his lips tightened. He folded his arms across his chest.

"Or Juanita? What about who broke into my apartment? Anything on any of these cases?"

Pellner narrowed his eyes and pointed toward the chairs, so Stella and I walked over to them.

Awesome stopped by Pellner's desk. "Are you sure you want the two suspects sitting together? They could be getting their stories straight."

"When it's those two, it's fine. You can head back out. Take someone with you and move Rosalie's car."

Awesome got an "Are you serious?" look on his face.

"You can put it in one of our parking spots," I told him and rattled off the address.

Awesome looked at Pellner, who nodded. He shrugged and took one more good look at us. I waved, and he headed out the door.

"Jeez, he's suspicious," I said to Pellner.

"You would be too if you were used to policing in New York City."

"What's he doing here?" I asked.

"I guess he got tired of big city problems," Pellner said.

"He's not a Yankees fan, is he?" Stella asked. She looked disappointed at the thought.

"I don't think that's on the list of questions on the application," Pellner said.

"Maybe it should be," someone said. That got a good laugh.

"Okay, let's get back to work. We have multiple cases to work on and a storm."

People's faces became grim, and everyone returned to their work.

Stella and I both whipped out our phones and pretended to concentrate on them while we strained to listen to bits of quiet conversations. But mostly, we heard the clatter of fingers on keyboards. Computers sure made it difficult to snoop at the police station. I picked up a word here and there:

Frieda, boot prints, cigarette butts in the woods, house unlocked, Juanita. Stella checked her e-mail, and I Googled "bait cars." Police departments parked them in areas where lots of thefts occurred. They had audio and video equipment to tape the events, along with kill switches. That explained why the car had stopped and locked. There was even a television show about them.

We sat for about forty-five minutes before Rosalie called. Pellner hung up the phone. "You're free to go."

Stella and I sat there. "We don't have a way home," I said.

"I'll get Awesome to swing back by."

I let Stella sit up front on the way home. The snow wasn't as heavy as it had been, but the roads were still slick. Stella and Officer Awesome laughed and joked the whole way back. I tried to make sense of the few bits I'd overheard at the station. Once I was up in my apartment, I looked out my window. The squad car was still outside, and Stella was still in it.

Chapter 23

In the morning I tossed aside my bedroom curtains and, squinting in the sunlight, looked out over the common. The nor'easter had blown through quickly and had left only about an inch of snow. It had seemed like there'd be a lot more when I went out in it last night. Great Road was already down to bare pavement, as was my street. Given the sun, all the snow would be melted by noon. The sun was shining a little too brightly for how late I'd been up last night. My phone rang.

"Are you okay?" Seth asked.

"Other than being sleepy, I'm fine. Why?"

"I heard you met Officer Awesome," Seth said. "He loves his new nickname."

I wondered how he knew this already. "I didn't think I'd ever laugh because I was picked up for stealing a car."

"And I didn't think I'd be laughing because someone did."

"So there's really a problem in Ellington with car

thieves?" It seemed so unbelievable, even if CJ had mentioned it to me.

"Not just in Ellington, but around the county. We want to stop it as quickly as we can. So we park the unlocked bait car with the keys in it. Someone steals it, and we've got them, as you well know."

"Isn't that entrapment?"

"The car isn't yours, whether the keys are in it or not. You have no right to take it. It's like if I helped myself to something you had out at a garage sale. It's stealing."

"You're right. Thank heavens they got ahold of Rosalie and that her car was there to prove my point."

"How'd Stella take it?"

"Fortunately, she has an excellent sense of humor."

"I've got another call. I'll talk to you later today." Seth hung up.

I heard a commotion outside my door and shuffled over to see what was going on. I still had bed head and wore a ratty thermal shirt over yoga pants, but I just didn't care this morning. I cracked open my door. Mike stood in the hall with a suitcase in his hand.

"Where are you going?" I asked, opening the door the rest of the way.

"Back to the North End, where I belong." He moved closer as his two brothers carted the poker table down the steps.

"Will you be safe?" I'd gotten used to having Mike and his security team around.

"We found out who threw the disk. That person is swimming with the fishies."

I took a step back and felt the blood drain from my face.

"Whoa. Don't believe everything you've heard about me." Mike laughed. "The girl that did it, Daniella, is down in Venezuela on a snorkeling adventure. I don't think she'll be coming back anytime soon."

I patted my heart. "Oh."

Mike set his suitcase down. "If you ever need any cheese or you're down in the North End for some reason, stop by and see me."

"I'm going to miss having you and the guys around." I gave Mike a hug.

"Stella's a good kid and took me in on short notice. I owe her one." He picked up his suitcase and trotted down the stairs.

A few minutes later I went down to visit Stella. "Mike's gone," I said. "He said he owed you one." Having a mobster owe you was probably a lot better than the other way around.

"I kind of got used to him being here," she said. "Come on in. Want some coffee?" She poured us cups without waiting for my answer. She knew I liked my coffee. My cup said I'LL BE BACH. Music humor. We sat on the couch and turned the volume down on her television.

"Tell me about Officer Awesome," I said. Tux sprawled in a sunny spot on the floor. It almost looked like it was raining out, because the snow was melting so quickly.

"He *is* a Yankees fan, but everyone has their flaws."

"Does he like music?" It seemed like an important part of Stella's life.

"He can't sing a note on key to save his life, and his taste in music includes rhythm and blues. He's never been to an opera." Stella smiled as she said it. "Oh, and he detests scotch."

"So in other words, you have nothing in common and won't be seeing each other again," I said.

"Yes and no. We don't have anything in common, but we're going out to dinner tonight."

I shook my head.

"Just think of us telling our kids how we met."

It surprised me that Stella wanted kids. CJ and I had wanted them, but it had never happened. "That he arrested you for stealing a car?"

"Yes! It's a great story."

I laughed. "An excellent foundation for a relationship." But who was I to judge? I had almost knocked CJ over and had spent the night with Seth the first time I met him.

Stella pointed to the TV. "There's CJ." She turned the volume up.

"We have a person of interest in the murders of Margaret More and Juanita Smith," CJ said.

"Are the murders related?" a reporter asked.

"I can't comment on that."

Several other people asked CJ questions, but all his answers were, "I can't comment on that."

Stella flipped the television off, and we stared at each other. Tux lifted his head and looked at us before deciding we weren't that interesting.

"Have you heard anything about this?" she asked me.

"Not a word, and I talked to Seth this morning. He must have known."

"Or they just found something out."

"I guess that's possible. I wonder who it is."

"I wonder how you can find out," Stella said.

"Do you think it could be me?" I really, really hoped I was wrong.

Stella's green eyes got larger. "Wouldn't Seth or CJ mention it to you?"

"I don't know." I stared into my coffee cup, wishing it would have some answer for me. There were so many things that both of them kept from me.

"I can't imagine that Seth would spend time with you or call you if you're a person of interest in a murder case."

"He didn't sound any different this morning."

"There you go. You're worrying for nothing."

"You're right. You must be right."

Preparations for the February Blues garage sale were the perfect counterbalance to everything going on in my life. I met Laura at the community center not long after I left Stella. Working was so much more fun than sitting around worrying about being a suspect in two murders.

"I'll use masking tape to mark off where each table will be," I told Laura.

"I've got a truck full of stuff from the thrift shop sitting outside for the sale. I'll start hauling in the lighter-weight items." As the base commander's wife, Laura ended up working at the thrift shop, since volunteers could be hard to come by. I volunteered when I could, even though I no longer had any official standing on the base. One of the advantages of organizing the sale was I put my table in a prime location—to the right as people came in and next to what would be the large space for the thrift shop, which would be a big draw. I supposed people would grumble, but I could probably stick myself in a back corner, and people would somehow think that was an advantage.

"Want to see if we're strong enough to get a couch off the back of the truck?" Laura asked after we'd worked for a couple of hours.

I flexed my arm to show her my muscles. It wasn't from working out, but from years of hauling stuff around for garage sales. "Let's give it a try."

We donned our coats and headed out. I blinked in the bright sun, amazed that almost all traces of last night's storm were gone. Laura got on the bed of the truck and pushed as I pulled on the couch. I balanced it on the edge of the pickup while she hopped down. She ran around to the other side, and we lifted. It dropped like a rock on her side, and I barely managed to jump out of the way before my side crashed down.

"Whoa. That thing weighs a ton," I said.

"It's a Hide-A-Bed."

"We're going to need more help."

"Let's go have lunch at the bowling alley and see if we can find somebody to help us move this monster. The couch is out of the way, and it's sunny, so it should be fine if we leave for a bit."

"You're the boss," I said.

Laura smacked my arm.

We walked into the café at the bowling alley. The crack of pins being knocked down rang out, even though it was 11:30 a.m. on a weekday. But it could be the Spouses' Club league or one of the retiree leagues. I used to bowl with the Spouses' Club but hadn't been able to since the divorce. We both ordered burgers and decided to share fries. Ordering food made me wonder when DiNapoli's would open again and how Stefano was doing.

We found a table near a TV and waited for our food.

"What have you been up to?" Laura asked me.

"I got arrested last night."

Laura's jaw dropped, but pretty soon I had her laughing so hard, other people stared. They called the number for our order. I leaped up.

"I'll get it," I said.

When I came back, Laura was still grinning. She chatted about the base book club, her boys, who both played hockey, and the upcoming possibility of her husband getting promoted to general.

Tables filled as we ate, and I noticed a couple of guys who were both with the security forces. They'd worked for CJ before he retired. I pointed to their table. "Maybe they can help us with the couch," I told Laura. She nodded.

I walked over to them, and they agreed to meet us at the community center as soon as they finished eating.

Laura and I were walking back to her car when my phone chimed, telling me I had another PopIt. "Laura, I know this is going to sound silly, but I want you to look at this PopIt with me."

"Why do you even have PopIt?"

"I use it a lot for my business. But I've gotten a couple of creepy photos lately. No one is ever around to see them."

"Really? Creepy photos? Let's look."

I clicked on the app. A picture of Lindsay making a sad face at the food in the school cafeteria popped up and disappeared.

Laura shook her head. "That's weird but not creepy."

I laughed. "Lindsay's pictures make me smile. Let's take one to send back to her." We posed with our tongues sticking out. "That will make her laugh."

My phone chimed again. I pushed the button. A picture of the couch by the community center popped up. A crudely written sign on the couch said DIE, SARAH WINSTON. Beside the sign was a little cat that looked like Stella's cat Tux.

"Laura, look." I held my phone out, but the picture was already gone. This time I'd noticed the user name. It was DieSarah.

Chapter 24

"What is it? You're as pale as that cloud up there," Laura said.

"We've got to get back to the community center. I'll tell you on the way."

We hurried back to Laura's car, and she drove over the twenty-five-mile-an-hour speed limit by a daring five miles. The base wasn't like the rest of the world. Here you really might be pulled over for exceeding the speed limit by five miles an hour—even by one on some occasions. The military meant business when they posted a sign. Maybe having security around wasn't such a bad idea. I filled her in as she drove up Travis Road, the main road that cut from one side of the base to the other.

"Call security," Laura urged. "We don't know what we'll find up there."

I called the nonemergency number, which I knew by heart from the days when CJ was the squadron commander. Even as I explained what had happened, I knew how strange it sounded.

"We'll send a car right away, Mrs. Hooker," the airman who answered the phone said.

Even though I identified myself as Sarah Winston, people from the base often forgot I'd gone back to my maiden name. Laura and I beat the security forces to the community center. We pulled up near the couch. The sign and the cat were both gone. A squad car screeched up beside us. I was happy to see that James was the first one here.

"Stay in the car while I look around," he told us.

We nodded gratefully. A couple of other cars pulled up, one belonging to the two guys from the bowling alley who'd said they would help us move the couch. The troops started to scatter.

I rolled the window down. "Please look for a small black and white cat," I called after them. I couldn't bear to think that Tux or his twin was roaming loose.

From past experience I figured the photographer was long gone. Focusing on the cat was a lot easier than focusing on the reality of getting another picture. First, a photo of me finding Margaret, then the creepy photos commenting on my clothing, then the one of me heading into my apartment, and now this. A direct threat. Did someone really want me to die? Who? Why? A thousand other questions tumbled around in my head like laundry in a dryer while I sat there. I shot off a text to Stella asking if she was still home and if Tux was there. She wrote right back answering yes to both. *Whew.* Laura called her husband to let him know what was going on. A few minutes later James came back and motioned for Laura and me to get out of the car.

"Do you have any idea where the picture was taken from?" he asked.

I looked at the couch and then turned my back to it. I faced the TLF, the temporary lodging facility, a hotel of sorts for military people, which was surrounded by woods. I pointed to a spot near a Dumpster that seemed like it would be at the right angle to photograph the couch. And there were plenty of trees, along with the Dumpster, to hide behind and easy access to parking to get away. Talk about déjà vu. "I got a picture . . . the day I found Margaret More. It was taken by someone hiding in the woods, too." What the heck was going on? I was not sure why, but I didn't want to tell James about the other photos.

James's eyes lit in recognition.

"The police said there were some cigarette butts near a tree. Maybe someone should check for some here." I pointed again toward the spot the photo seemed to have been taken.

James spoke into the radio on his shoulder. A guy and girl hurried from the community center to the woods. At least with James on the case, I might have a chance of finding out what was going on.

"Let's go take a look inside the community center," James said. "We've already been through it, but you ladies might have a better idea if anything is out of place."

"Can you help us carry the couch in?" Laura asked. "We can't do it alone."

James picked up one end, and Laura and I took the other. With a bit of huffing and puffing, we managed to get it inside the room. The community center was empty, and there weren't any threatening signs lying around.

"I probably should go tell someone in the Ellington Police Department about what happened," I said.

"I can do it for you if you'd like," James said.

"Thank you. That would be great." If James told them, I could avoid any lectures or questions that might arise from this latest incident. It would give me time to think the whole thing through.

James's radio crackled, and we all heard someone say, "Found something." We followed James out, and Laura locked up. Several of the security policemen were standing by one of the trees, looking down.

"Stay here," James told us before trotting over to join the others.

He talked to them for a couple of minutes, and I saw one of the guys bag something. James trotted back over. "You two can take off."

"What was it?" Laura asked.

"Sorry, ma'am. I can't tell you," James said.

Laura gave him a steely look, but James held her gaze. She turned to me. "I'm going. Call me later. We'll finish our prep work tomorrow."

I nodded and waited until she was out of sight. "What was it, James? Please tell me. I'm scared."

"A couple of cigarette butts. Nothing else."

"So whoever is doing this is pretty dumb."

"And has access to the base," James said.

"That doesn't narrow the field by much." The base employed hundreds of people. Lots of retired military people lived in the area and used the base facilities. Then there were delivery people and guests. "Thanks for letting me know."

"Don't rat me out," he said with a grim smile.

"Never."

At 1:30 p.m. I walked over to DiNapoli's, which, happily, had reopened. I walked in, and the place was still pretty full. Ryan waved to me from the back as he bused a table. Rosalie looked up from taking an order.

"Hold on a minute," she told the person. "Lois, can you finish taking this order?" Rosalie came around the counter and hugged me. "I'm sorry we got you in trouble last night."

I shook my head. "I should have paid more attention. All cars look alike to me. How's Stefano doing?"

"Much better. Thanks." She went back around the counter. "Angelo made a new soup. Italian sausage, potatoes, white beans, kale. It's delicious."

"Sounds perfect."

I sat at a table, and Ryan brought over a basket of garlic bread. "It's great with the soup."

"Thanks, Ryan. Did you ever find a gift for your girlfriend?"

"No. I'm still looking, when I have time. I've been doing a lot of extra handyman jobs lately."

"The base is having a community sale on Friday.

Maybe you could find her something there. Do you have a way to get on?"

"I do. One of my buddies works on base." A group behind me left their table. Ryan grinned at me. "No rest for the wicked."

Angelo brought over my bowl of soup. He sat in the chair across from me and gestured toward the soup. "Tell me what you think."

I reached for the pepper.

"Really? You're going to add extra seasoning before you even taste it? I put just the right amount of pepper in it. You add more, it will upset the balance of the flavors."

I withdrew my hand. Angelo was rarely wrong when it came to food. I dipped my spoon in the soup. Chunky pieces of sausage and potatoes, spiked with pepper, steamed on the spoon. I blew on it before taking a bite. "Mmm. You're right. It's perfect."

Angelo nodded in an "Of course" motion.

"Kale seems kind of trendy for you, though."

"Humph. My mother used kale in this recipe long before it became trendy. She grew it in her own garden. I had to pick and clean it. It ain't easy to clean. Everyone looked down on us for having kale instead of iceberg lettuce." He waved his hands around. "Now everyone wants to eat kale. Until the next big thing comes along."

"Did you hear about Juanita?" I asked him.

"It's a sad business."

"Do you know if Margaret and Juanita knew each other?"

Angelo turned in his chair. "Rosalie, you got a minute, honey?"

Rosalie was wiping down counters but put the cloth down and joined us. I repeated my question.

"Margaret came in a few months ago, talking about needing a new cleaning lady. I mentioned Juanita because I'd seen her ad on your garage sale site."

I almost dropped my spoon in my soup. "Do you know if she used her?"

"No idea," Rosalie said.

"I saw CJ on TV this morning, saying they had a person of interest. Do you know who he was talking about?" I asked.

"With Stefano sick and getting caught up here, I haven't heard a thing," Rosalie said. Angelo nodded his agreement. "What have you heard?" she asked.

That was disappointing. "Nothing. It's just since I found Margaret, I'm worried he was talking about me."

Angelo frowned. "He'd better not be. You need me to call Vincenzo? I'll call him right now."

I smiled in spite of my worry. "No. It's okay."

"Eat your soup, before it gets cold," Rosalie said.

They left me alone with my thoughts. I used the bread Ryan had brought me to mop up the last bits of soup in my bowl. It wasn't like I could call Margaret's relatives and ask if they knew who her cleaning lady was. I didn't have access to her accounts or books. CJ might, but he wouldn't be answering any of my questions. Seth had said he'd call me later. Maybe he'd know. But I should probably notify the EPD about this development. The more they looked at someone else, the less they'd look at me. In the meantime I'd look through old posts and notifications on my Web site to see if I could find a connection there.

As I walked home, I realized maybe I could ask Nancy Elder if she knew anything. I'd go under the pretense of talking about the second annual New England's Largest Yard Sale, which we were planning for next fall. Since Nancy was engaged to one of Margaret's sons and she was the town manager, she just might have some information and not even know it.

Chapter 25

Minutes later I stood in front of Nancy's desk in the town hall. Her office was cramped and old, with a rusty pipe in one corner, but it had fabulous light pouring in through a large window. You'd think the town manager would have a nicer space. She'd brought in her own area rug, beiges and greens, along with a couple of chairs for her visitors to sit in. I took one of them, careful not to get my wet boots near the cream-colored upholstery.

"I wondered if you had gotten all the permits for the community yard sale next fall," I said.

"Yes. I e-mailed them to you last week." Her tone indicated she didn't think I was on top of things.

"Hmmm. It must be buried somewhere. The virtual garage sale sometimes overwhelms my inbox." I'd actually seen the e-mail but, fortunately, hadn't responded. "Great. Then I can start putting out the word to the vendors."

"This early?"

"Yes. These people plan ahead. There are lots of

festivals in the fall, so I want to make sure they don't forget ours. Plus, that way I can start laying out a map of whose booth will go where."

Nancy nodded. Her short hair swung around her ears. She'd draped her suit jacket across the back of her desk chair, and her shirt was a no-nonsense white.

"How's Margaret's family doing?" I asked.

"They're mad as heck someone took her life." She picked up a pen and twirled it around with a slight smile. "And there's a lot of jockeying to see who will be the next top dog."

"Filling her shoes won't be easy."

Nancy grimaced. "That's for sure."

"Do you happen to know who her cleaning lady was? She mentioned her one time, and I have a friend who's looking."

"She changed cleaning ladies like other people change shoes. No one was ever quite up to snuff with her."

"Oh, I thought she had someone she loved."

"She did for years, but Frieda Chida quit abruptly last spring. No notice. She just quit coming."

Frieda had told me she'd been fired. I wondered which story was the truth, but figured I didn't have any way to find out, since Margaret was dead and Frieda was none too fond of me. "I've heard some really good things about Juanita," I said.

"And I'm guessing a lot of complaints. But still, her death is such a pity."

"From what I've heard, it's like Juanita was the

little girl with the curl of cleaning ladies. When she was good, she was very, very good. But when she was bad, she was horrid. Did you ever use Juanita?"

"I did." Nancy leaned back in her chair. "I've heard the rumors. Pellner was around, asking questions. But I never had a problem. Not one."

Back home I opened my laptop and sent a private message to Frieda, asking her to call me. I didn't know her well enough to ask her a bunch of questions, and I was guessing she wouldn't answer me, anyway. But if I had her come over and clean, then she might be more inclined to talk. As I waited, I finally thought about the picture of the couch, and suddenly Angelo's soup was roiling in my stomach. I didn't have to wait long before my phone rang.

"What do you want?" she asked.

"I'm looking for a cleaning lady." I looked around my tiny apartment, which was pretty neat and clean.

"Give me your address. I'll be there at nine in the morning."

"How much will it cost?" I asked her after giving her my address.

"I'll tell you when I see the place." She hung up before I had a chance to agree or disagree. Maybe that was why she had been fired and/or had quit— her grating personality. But nine in the morning was fine with me. Fortunately, I hadn't dusted in the past week. I'd fix something for dinner tonight and make as much of a mess as I could when cooking for one.

I kept thinking about what Nancy had said about Margaret's family fighting over who would fill Margaret's shoes. How could I find out which of her siblings wanted to? I decided to call Orchard House and see if Kathy Brasheler was working. Hopefully, she wasn't giving a tour right now and would have time to talk.

"It's been the main topic of conversation around here," Kathy said after I explained what I wanted.

"Why?"

"Three members of her family have been contacting every board Margaret was associated with, saying they were the one she wanted to take over for her."

"So what's the Orchard House board going to do?"

"Right now we're on hold, trying to wait to see how things shake out. No one wants to offend any of these people."

"Who would you pick if it was up to you?"

"I'd rather not say. But no one should assume that family position gives you power or that you can buy a position on this board. I'll take smarts anytime."

I couldn't put off buying groceries any longer. If I kept eating fluffernutters and food at DiNapoli's, I was going to have to buy a new spring wardrobe. So I drove over to the Stop & Shop. I decided I'd make pasta tonight. That ought to make a mess in my kitchen. I pushed my cart around the store and tossed in a baguette to make garlic bread, some candles, bubble bath, broccoli, and fusilli, instead of plain old spaghetti. I was reaching for a jar of sauce when someone tapped my shoulder. Seth.

He looked at my cart and picked up a candle and the bubble bath. "It looks like you have a fun night planned."

"Dinner and a bath for one," I said. I didn't want to hurt anyone. Seth deserved better, and so did I.

"Sure you don't want to make it for two?" He gazed at me with his incredible eyes, and I almost blurted out, "Yes, yes, I do."

"Dinner, maybe. Bath, no way."

"What about reversing that?"

I shook my head, lips firmly pressed together, to keep the blurting in. I reached for the sauce again.

"Let me teach you how to make a very simple marinara. It's way better than that stuff." Seth pointed at the shelf.

If Seth was willing to come over and spend time with me, that must mean I wasn't the person of interest CJ had mentioned on the news. I was still ready to say no to all of it but since Seth's family and Margaret's family had been intertwined for years, I'd feed him and then pick his brain. "Okay. What do I need for the sauce?"

"I'll bring the ingredients."

"Seven?" I asked.

"See you then."

* * *

Every time Seth was in my kitchen, it seemed smaller than normal. Seth and I kept bumping into each other as we prepared dinner. Maybe part of the bumping wasn't by accident. I managed to chop the onions and mince the garlic without cutting myself. After sautéing the onions and throwing in the garlic for a minute, Seth added Chianti.

"That jarred sauce you buy won't have Chianti in it," Seth said. He poured each of us a glass while letting the wine cook off. He added tomatoes and turned down the heat to let it simmer. "We have fifteen minutes. What do you want to do?"

"Boil the pasta and fix the garlic bread."

Seth grabbed me and whirled us around. "That's no fun."

I laughed but pulled away. "Neither is having just marinara sauce for dinner."

Seth sliced the bread, which I arranged on a baking sheet and slathered with olive oil. He popped it in the oven, while I added the fusilli to the boiling water.

"Now we have ten minutes," Seth said. "I can make you very happy in ten minutes."

"Seven. The bread will be done then." I set the timer. "Not enough time to make me *very* happy."

We sat on the couch with our wine.

"So what's on your mind?" Seth asked.

"Why do you think there's something on my mind?"

"Very few women would pass up seven minutes with me."

I didn't want to think about Seth and other women. "Does your bio say 'incorrigible'?"

"No, but my mother always has. I could see you wanted to ask me something at the store when I offered to make the sauce."

"I thought people around here called it gravy instead of sauce."

"Some Italians do. My family isn't Italian. Nice try changing the subject."

"I've just been hearing rumors about infighting within Margaret's family."

"No surprise there. Who in her family wouldn't want to be the next Margaret? She's made quite a name for herself. People love power."

That was what Kathy and Nancy had said. "Do any of them have financial troubles? Something to gain from Margaret's death?" I couldn't imagine that any of them did, but I was using my "Leave no stone unturned" philosophy.

"Not that I know of."

"What about Nichole?"

"She's doing fine on her own. Why ask about her?"

"I'm just trying to figure out what's going on around here. Did Nichole use Juanita as a cleaning lady?"

"I have no idea. You'd have to ask her." Seth looked at me, eyebrows drawn together. "Why are you so focused on the cleaning lady?"

I thought about it. "I'm not sure. It just seems like something is off with the woman who used to be her cleaning lady." But why *had* I been so focused on Frieda, Juanita, and Margaret? My original idea had been to figure out who my stalker was. How had I let that slide? Because no matter what I thought about the cleaning women, I didn't think they had anything to do with my stalker. I sniffed the air and leaped up. "The bread."

I ran into the kitchen, grabbed a mitt, and hauled the baking sheet full of blackened garlic bread out of the oven. I looked at the timer. I had set it but hadn't turned it on. Seth scraped the burnt parts off the pieces of garlic bread and handed them off to me. I rubbed a clove of garlic over them. "I can't ever manage to pull off a dinner without something going wrong."

"It'll be fine."

I threw together a salad, while Seth drained the pasta. He reserved a little of the water and added the pasta and a bit of the water to the sauce. We crammed everything onto my small table. Seth held my chair out for me, and I sat. He pulled his chair next to mine, and we dug in.

"Better than that grocery store stuff?" he asked.

"Way better."

Chapter 26

After Seth left, I started to fill up the tub. I put my hair up in a sloppy bun and threw my clothes in the hamper. I had resisted Seth's comments about how my tub was the perfect size for two and had pushed him out the door after a long sizzling kiss. A cold shower might be a better idea than a bubble bath. But really, he hadn't pushed me that hard.

I tested the water with my hand before climbing in and sinking into the deep tub. I played with the bubbles, making bubble sculptures, and wondered about Seth. I leaned back, resting my neck on the edge of the tub and floating as much as I could. Seth and CJ were kind of alike. Both had good sides; both, because of their jobs, had things they kept from me. But maybe it wasn't only their jobs. That was the problem: I didn't completely trust either of them. I'd been so shaken by what happened between CJ and me last year that I still didn't trust myself. Margaret had trusted someone too much, someone she had let get close enough to kill her, but who?

I soaked until the water cooled. After putting my plaid pajamas on, I flipped on the TV but didn't really pay attention to the singing competition that was on. I thought again about the connection, if there was one, between the person stalking me and Margaret. The problem was I couldn't picture anyone I knew sending me the pictures or threatening me. James flitted into my mind, but I tried to push the thought away. Yes, I'd thought he might have feelings for me on occasion. Yes, he'd changed since he came back from his deployment. But I didn't believe he'd changed that much.

I sat straight up and turned off the TV. James had said he'd report the most recent photo to the EPD for me. But Seth hadn't mentioned it when he was over. And since Margaret had died, he'd been keeping pretty close tabs on anything concerning the EPD and me. I had no idea what any of that meant, except that I probably wouldn't sleep well tonight, wondering.

Before I went to bed, I still had some work to do on the apartment. Even with the kitchen messy, the place still didn't look like it needed much cleaning. Seth had offered to clean up after we ate, but I'd refused. The sauce splashed on the stove and the dishes in the sink worked for my visit from Frieda tomorrow morning. I got some dirt out of the pot with the indestructible plant a friend had given me a cutting of when she'd moved. The plant had stood up to large amounts of abuse, such as a lack of water. I rubbed the dirt onto the tub with the remaining bubbles until it looked a lot like a soap ring. I spilled a little more of the dirt on the floor and tracked it around a bit, carefully avoiding my oriental rug.

When I heard a knock on the door at nine in the morning, I gave one last look around the place, a bit proud of myself for the mess I'd made. I'd never had a cleaning lady before, so I wasn't sure of the protocol. Should I leave or stay? There was another sharp rap. I opened the door, and Frieda brushed past me, lugging a bag full of cleaning supplies. She looked very different from her online photos. Yes, her hair still had the purple ends, but she was large enough to be a tackle for the Patriots. Maybe she'd been stress eating since her online pictures were taken.

"We didn't finish discussing your prices on the phone yesterday," I said.

"Well, if you expect me to be as cheap as that Juanita woman was, I might as well just go."

"No. I didn't—"

"She undercut me every chance she got and stole my customers."

Interesting. "I heard there were a lot of problems with her, though."

Frieda went into the kitchen and started unpacking her bag of industrial-strength cleaners on the counter. "You get what you pay for." She looked around the room. "You really can't take care of this place yourself?" She frowned at me, her heavy brows twitching on her protruding forehead. The word *Neanderthal* came to mind.

"Normally, I do, but I'm really busy with the February Blues garage sale on base. Things just got away from me."

"Compared to most of my jobs, this place is spotless. You wouldn't believe the condition of some people's homes. They drive their fancy cars and wear their fancy clothes, but their bathrooms . . ." She paused and shuddered. "I'm not sure how they can live like that."

"Would you like a cup of coffee while you work?"

Frieda looked surprised. "Sure, if you don't mind. That's nice of you. Some people don't even want you to take a drink of water. Treat you like the dirt they've swept under their rugs."

I busied myself making coffee. Frieda sure had a lot of anger built up. "Do you take cream or sugar?"

"No. Black is good. I can't always afford the cream, so I stick with black so I don't miss it."

I filled two mugs and handed her one. "I'll work on my computer and move around so I'm not in your way."

Frieda took a sip of her coffee. "You don't have to stay."

"Thanks, but it's easier to stay here."

I went into the living room and fired up my computer. I approved a bunch of new members and banned a couple of people who weren't following the rules. I was glad to see the new members. At first, after Margaret's death, people had left at an alarming rate. But now there seemed to be a bounce back. I wasn't sure if it was the whole "Everyone wants to see the train wreck" or if it was because I was the only online site in Ellington.

I had a request from James to join the group. *Interesting.* I'd be curious to see what he bought and sold. You could figure out a lot about the members just from their buying and selling habits. Who had kids, who liked antiques, who was into fitness, who always said they had money problems. Some really did have financial problems, and some didn't. A lot of people seemed more interested in the bidding game than in the actual item being sold. I called it the "I'm a winner" syndrome—it made people feel good about themselves to get the item.

I'd been toying with the idea of setting up a site that was only for furniture and antiques. Sorting through all the clothing posts and toys to find things I was interested in wasn't easy and the search function wasn't optimal. The group was large enough that members had to scroll through a lot of posts to find what they liked. I just wasn't sure if I had time to manage two different sites. It wouldn't be so bad now, but once spring hit and I was doing more outside sales, it might be a problem.

A couple of hours later Frieda announced she was done. My apartment was filled with fumes, and my eyes were watery. As soon as she left, I'd fling open the windows, heating bill be damned. I wasn't sure it was entirely Juanita's practice of undercutting prices that had made Frieda lose business.

"Would you like another cup of coffee?" I asked her.

"Might as well. I got nothing better to do." She eased onto one of my two kitchen chairs and rubbed her knee before scooting closer to the table. I glimpsed her swollen ankles before she stretched her feet out under the table. If it wasn't for getting half of CJ's retirement pay and the alimony he'd insisted upon, I might be doing some kind of hard labor myself. Although I tried to stick most of it into savings, over the winter I'd had to use some of it. My dream of returning it all to him someday had faded just a bit.

I poured two cups of coffee and took them over to the table before sitting across from Frieda. She traced one of the flowers on the vintage tablecloth covering the table with her finger.

"Do you collect these things?" she asked.

"Yes. I like them. They're cheery. Especially on a gloomy day."

"I don't have the money to collect them. It's why I wanted the one like my grandma's so bad."

It made me pause. For all of Frieda's complaints about money, she had doubled the price of the tablecloth Margaret was selling without batting an eye, as far as I could tell, and had ended up paying far more than the actual value. It made me wonder if that was really why she'd wanted it or if she had just needed an excuse to go see Margaret.

"Why did you quit cleaning for Margaret?"

"I told you she fired me. For all her money, that woman was tightfisted when it came to her own expenses. She might gift this person or organization some huge sum, but she clung to her personal budget like she didn't know where the next dollar was coming from." Frieda took a long drink of her coffee. "She figured out if she kept changing cleaning companies, she could use their specials and coupons so she didn't have to pay as much." Frieda scooted her chair back and pushed off the table to stand up.

"Then once she saw Juanita's ad on your site, she kept on using her." Frieda scowled. "I stopped over once a couple of weeks ago, after Juanita left. I tried to convince Margaret to take me back on. I pointed out to her how much more I did and what Juanita had missed. Let me tell you, Juanita did half the work I did. And the place didn't smell good and clean, like yours does."

"Have any guesses as to who would be mad enough to kill Margaret?"

"Maybe Juanita. Margaret agreed to take me back."

Chapter 27

I watched out the window as Frieda made her way down the sidewalk. She was the first person I'd found who had a connection to both Juanita and Margaret. She seemed pretty angry. Had Margaret really agreed to take her back, or had Frieda killed the competition? I knew that the police had spoken with Frieda after the murder, but I wondered if she'd shared any of this information with them. Frieda climbed into a nice-looking black SUV. As soon as she pulled away from the curb, I flung open the windows to alleviate the fumes.

I realized I probably needed to tell CJ all of this. I knew I was being paranoid, but on the off chance that I was the person of interest mentioned in the news report, I didn't want to go to the station. I called CJ but couldn't get through, so I left him a message. I also mentioned the incident on base yesterday, just in case. *Just in case what?* I asked myself. *Just in case James is your stalker? Just in case James hasn't reported it?* I was beginning to think *I* was the demented one. Then I left a message on CJ's cell phone, which I didn't normally like to do. While I waited for him to call back, I updated the garage sale site.

If CJ wouldn't talk to me, I really had to be the person of interest. *Get a grip. He's probably busy.* Half the time he didn't tell me stuff, anyway. But just in case, I had to track CJ down. I had to force him to listen to me, in person and alone. That way I'd have a chance to point him in other directions. I looked online. The Ellington Police Department basketball team was playing the Bedford firefighters tonight at Bedford's middle school. I'd go there to see him.

At eight o'clock that night I sat in my Suburban in a far corner of the middle school parking lot. The basketball game should be over soon. I'd parked out here in hopes that CJ would spot me and that no one else would. People started trickling out of the school. CJ came out a few minutes later with a large group of laughing people. Either they'd won or they were really good sports. I willed CJ to look over in my direction as the group started to break up and the people headed to their cars. If worse came to worst, I'd follow him home, but I preferred not to do that. If I was the person of interest, it wouldn't look good for him to be getting phone calls or visits from me. And I really hoped he was alone. I'd abort the mission if anyone got in the car with him, especially if it was the redhead Carol had mentioned.

As the group broke up, CJ spotted me. But instead of coming over, he shooed everyone toward their cars. I slid down in my seat, hoping no one else would notice me. A few minutes later there was a tap on my window. I popped back up to let CJ inside the car.

"What's with the subterfuge?" he asked as he climbed in the passenger seat.

"You didn't answer my calls, and I didn't want you to have to be seen with me if I'm the person of interest you mentioned in the press conference." CJ's warm presence seemed to fill the car.

CJ shook his head. "I've been busy. What do you need?" He didn't do anything to reassure me that I wasn't the person of interest.

"Why do you assume I need something?"

"Because that's how it's been between us."

Was that true? I thought over our interactions of the past few months. He wasn't being fair, but that wasn't why I was here. I held in a sigh. "I'm here because I stumbled across a connection between Frieda Chida, Margaret, and Juanita." I filled him in. "I just wanted to make sure you knew. And I was worried about how angry Frieda seemed."

"You can afford a cleaning lady now?"

"That's your takeaway from what I just told you?" I stared at him. "It was a one-shot deal. The garage sale on base is taking a lot more time than I expected. As is the virtual site." I knew he wouldn't like that my real reason for having Frieda come over was to find out what she knew.

CJ leaned back against the seat and blew out a breath. "Thanks for the information. I didn't know how angry she is." He opened the door, climbed out, and looked back at me. "I miss you."

He closed the door and walked to his car. He folded himself into his little red Sonic. Without looking back at me, he pulled out.

"I miss you, too."

"He said he missed you?" Carol asked. Her last class had just let out as I pulled up into my driveway. I'd hightailed it over to her shop to talk over my conversation with CJ. We both held glasses of wine and sat in her studio behind the classroom section of her shop.

"Yes. I don't get it. First, he's short, then he's Mr. Official Police Chief, and now this." I took a large gulp of wine. "I'm so confused."

"I'm guessing he is, too. You tell him to stay away. Then you look all hot when he's taking you out to dinner. And now you lurk in a dark parking lot to talk to him."

"Whose side are you on? You're the one that wanted me to go all out the night we went to dinner."

"I'm on your side." Carol smiled. "CJ needed a reminder of what he was missing. And it looks like it worked."

"I envy you and Brad."

Carol's smile slipped a little.

"You two are okay, aren't you?"

She took a drink of her wine. "Yes. It's just that between the stresses of both of our jobs and the kids, we don't have much time."

Brad worked at the Veterans Administration hospital in Bedford. "He must be under a lot of pressure with all the scrutiny and accusations about the VA," I said.

"That about sums it up. Things have picked up a lot here, which is good, but it keeps me busy on the weekends and evenings, when he's home."

"Do you want me to babysit the kids or the shop some night?"

"That would be lovely. Why did you go see CJ in the first place?"

I told her about the connection between Frieda, Juanita, and Margaret. "I'm trying to find other connections between them."

"I might know of one."

"How do you even know who Frieda and Juanita are?" I figured everyone knew Margaret, so asking about her wasn't necessary.

"With my schedule, I've been using cleaning ladies. Frieda uses too many strong chemicals. I had to air the place out."

I nodded.

"Then I saw a coupon from Juanita. And who can pass up having your house cleaned for fifty dollars?"

"Did you have any problems with her?"

Carol stared into her wineglass for a second. "It wasn't exactly a problem."

"What happened? Doors unlocked? Windows open?"

"The bathroom smelled a little like cigarette smoke. But maybe it was just my imagination. Then, a couple of weeks ago, I stopped for coffee at that place off Great Road, Ellie's Deli."

I leaned forward.

"As I parked, Frieda and Juanita stomped out at the same time. Both looked angry. When I went in, Margaret was sitting at a table in the corner, looking like she was holding court."

"Was she by herself?"

"Someone else was there, but I didn't recognize her. Why do you care?"

"I think I might be a person of interest. The one CJ called a news conference about. I found Margaret and Juanita. That sounds fishy, even to me."

"Oh, no. I know how that feels."

"I flat out asked CJ, and he avoided answering."

"Have you talked to Vincenzo?"

Vincenzo had represented Carol last fall, when she'd been arrested for a murder. "Not about this. I didn't think I needed to. Yet."

"Have you asked Seth?"

"No. But he called me this morning and said he'd call back, and he hasn't."

"The night's still young."

I looked at Carol's wall clock. "Holy crap. It's almost nine. I should go so you can get home."

* * *

I pulled up in front of Seth's house at 9:20 p.m. A sleek black sports car that definitely wasn't Seth's was parked in the drive. But at this point I didn't care who he was entertaining and hurried up the drive. The door opened, and Nichole strolled out, looking very satisfied with herself. She stopped short when she saw me walking toward the door. I didn't think she liked seeing me here one bit. Before acknowledging me, she opened her purse and pulled something out.

"Here's my business card. Call me if you need representation."

She thrust it at me, and I grabbed it without thinking. *Oh, no.* She thought I needed a lawyer. Why did she think that?

"I . . . I . . . I don't need a lawyer," I said, actually stammering. *Darn it.* If she was right, I'd be calling Vincenzo, not her, anyway. I tried to hand the card back, but she brushed by me and got in her car. I rang Seth's doorbell and turned when I didn't hear the car start. Nichole lit a cigarette. *Yeesh.* I'd never realized how many people still smoked. She rolled down her window and waved as she pulled out.

The door opened behind me. "What now, Nichole?" Seth didn't sound happy. I turned back. He looked tired and none too pleased to see me. That couldn't be good. He ran a hand over his stubbled face. He stepped out on the porch, instead of asking me in, so I knew things were bad.

"Am I the person of interest CJ talked about in the news conference yesterday?"

Seth looked down at the porch. "I can't talk about it."

"But you could with Nichole? She just asked me if I needed representation."

He met my eyes this time. "She's a salesperson. She hands out her cards to everyone. Don't let her play mind games with you."

"You didn't answer either of my questions."

"I can't talk to you about the first one. And Nichole's good, if you need a lawyer."

I trotted down the steps and hurried to my car.

"Sarah, wait," Seth called out.

But I didn't. Tomorrow I had to work even harder to find out who killed Margaret and Juanita.

Chapter 28

Thirty minutes later I stood in front of my living room window, looking over the dark town common. Light reflected off the four stories of church windows. Maybe I should call Vincenzo if I was a person of interest. But there really didn't seem to be any reason to call him right this minute. I'd wait until the morning.

Through the floor I heard Stella singing a song from *South Pacific*. The one about being in love with a wonderful guy. I'd been so caught up in my own drama, the words just now registered. I'd noticed Officer Awesome's car parked in front of the house when I came in. *Wow.* That was fast. I hoped for the best for Stella, but, boy, romance certainly had more downs than ups. She'd probably be singing the one about washing him out of her hair in no time.

My phone chimed. I wondered if it was Seth, with an apology. I was pretty angry and was not sure I felt

very forgiving right now. I walked over to the couch
and dug my phone out of my purse. If it was Seth
with one of his sad face photos, I might throw the
phone out the window. But it wasn't. It was me.
Standing in my apartment window two seconds ago.
I swallowed a huge lump in my throat. Whoever
had sent it had made it look like a drop of blood
was dripping from my chest. The black heart was
back, too.

Freaked out, I ran to the window and yanked at
the curtains, desperate to get them shut. I jerked so
hard, I pulled them and the flimsy curtain rod
right off the wall. Now I was really exposed. I hugged
the whole mess to me, staring out into the dark-
ness. Was someone out there? Watching all this?
Laughing?

I flung the curtains and rod down and one-finger
saluted whoever was out there. *Take that, you crazy
stalker.* Then I came to my senses and ran over to
shut off the overhead light. Now I missed Mike
and his brothers and wished they were still next
door. I dropped to the floor and crawled back to
the window. I peeked over the sill, but I didn't
see anyone moving or any cars driving away. Up
until right now, I'd loved looking at the common at
night. Loved the way the moonlight lit the church.
The way the trees looked silvery without their leaves.

Awesome's car was still parked down below. I
scurried across my apartment and tore downstairs
to Stella's. I shoved open her door, thinking she
really should keep it locked. A startled Officer

Awesome leaped off the couch, holding a beer in his hand. Stella whipped her head toward me, mouth open. Thankfully, they were both fully clothed.

"Someone sent me another picture. Me standing in my window."

Awesome leaped up and was out the door before I said more.

"Are you okay?" Stella asked.

I wasn't sure if I was okay. I wanted to be, but that photo with the drop of blood, of me in my own apartment . . . Some freak had been spying on me here, in my own home. And his intentions clearly weren't good.

"Come sit," Stella said. She poured me a glass of wine and herself some scotch. "Here. This will help. You must be scared."

I thought about that while I took a drink of the wine. "Scared? Yes, I'm scared, but now I'm mad, too." I tried to convince myself that anger was the stronger of the many emotions circulating through my head. "I'm going to figure out who's messing with me. Sending me all these disappearing photos . . . I almost wonder if it's more than one person."

"Why?"

"Because some of them are nice pictures complimenting my clothing. Then others are dark. Scary. Threatening." I tried to hold on to the anger but felt myself slip back to scared. I set my wine on an end table. "I'm an idiot. The angry pictures always come after I've been with Seth."

"Are you sure?"

"Yes. I should have realized it before. Except for the other night. He came over for dinner, and there wasn't a photo after that. I wonder what was different about that night." I hugged my arms to my waist. "So now I just have to figure out who doesn't want me to be with Seth."

"I don't have a clue. Do you?"

"Seth's mother, but I can't picture her doing this. Nichole. And . . ." I didn't want to say it out loud.

Stella looked at me. "And CJ. He wouldn't want you to see Seth."

"No way it's CJ. Do you remember meeting James last fall? He's with the security forces on base."

"Yes. Do you think it's him doing all this?"

"I don't want to. But he's different since he came back from his deployment." I stared into the glass of wine. "Maybe there's someone we aren't even thinking of."

Stella nodded but didn't look convinced. "What about Seth? Doesn't he seem to be a little too good to be true?"

"No." I shook my head so hard, it hurt. "I can't think about this anymore. Let's talk about something happy. Are you in love with a wonderful guy?"

Stella looked at me like I'd just spoken Russian.

"You were singing about it."

"Yuck, no. I was practicing. I'm singing at an

event to honor Rodgers and Hammerstein. They did a drawing, and that's the song I got. Trust me, after the last debacle, I'm not in any hurry to fall in love."

Awesome came back in, frowning. "I didn't see anyone, but I'm guessing between the time of the picture and the time you got down here, they had plenty of time to get away."

I sighed. "Figures. No one's seen who's doing this. Not once. Not even me."

"I found some cigarette butts by a tree. I read the reports that there have been others in scenes involving you. They could have been there awhile. It's not like they were warm."

Yeesh. Scenes involving me. Reports about me. I stood. "Thanks."

"I bagged them, just in case."

Stella hugged me and insisted I take the glass of wine with me upstairs. I looked back at her as I left. "Keep your door locked," I told her.

Back in my apartment I got out my drill and reattached the curtain rod to the wall and re-hung my curtains. Then I deleted the PopIt app from my phone. I'd been reluctant to do it until now since I'd used it to promote my business. But I didn't want to see one more picture of myself being watched. It was like living with a bogeyman, and I was tired of it. I couldn't keep on like this, jumping every time my phone went off or constantly worrying I was going to be arrested for not one, but two murders. I needed to do something. I thought about the night I met Awesome and the bait car, about how the car lured the criminal to them. Maybe that was what I needed to do. Make myself the bait.

Chapter 29

The first thing I did when I woke was download the PopIt app again. The sun had chased away the bogeyman and my fears. I might need PopIt for my plan to work, and I certainly needed it for my business. What had I been thinking last night? I made a cup of coffee and opened my computer. I sat with my fingers poised over the keyboard. I'd come up with a plan, and I'd looked at it from every angle I could think of. It should work. I opened my garage sale site and posted a note: *Cleaning and other services available. Introductory offer $50.00. Willing to take on any job.*

I took a deep breath and hit SEND. This seemed like a safe way to find out what was going on. The way I figured it was that the person hiring the cleaner was an innocent victim. It was the cleaning person who was caught up in some kind of crime ring. I hoped by putting myself out there, I might flush him or her out with no risk to myself. Since I was undercutting the competition and saying I'd do any job, he or she might think I was the perfect person to replace Juanita. If I got any creepy notes or threats, I'd be at the police station faster than you could empty a wastebasket. Now all I had to do was sit back and see what happened.

Two people answered almost immediately, saying they'd sent me private messages. A third message was from Frieda, and all it said was, WTH?

I chose to assume she meant "What the heck?" and decided that responding wouldn't do any good. I looked at the other two private messages. One woman asked if I could come today, and the other wanted someone tomorrow. I said yes to both. I gathered what cleaning supplies I had in my house and stashed them in an old galvanized metal bucket that had been sitting under the kitchen sink. I decided to run to the grocery store to pick up a few extra items before going to the first job.

This was kind of exciting. I'd earn some extra money, and how hard could cleaning be? I'd been cleaning up after myself since I was a little girl, my family being firmly behind the idea that a busy kid was a good kid.

Many hours later—which felt like several days— I dragged my weary rear end back into the house. It was only 5:30 p.m., but it felt like bedtime. Even my fingernails seemed to ache. I'd faced three thousand square feet of disaster, and I wondered if the woman had ever cleaned the place before. She had somehow seemed to think my title was miracle worker, not cleaning lady. Sharpie hadn't come off the painted walls no matter how many magic cleaning products I'd tried. Then she'd argued about paying me the full fifty dollars, for goodness' sakes. And I wasn't any closer to figuring out who had murdered Juanita and Margaret. Or who my stalker was.

I poured myself a glass of wine and eased down onto the couch. The only good news that had come out of the whole ordeal was that she had also hired me to run a garage sale for her in the spring. I'd upped my commission by 10 percent, and she hadn't blinked. My phone buzzed on the end table. It had been vibrating all day. I had updated the garage sale site when I took quick breaks but had ignored the new voice mails from numbers I recognized. I took a deep breath and looked at the list: CJ, Seth, and Carol. I listened to Carol's message first.

"Have you lost your freaking mind? You're cleaning houses now? Come work for me if you need money."

Next up, CJ. "Do you need money? I'll increase your alimony or give you all my retirement pay. This housecleaning nonsense better not have *anything*— let me say that again, *anything*—to do with Margaret's and Juanita's murders." There was a pause. I could picture him pinching his nose. "Just stop it now. Whatever it is you're doing."

Seth. "I heard a wild story that you started a cleaning business. Call me."

On the bright side I was flattered that three people cared about me in varying degrees. But now seemed as good a time as any to put my moratorium on seeing CJ and Seth back in place. I called Carol. Fortunately, my call went straight to voice mail, so I left her some flimsy excuse about why I was now in the housecleaning business. Then I stumbled into the bathroom, took a long shower, flopped on my bed, and conked out.

Thursday morning I perused my garage sale site as I drank my first cup of coffee and ate a fluffernutter. I considered myself a strong person after all the years of garage sales and hauling things around. But this morning I still ached, and I already hoped that the job today wouldn't be as bad as yesterday's. I didn't know how long I could keep this up.

Frieda had posted her own cleaning ad. It cost ten dollars more than mine, and she emphasized her twenty years of experience and her triple A rating with the Better Business Bureau. Her "Don't hire an unknown person" was a direct strike at me. Even though I wasn't in this for the long haul, I still felt annoyed, not just for myself but for Juanita and all the other hardworking cleaning people out there.

I decided to drop by Ellie's Deli, the place where Carol had seen Frieda and Juanita together, on the way to my morning cleaning job. By the time I got to Ellie's, the work crowd was gone and the moms whose kids were in school had arrived. There was a banner by a corner table that read WE MISS YOU, MARGARET. FOREVER IN OUR HEARTS. It didn't take a genius to know there was some story here. I just hoped I could find out what it was.

I ordered chai tea and a scone. If it wasn't Dunkin's coffee, I really wasn't interested. I found a small table and watched Ellie work. I figured when things slowed down, I'd ask her to join me. I was on my second cup of chai, and a "chai high" was kicking in. I'd never figured out if it was the caffeine or the sugar, but when I drank this stuff, I got a boost, one that would have me cleaning like a whirling dervish when I got to my job today. I thumbed through my phone, approving and disapproving various posts for the garage sale site. By the time I finished, there was a lull, and so I went up to Ellie.

"Do you have a minute?" I asked her. We'd met when she'd catered some breakfasts for Spouses' Club activities on base.

Ellie swiveled her head around, taking in the scene. A little smile played over her lips as she observed her domain. "Sure," she said, turning her "so blue they were almost violet" eyes on me. "Let me grab some coffee. Do you need a refill?"

"No, thanks." A third cup of chai would probably have me levitating.

I sat, and a couple of minutes later, Ellie set a cup

of coffee and a plate of cookies on the table before sitting across from me. Her light brown hair was in a tight bun.

"What can I do for you?" she asked.

"I wanted to ask you about Margaret." I pointed to the sign by the corner table.

Ellie took a sip of coffee and relaxed into the chair. "Why?"

I leaned forward. "I'm the one who found both Margaret and Juanita. I'm scared the police are looking at me as a suspect. And a friend told me they saw her here with Frieda Chida and Juanita a couple of weeks ago. I feel like I need to find out what was going on in Margaret's life. Who might have wanted to kill her."

"Frieda and Juanita used to be here together a lot. Thick as thieves."

Hmmm. Interesting way of putting it. "When did that change?"

Ellie thought about it as she munched on one of the cookies. "A few months ago. I'm not even sure when."

"I heard they had a fight here the other day."

"They weren't happy with each other. I know that much."

"Do you have any idea why?"

Ellie reddened. "I don't like to seem like I eavesdrop on my customers."

"Trust me, I understand. You can't help but overhear things."

"Most of it I wish I could un-hear."

"Happens to me when I throw garage sales sometimes."

"They were arguing about money and who owed whom what. It stuck in my mind because I know Margaret didn't have money problems."

And I knew Frieda did. "That's odd."

"At first I figured it was just about the whole cleaning lady thing. Do you know about that?"

"Frieda gave me an earful about it. Was that all you heard?"

Ellie looked around and leaned forward. "Frieda told them they were both liars and cheats."

"Both of them?" Maybe this wasn't some big mystery. Maybe it was just Frieda still being angry about Margaret replacing her with Juanita.

"I'm sure of it."

"Ellie?" called one of the women behind the counter. "The modem's on the blink again."

Ellie stood. "Sorry. Duty calls."

"That's fine."

"I'll have the cookies wrapped for you to take whenever you're ready."

"Thanks. One more question. Do you know if any of them smoked?"

"Frieda does. Like a chimney."

Chapter 30

I'd spent a lot of my time cleaning thinking about Margaret, Juanita, and Frieda and focusing on Frieda as the killer. It seemed plausible. She had had an axe to grind with Margaret and Juanita. She had obviously been angry with them. Maybe she'd lied to me about Margaret rehiring her to throw me off. No one could contradict that. But why would she stalk me? All I'd done was let Juanita post an ad. Was that enough to make Frieda go berserk?

At the end of my second day of cleaning, I was beginning to think my theory that somehow the cleaners were involved in a crime ring was wrong. Maybe I was just overeager, or maybe I needed to post another ad, a more desperate-sounding ad. On top of that, I was already losing faith in humanity. The house was a small cape; the owner a perky, small woman who, if she'd been a dog, would have been a whippet, sleek, energetic, and alert. The place had looked pretty clean, no Sharpie-covered walls. After I'd finished cleaning, she'd asked me to organize the closet in the master for an extra fifty. No problem. Sorting clothes into categories was easy, and everything had gone smoothly, until I reached for a box on the top shelf. The lid had flown off, and I'd got showered with racy clothing and pictures of the owner in them. *Yuck.* She wore stuff I wouldn't dream of wearing, let alone owning or being photographed in.

Even now as I drove to the base to help with the final setup for the February Blues sale, I shuddered at the images I'd seen. Telling her good-bye and accepting money from her had required my best acting skills. I'd channeled my inner Hennessy. The woman had asked me to run a garage sale for her. I wasn't in a position to turn down business, so of course I'd said yes. I grinned to myself. It might be one of the more interesting ones I'd ever do. Thankfully, tomorrow was a day off from cleaning, and I was back to the fun of running the base sale.

I pulled into the community center parking lot. There was only one other car there, and it wasn't Laura's. Where was she? I walked into the community center and hollered hello. No one answered, so I took a few tentative steps and yelled again. James popped out from around the corner, which made me jump.

"Sorry," he said. "I was trying to keep from scaring you. You must not have heard me yell back."

"It's okay. Where's Laura?"

"She's at some meeting and will be over as soon as she can. I came to help in the meantime."

"Great." It was great, wasn't it? I didn't get any creepy vibe from James when I was with him. He was different, yes, but not creepy. "Let's start hauling the tables out and setting them up. You're probably stronger than Laura, anyway."

Forty-five minutes later all the tables were set and ready to go. Laura walked in. Her timing was so convenient, I wondered if she'd arrived earlier, seen us working, and scurried out. *Yeesh.* I was becoming cynical.

"Sorry, I'm late." But she grinned and didn't appear all that sorry. Maybe I was right. She looked at me closely. "You look beat. Why don't you go on home?"

"Because I promised you I'd stay while people set up their tables." The room was going to be open for the next two hours so the sellers could arrange their things this evening instead of early tomorrow morning.

"As long as you give me the list for who has what spot, I can handle it."

I hesitated. Food and a bath tempted me.

"Really," Laura said, giving me a push toward the door. "I've got this."

I handed her the list and kissed her cheek. "Thanks."

James walked me to my car. "Want to grab a pizza?" he asked.

I had to eat, I didn't want another fluffernutter, and I did want to find out what was going on with

James. I liked James but was worried about him. He had always been one of those "the nicest guys you'd ever meet" types. Or at least he had been before his last tour in Afghanistan. Today he was showing his nice side, but lately, I'd seen his harder side, too. I hated to think his deployment had changed him, but he wouldn't be the first it had happened to or, sadly, the last. So yes, I wanted to have pizza and talk with him. Find out how he was. And I had another reason. I wanted to get to the bottom of these silly concerns about him and being with him in a public place seemed to be the best way.

"Okay. DiNapoli's?" I said.

"Sure. I'll meet you there."

Thirty minutes later we sat across from each other at DiNapoli's. My being here with James raised a few eyebrows. Okay, a lot of eyebrows. Everyone from Rosalie to Angelo to Ryan to Lois to some of the diners had done a double take when we walked in. I couldn't exactly shout out that we were just friends. But I had introduced him that way as we ordered a half-pepperoni, half-cheese pizza.

James deflected my attempts to find out more about his deployment as we drank water and waited for our food. I ended up talking about myself more than I had meant to. When the pizza arrived, we started to eat, and our conversation was more about "Pass the hot peppers and the Parmesan cheese."

After my third piece of cheese pizza, I pushed my plate away. "That was good."

"Mind if I eat the rest?" James asked.

I shook my head no, relieved that with whatever was going on, at least he was eating. "Have you heard anything about Margaret's or Juanita's murders?" I asked.

"Is this why you wanted to eat with me?"

"No." It wasn't the only reason. "I wanted to see how you were doing, but you aren't talking."

"Since the victims have nothing to do with base, I haven't heard much."

I was disappointed. "I guess that makes sense."

"But I saw on the garage sale site, you started a cleaning business." James watched me intently.

I tried my best not to squirm. "I needed the extra money. There aren't a lot of garage sales in New England in the winter. The garage sale site takes a lot of time and produces very little income."

"Do you want to come clean my place?"

I laughed. "You live in one room in the dorm on base." Single enlisted troops could live in dorms on base for far less than they could out on the economy or, as civilians would say, in town.

"Not anymore. I moved off base a few weeks ago, to an apartment not too far from here."

Well, this was awkward. I hadn't thought about someone I knew asking me to clean for them. And beyond being awkward, James lived in town now. Which meant he'd could have been around, taking pictures a lot more easily, but I still didn't want to believe James could be my stalker. "I'm pretty booked right now." It sounded like a lie, and judging by the frown on James's face, he thought so, too.

"Did you stop to think it might look like you killed your rival and then took over her business?"

Oh, no. I'd never dreamed anyone would think that, but if James did, others might. By trying to draw out the killer, I'd just completely screwed myself. "You know that isn't true."

"I know that, but the state police might not."

Chapter 31

After a restless night's sleep, and having no solid answers either way about James, I roamed around the community center at eight in the morning. The sale would start in an hour. Tables lined the outside walls, and there was another square of them in the middle of the room, allowing just enough space to maneuver around everything. Laura and I were the only ones here. She'd helped me set up my table. We had eaten the donuts I'd brought along, and now we sipped coffee as we walked around the room.

"Laura, look at this bench." The curved arms of the bench were upholstered in burgundy leather that had cracked in several places. The seat was burgundy velvet, which I suspected was added later. I tipped the bench over and saw that the thin cheesecloth-like fabric covering the bottom was still intact. I stuck my nose as close as possible to the bench and sniffed. It smelled fine. I was leery when things smelled of air freshener or Febreze.

"Where would you put it?" Laura asked when I stood back up.

"It would just fit at the end of my bed." Where it would really look beautiful was in Seth's bedroom in his house in Bedford. The previous owners had turned the attic into a spacious master. I blushed a little as I thought about that. I'd done some decorating for him, and he'd asked me to do more, but with the moratorium on seeing him, I hadn't. Although I'd broken that well and good more than once recently. "I'd have to re-cover it, but you don't see these every day."

"The carving along the bottom and on the legs is beautiful."

"I told myself I could spend fifty dollars today." Even though I wasn't in desperate straits financially, I tried to watch my spending. It was kind of like going to a casino with a set budget and quitting when you hit your limit. But unlike from a casino, I usually walked away from my bargain hunting expeditions with something that delighted me.

"There's no price on it," Laura said.

"I'll watch and make them an offer as soon as they come in."

Half an hour later a couple showed up and stood behind the table with the bench. I rushed over and realized I was breaking my own rule about trying to act casual to get a better deal. "I love your bench." *Yikes.* What was with me this morning? I seemed to have lost all my bargaining skills.

The couple exchanged a glance. "It's not in very good shape."

Oh, be still, my heart. They didn't realize how hard it was to find a bench like this. I had been looking for a long time and knew it was worth several hundred dollars, even in its current condition. "I know. I'd have to have it reupholstered. And I'm not sure I want to put that kind of money into it." I hoped they bought my story. "What are you asking for it?"

"Two hundred."

My heart dropped. That was way out of my price range. "Thanks, anyway." I turned.

"You can make us an offer," the man said, with a quick glance at his wife.

Yeesh. I should have done that automatically. "Would you take fifty? Since it's going to require a lot of work?"

The woman shook her head and shot a "Don't say yes" look at her husband. From the looks of things, he was lucky to escape with a look and not a swift kick. "One-fifty. It does need work, but we've priced it with that in mind," the woman said.

"I can't. Fifty's my limit today."

"If it lasts through the day, we'll consider it," the man said.

I smiled. "Thanks. I don't think it will."

"I don't, either," the woman said.

I hated losing out but brightened at the thought that if I sold enough today, maybe I could buy it. I put some finishing touches on the things on my table. I found a plug, so the blue and white lamp glowed. I arranged the atomic starburst dishes, and I gave the small end table a final dusting. After making sure everything looked as good as it could, I waited for the doors to open.

The crowds were great, and I was so busy selling items that when my stomach rumbled, I was surprised to see it was 12:30 p.m. Since there seemed to be a lull, I ate the fluffernutter sandwich I'd brought with me. Just as I swallowed the last deliciously sticky bite, Ryan from DiNapoli's walked in.

"Ryan, hi." I reached over the table and gave him a little hug. "You look nice today." He had on a collared dress shirt and dark slacks. A wool overcoat was folded over his arm.

"Thanks. I don't always wear my work clothes."

"You made it," I said.

"A friend of mine brought me. We did a tour in the air force together years ago. It wasn't for me. They sent me to a small town in New Mexico, and I thought I'd never leave that place. Have you ever been there? It's so . . . so . . . different." He smiled, and we both laughed. "Although, I guess I should have stayed in. My buddy has done well, and I'm still working at DiNapoli's."

"I thought you liked it there. Angelo would be lost without you. He says you can fix anything."

"They're like family. My own handyman business is really taking off, and it's hard to do both."

"You should be proud of yourself. I know how hard it is to start your own business. Are you here looking for anything in particular?"

"My girlfriend likes old stuff. I thought I might find something for her."

"Does she collect something or have a specific era of things she likes?"

"I'm not sure." He picked up and set down several things on my table.

"What about a favorite color?"

"She has a lot of blue in her house."

"A woman after my own heart. It's my favorite, too." I showed him a couple of cobalt-blue glass bottles from the forties. One was shaped like a violin. I had found them at a garage sale last summer and couldn't resist them. But I'd realized I didn't really have anywhere to put them.

"I'm not sure," he said.

"What about this?" I picked up a blue and white porcelain jar. The writing on the front said MAGDA TOILET CREAM C. J. COUNTIE & CO. CHEMISTS. The top lid said COUNTIE OF BOSTON. "It's from around eighteen-ninety. I did some research and found out the company was bought and it became Pond's Cold Cream."

"She'll like it because it says Boston on it," Ryan said. "How much is it?"

"Thirty," I said.

"Okay." Ryan pulled out his wallet.

"Wait. You're supposed to bargain."

"But that seems like a fair price for what it is."

"Always ask at these kinds of events or at antique stores if they'll take anything off. Most dealers will. If they don't, you have to decide if it's worth full price or not."

Ryan handed me three tens. I gave him three dollars back.

"You're taking all the fun out of my day. I like to bargain," I said. I wrapped the lid and the base in tissue paper and then stuck them in a plastic bag. "I hope she likes it."

"Me too. See you around."

Right after Ryan left, I saw a couple carrying out the bench I wanted. *Darn it all.*

The afternoon continued to be busy. James stopped by. "I'll swing back by at five and help you put the tables away."

I nodded and waved, then turned to negotiate the sale of a chair I loved but didn't have room for. It was a sleek leather chair from the fifties. I had found it on the curb one morning on base, set out next to the garbage cans. The red leather went with nothing I had, so I had decided that keeping it under the eaves was selfish. The young couple I was negotiating with was so excited about it that when they gave me a lowball offer, I took it. Part of me envied their young love, and the other part didn't want to have to drag the chair back up the stairs.

I never did have time to go back around and take another look at what people had for sale. By five o'clock I had sold 90 percent of what I'd brought with me and had made three hundred dollars. I decided to donate what was left to the base thrift shop. I put what I could in boxes and carried it over to the thrift shop space.

Laura looked a bit frazzled. "We sold a lot, but people keep dropping off stuff they didn't sell."

I held up my box. "Here's more. It will be good for business."

"Yes, but I don't want to have to haul this all back tonight."

"I could come back tomorrow and help."

"I could, too." I turned, and James was standing behind me.

"That would be great. One-ish?" Laura asked.

Laura's husband stopped by, and between the four of us, we got the community center looking almost like it had when we started.

"I'm going home, putting up my feet, and having a large glass of wine," Laura said. "Anyone want to join me?"

James shook his head. "Thanks, but I can't."

I wanted a shower and a good night's sleep. Although, now that the sale was over, all my worries started swarming me. I hugged Laura. "Thanks for the offer, but I'm beat."

After a shower, I sat on my couch, flipping through a magazine full of decorating tips for flea market finds. It was only seven, but it felt more like midnight. Someone knocked on my door. As I went over to answer it, I yet again missed having Mike and his brothers next door to prescreen my visitors. And since the photo from the other night had me on edge, I called through the door, "Who is it?"

"It's Seth."

I leaned my forehead against the door, not sure if I was ready to see him.

"Please, Sarah."

I opened the door and stepped back to let him in,

but I didn't move from the door or close it. As far as I was concerned, this was going to be a very short conversation.

"I'm sorry about the other night. I should have answered your question."

"You told me last fall the difference between you and CJ was that you wouldn't let me go. But you did."

"You're the one that took off. Couples have disagreements."

"It was more than a disagreement. It was trust. It's about you having a job that's complicated. I think I need easy right now."

Seth took my hand. "Move in with me."

I stared at him, in shock.

"I'll take care of you."

A million thoughts swept through my mind. "But I want to take care of myself. I have to for a while."

"I love you. Please. Move in with me."

A creak sounded from the stairway. CJ stood on the landing. Instead of turning and leaving, he trotted up the rest of the steps.

I looked from Seth to CJ and bolted.

Chapter 32

I ran past CJ, down the steps, and out of the building. It was snowing, and a fierce wind blew. I didn't have a coat or keys. I knew it wouldn't be long before one or both of them came after me. So I ran, slipping on ice patches, to Carol's shop. I burst in the door, freezing cold and covered with snow. Her entire class turned around and stared. I fled to her back room and heard Carol excuse herself.

"What's wrong?" she asked.

"Seth asked me to move in with him."

Carol's jaw dropped. "What did you say? I'm guessing no, since you showed up here looking like you'd seen a ghost."

"Let me finish," I said. "CJ showed up right when Seth asked me. I had to get out of there."

Carol burst out laughing.

"Really?" I asked her.

"I'm sorry." She tried hard to look serious but laughed again.

I stared at her for a minute and laughed, too. I doubled over, I laughed so hard I cried. I straightened up. I couldn't decide if I was crying because I was laughing or if I was laughing to try to keep from sobbing.

"Take my keys," Carol said.

"Are you sure?"

"Go to my house. I'll call you when I'm done. It shouldn't be more than an hour."

"Thanks."

"I'm parked in the back." She found her keys and tossed them to me. "And take this coat. You'll freeze otherwise."

I started Carol's SUV and hit the button for the seat warmers. The coat she'd given to me was thin wool, but purple and really cute—more for fashion than warmth but better than nothing. Instead of heading toward Great Road, where I could easily run into CJ or Seth, I turned right into the residential section of Ellington. I wended my way along back roads but decided against going to Carol's house. I didn't want to have to explain anything to Brad or have him call CJ, which, I was guessing, he would do. Brad and CJ were almost as good friends as Carol and I were.

I drove to Billerica and stopped at a family restaurant and bar. I slipped into a booth at the bar and ordered a Coke. The last thing I needed right now was alcohol, even as tempting as it sounded. The Celtics were playing the Knicks on a big-screen

TV in the corner. It gave me something to think about instead of either the funniest or the most surreal moment of my life. I thought Seth and CJ might look at it differently. Both had texted and called, but I hadn't bothered to see what either had to say. If I weren't waiting for Carol to call, I'd turn the darn phone off.

My life had become a three-ring circus. CJ in one ring, Seth in another, and my stalker in a third. I was on a tightrope high above them, trying to stay balanced but wobbling seriously and at my peril. I had no safety net, and the wrong move could be my last. I wondered if I *should* get some rum to go with my Coke.

Thirty minutes into my wait, Seth slid into the booth across from me.

"How did you find me?" I wondered if he had some kind of tracking device.

"I drove around looking for Carol's SUV."

"How did you know I'd have her car?"

"Yours was at home. So was Stella's. I heard the front door slam and knew you'd left the building. I stopped at DiNapoli's, but you weren't there. I figured you must have gone to Carol. She denied seeing you, but I could tell she was lying."

I narrowed my eyes. "But how do you know what kind of car she drives?"

Seth smiled. "It's hard to miss a vanity plate that says 'Paint,' with a holder that says 'Paint and Wine.' And you mentioned this place to me once. That narrowed down my places to look. I figured Gillganins was too obvious, and Lowell too far. Some place familiar would be more comforting if you were upset."

No wonder he was such a successful lawyer.

"I withdraw my suggestion that you move in," he said.

"What if I was going to say yes?"

"Were you?"

"No."

"I played my hand too soon." He smiled as he said it.

"Dealt too early."

"I laid all my cards out on the table before I should have."

We were both grinning. And this took me back to my whole dilemma with Seth and CJ. I had so much fun with Seth. I liked him. A lot. But CJ and I had a history, a deep love that had been twisted by a sadistic young twit. We hadn't been able to recover, since neither of us was ever on the same page at the same time. And we had a problem with trust. At least I did.

"You okay?" Seth asked. "Your smile left, and then you seemed to, too."

I nodded. "What happened after I left?"

"There was a little yelling. A lot of yelling. Until Stella stomped up the stairs, with Awesome at her heels, to find out what was going on. She told us to quit thinking about ourselves and to think about you. So we both left. Stella locked up for you."

"It must be awkward for you two to have to work together."

"It can be, but so far we've both been able to put that aside and remain professional."

"So far?"

"I think CJ was pretty close to decking me tonight."

"I'm sorry."

"It's not your fault. I'd have wanted to do the same if the situation was reversed."

I wasn't sure that was true. If I'd just cut Seth out of my life as soon as I realized who he was, none of us would be in this mess. "Thanks for coming by, but I just need to think through things."

"Okay." He stood, but instead of leaving, he pulled me out of my booth and into his arms. He kissed my hair, then let me go. "Take care."

I sat across from Carol in her now empty shop. We each had a glass of Merlot. I could drink now that I didn't have to drive. "How'd the class go?"

"It was a fun group. A fiftieth birthday party and they picked a row of wine bottles to paint. My favorite part of doing this is seeing how excited everyone is at the end, when they've finished their own painting. Although, the guest of honor drank so much, we dubbed her painting *Wine Bottles in Abstract*. Did I tell you I'm starting a new after-school kids' club?"

"That's a great idea."

"How did your evening go? I take it you didn't go to my house."

"What makes you say that?"

"I talked to Brad. CJ was there."

Busted. "That's exactly why I didn't go over." I

took a drink of my wine. "I went to that little family bar and restaurant in Billerica. Seth showed up."

"What? How?"

"He used that lawyer brain to track me down."

"Pretty impressive." Carol's face belied her words. Even though she'd been on my side all this time since CJ and I split, I think when push and shove met, she wanted me to be with CJ. "What are you going to do about the two of them?"

"Nothing for now. I'm not going to make hasty decisions or let anyone pressure me."

"That's good. Want me to drop you home?"

I finished the last of my wine. "Yes, please."

I went home and put on my plaid flannel pajamas; then I logged on to my virtual garage sale site. I went through my usual routine of approving and disapproving posts, reminding people to remove old posts, and then I started going through the long list of private messages from people with questions and comments. They were innocuous until I opened this:

I know where you live. You won't see me coming. No one ever saw me coming.

Chapter 33

My fingers froze over the keyboard. I started to ban the person. But first I went to his page to see what I could find out about him. There weren't any real posts. He belonged to a few other buy-sell groups. He didn't have any photos posted, other than a cartoon character named Dr. Doom that he used as his profile picture and header. The account was obviously fake, but someone had added him to the group. I forwarded the message and the account name to Pellner. Not that there would be much he could do. I'd had it with these jerks, whoever they were. I banned him and posted a reminder on the board not to add people unless you knew them personally.

A knock on my door made me jump, but I figured Dr. Doom wouldn't be knocking.

"It's me," Stella called. When I opened the door, she looked over my pajamas. "You're one hot mama."

"Very funny. I happen to like plaid. Come in." We sat on the couch and turned toward each other.

"If only they could see you now."

"CJ and Seth? They'd see beyond the pj's."

"At least they'd like to."

I laughed. "That's not what I was talking about. I heard you tossed them out of here."

"How did you hear that?"

"Seth tracked me down."

Stella's beautiful green eyes widened. "Interesting." Stella said it with a neutral tone. She was more neutral than anyone else I knew. While I'd met Carol soon after I'd met CJ and when we were madly in love, Stella had met me as a wounded, lost soul. Her first impressions of CJ were as the cheater who'd hurt me.

"When I was a teenager, I would have swooned at the thought of two men fighting over me. The reality of it sucks," I said.

Stella laughed. "Is something else bothering you?"

"Just the trolls on my garage sale site."

"Is it more than that?"

Maybe it was time to tell someone what had been rolling around in my mind for the past few hours. "I've been running around, finding connections between Juanita, Margaret, and Frieda." I played with the button on the front of my jammies. "But maybe I should be looking at a connection between them and me."

Stella sat up a little straighter. "That makes sense, but do you think there is one?"

"It's going to sound crazy. Even worse than when I told you I thought I had a stalker."

"Try me."

This was what I loved about Stella. She'd listen without judging. "Margaret and I had a public disagreement on my garage sale site about Frieda getting a vintage tablecloth instead of me."

Stella made a "Go on" motion with her hand.

"When I found her body, the tablecloth was stuffed down her throat." I shuddered as I pictured the scene again.

"What about Juanita? Do you think there's a connection there, too?"

"I was attacked the day she came to my house. It created a commotion outside, was in the paper, and on the police blotter."

"But she didn't hurt you."

"I did some digging through the police call records in Lexington, Concord, and Bedford. And I compared them to what I could find out about Juanita's cleaning business. I think her business was some kind of front for a burglary ring."

"You do?" Stella had a little worry crease between her eyebrows.

"Yes. First, there were the odd complaints of people finding a door or window open. Then I compared the places she had cleaned to the police logs."

"Why didn't anyone else figure this out?"

"Maybe the police have, and they just aren't saying anything about it. Someone else could be involved, but they don't know who yet. Or maybe the incidents have been far enough apart time-wise and location-wise that they haven't figured it out."

"So you think that someone, maybe your stalker, is killing people that they perceive have hurt you?"

"It sounds even crazier when you say it than when I thought it."

"I'm going to stay on your good side, just in case. You can live here rent free from now on. And I'll be your chauffeur. However, I draw the line at cooking and cleaning. Just make sure you put it out there in public, so your crazy stalker person knows how good I am to you."

I swatted Stella with a throw pillow. I gasped.

"What?" Stella asked.

"The day Hennessy embarrassed me at Di-Napoli's . . . Her tires were slashed that night."

"So you think it's someone at DiNapoli's?"

"The place was packed. It was the first day of Angelo's ten percent off for military. I'm trying to think if anyone stood out." I remembered how crowded it was. Could James have been there and I hadn't noticed? "I was so focused on Hennessy, I don't remember who else was around."

"Was James there?"

"Why ask about James?" Stella had met him last fall, when we were on Fitch one day. But since I'd been wondering about him, it worried me that his name was the first one out of Stella's mouth.

"Because anyone could tell from the way he looks at you that he likes you."

"In a romantic way?"

"Yes. Yeesh, how could you not know?"

"I've had my suspicions on and off, but nothing has ever happened."

"How about Seth?"

"No. I'd remember that. But why him?"

Stella lifted and dropped a shoulder. "Like I said before, sometimes he just seems too good to be true."

"No. It's not Seth. He's a great guy. He's the DA, for goodness' sake." Stella was such a terrible judge of men, I could disregard her line of thinking about Seth.

"I think thou dost protest too much."

"Okay, Mrs. Shakespeare." I bit my lower lip. I did worry a bit about Seth's association with Mike.

Stella and I sat in silence for a few minutes.

"But wouldn't CJ be in danger? Heaven knows, someone could think he's hurt you," Stella said.

"He'd be harder to get to, though. This sounds terrible, but others are sort of low-hanging fruit." I mentally added something to my list of things to do: find a way to ask CJ and Seth if they'd been threatened, without sounding insane.

"He lives alone, too."

"Yes. But he's armed, and investigations are different when a cop gets killed."

"Are you sure it's a man?" Stella asked.

"What? Of course." I thought for a moment. "It has to be, doesn't it?" Statistically, more stalkers were men than women—at least I thought I'd read that somewhere.

"You never saw your attacker's face," Stella said.

Another knock on the door saved me from spilling

my worries about Seth and Mike's relationship. It was a ridiculous thought.

"Stella?" It was Officer Awesome.

Stella winked at me. "I left a note on my door that I'd be up here. Are you okay?"

"Yes. And you two will be downstairs if I'm not."

She flew over to the door and threw it open. I waved at Awesome as Stella linked arms with him, and then they hurried down the stairs.

Pellner called me at 7:30 a.m. on Saturday. I'd barely pried my eyes open. It was still fairly dark in my room, so it had to be cloudy out. I hoped it wasn't snowing.

"Can you come down to the station?" he said.

"Why? Is CJ okay?" Since last night, when I shared my fears with Stella, I'd been worrying even more about what was going on.

"He's fine. I want to hear about the latest threat you received."

"Can't I just tell you over the phone?"

"Let's make it official," Pellner said. He paused for a second. "So we have a record."

"I guess so," I said. "I'll be there after a while."

"Make it sooner rather than later, if you can."

"Okay." I hung up, showered, did my hair and makeup, and got ready to leave. But something just didn't feel quite right. I worried that Pellner wanted to get me there without a fuss. So I called Vincenzo.

"I can meet you there at ten," he said.

"I told them I'd be there sooner than that."

"Were you specific about a time?"

"No, I just said a while."

"Why don't you go somewhere until ten? Let me know where, and my driver and I will pick you up on the way. I don't want them to get impatient and show up at your house."

"You think it's serious?"

"I'd rather err on the side of caution and not have the police trying to interview you without me being present."

Chapter 34

I drove through the Dunkin' Donuts drive-through and bought a dozen assorted donuts. Then I headed over to DiNapoli's, eating one of the donuts on the way. The DiNapolis didn't serve breakfast but would probably be there prepping for lunch. I parked in the wide alley behind their restaurant and sent a quick text to Vincenzo, letting him know I was here. As I hopped out of the Suburban, I glanced over at Herb Fitch's house to see if his curtain twitched. He was a retired police officer and kept an eye on the neighborhood. I was grateful that I didn't see a twitch. He might know if the police were looking for me and alert them about where I was. I knocked on the back door of DiNapoli's, and Ryan opened it.

"What are you doing here?" he asked.

"I brought donuts." I held up the box. Angelo had opinions about breakfast, but I knew bringing donuts was acceptable.

Rosalie and Angelo joined me at a table, bringing over a pot of coffee and mugs. Ryan and Lois were the only employees there. They both grabbed a donut but took them to the room behind the kitchen where the dishwashers and coolers were.

I took a coconut donut from the box. Angelo grabbed a Boston cream, and Rosalie took a simple glazed donut.

"Do you know anything about Nichole More?" I asked them. She'd been on my mind during my sleepless night. James, Seth, CJ, Nichole—thoughts of them had kept me up half the night.

They exchanged a look. Angelo took a big bite of his donut.

"Our boy, Tim, dated Nichole in high school, then on and off during college," Rosalie said.

Angelo swallowed. "Apparently, a kid whose parents make a decent living by hard work isn't good enough for the likes of Margaret More."

"Angelo," Rosalie said. "It was for the best. Nichole has a reputation."

"Broke our boy's heart more than once," Angelo said.

"What kind of reputation?" I asked.

"Drinking, partying," Rosalie said.

"Sleeping with anyone." Angelo sounded bitter. "The last time Tim caught her, he left. Quit college and came home."

Rosalie patted Angelo's arm. "But if he hadn't, he would have never met Beth. She's a sweet girl, and they have a lovely family."

"That's true, Rosalie. I just wish he hadn't gone through so much before he did." Angelo stood up. "Are you in some kind of trouble, kid?"

"Why would you think that?"

"Because you're here with donuts," Angelo said.

"The police want to have a chat with me."

"I'll go with you."

"I called Vincenzo. He's going to pick me up at ten. Do you mind if I wait here until then?"

Rosalie stood, too. "You wait here as long as you need to."

Lois came out a few minutes later and sat across from me. "Can you show me how your online garage sale works? I've got some stuff I want to get rid of." She frowned. "Need to get rid of. Living in this area costs a fortune, but I don't want to take my kid out of the school here if I can help it."

"Sure." I took my phone out. "You send a request to join this site. Do you want to do it now? I'll approve it right away."

Lois slipped a phone out of her black work pants. She sent the request, and I approved it.

"All you have to do is take pictures, post them, state the price and where they can be picked up."

"You want me to put my address on there?"

"No! Never. I mean put, 'Pickup in Ellington.' Technically, everything is supposed to be picked up in Ellington, but there are people from other towns who post on here." I gave her my safety briefing and showed her the site rules.

"What does *bump* mean?" She pointed to a post.

"If no one buys your item, once it's been on there for a week, if you type in the word *bump*, or any other word, for that matter, it will make it go back to the top of the site."

"What's this one that says 'ISO girls' five-T clothing'?"

"'ISO' stands for 'in search of,' so someone's looking for clothing for a little girl who wears size five-T."

I sipped my coffee as Lois continued to scroll through the site.

"What's this one?" she asked, turning her phone toward me. "It says the admin of this site sucks."

I paled and grabbed my phone. There was a long list of complaints. Someone had said they were going to start their own site. I had a lot of things I'd like to say to these people, but instead, I deleted the post.

"You worried someone else will start a site?" Lois asked.

"No. They're welcome to. It's a lot of work and headaches. If people have complaints, they can come to me or send a private message to the person they have an issue with."

I posted a reminder that I didn't allow drama on the page.

"How do you know how to price things?"

I looked at Lois. Lines of worry were etched around her eyes and creased between her brows. "I could help you."

"Would you? How soon?"

"When's your next day off?"

"Monday," Lois said.

I checked the calendar on my phone. "How about early afternoon?"

"That'd be great."

Thirty minutes later Vincenzo and I sat in an interview room at the EPD. He'd let me answer all of Pellner's questions about the threats I'd received through the garage sale site, and I had told Pellner about all the pictures I'd received. I hadn't mentioned that almost all the bad ones had come after I'd been with Seth.

"I don't think there's any way to trace who the threats are coming from, Pellner. People set up fake accounts on public computers. I don't think it's worth the time to try to track them," I said.

Vincenzo leaned forward. "At this time."

Pellner stood. "I'll be right back."

Vincenzo whispered in my ear. "Now we're going to find out why you are really here."

I stiffened.

"Relax. You haven't done anything wrong. They're fishing. I'll protect you. Keep your answers brief."

I tried to peel my shoulders back down from my ears.

A thin, wiry state patrol officer entered. I recognized him from the day Margaret had been murdered.

"Let's keep this brief," Vincenzo said, taking the offensive. "My client has been forthcoming with her information. I don't see the point of questioning her further."

"The day of the murder were you ever in Mrs. More's car?" the officer asked. His dark brown eyes were hooded making him hard to read.

I looked at Vincenzo. He tilted his head, which I took as an okay to answer. "No. As I stated in my report, the car was locked."

"Did you ever, at any time, ride in her car?"

I opened my mouth to answer, but Vincenzo interrupted.

"How can you expect her to answer such a broadly worded question? Ever?" Vincenzo shook his head.

The officer frowned. "Have you recently ridden anywhere with her?"

I looked at Vincenzo. He did the head tilt thing again. "No," I said. I wanted to tell him that I'd never ridden with her and to ask why he wanted to know.

The officer watched me. We all sat in silence. I knew the officer was hoping I'd crack and confess to something. Believe me, it was tempting. But the only thing I'd done wrong lately was eat too many donuts. And as far as I knew, that wasn't against the law.

"You've claimed that you've received numerous

photos through an app called"—he paused and looked at his notes—"PopIt. Has anyone else seen the photos?"

I'd wondered if the state police doubted the pictures' existence.

"No." I didn't add anything else but glanced at Vincenzo.

Vincenzo stood. "Unless you have anything else to ask Ms. Winston, we're leaving."

The man didn't look happy but nodded.

When we got back in Vincenzo's car and I'd snuggled into the soft leather seat, I turned to him. "What was that about?"

"I'm not sure." He looked a bit worried, which worried me. I'd never seen him ruffled. "Have you ever been in Margaret's car?"

"I don't think so. It's not like we were buddies."

"Then there's nothing to worry about."

"You think somehow my DNA showed up in her car?"

"You've been to her house before?"

I hated it when people didn't answer my questions. "Yes."

"So if your DNA was in her car, it could have been transferred from her to her car. Or it could be sloppy police work. You were at the scene."

The driver pulled up in front of my apartment. He got out and held the car door open for me as I stepped out. Vincenzo leaned over. "Don't worry about this. It's nothing."

Easy for him to say. I realized I'd left my car behind DiNapoli's and walked over to get it. I came around the corner of the alley and saw that one of my tires was flat. When I got up to it, I saw a piece of paper stuck to the tire, held in place by a knife.

Chapter 35

I knelt down to read the note, careful not to touch it. It said, *You won't see me coming.* I whipped around, but I had a feeling the person who did this hadn't waited around to watch me. But I looked around just in case, wishing I'd spot someone with a sign around his or her neck saying I'M YOUR STALKER. I was alone in the alley, very, very alone.

I tried to shake off the fear. "Oh, big deal. You killed my tire." My attempt at bravado didn't help. Not at all. What I wanted to do was take the knife out, toss it and the note, and try to pretend this never happened. Instead, I hurried over to Herb Fitch's house and knocked on the back door. I must have pounded harder than I thought, because a neighbor opened her back door and stuck her head out.

"Are you tryin' to wake the dead? I've gotta kid taking a nap," she said.

No, just Herb. I hustled over to her. "I'm looking for Herb."

"He goes to Florida every February." She said it with a tone that indicated if I didn't know that, I didn't know Herb.

Just my luck, when I really needed the guy, he was on a midwinter break. "Did you see anyone in the alley this morning?"

"Yes."

Oh, good. "Who?"

"Lots of people. There's always people coming and going from the businesses."

"See that Suburban? Did you see anyone around it? Someone stuck a knife in my tire."

"Someone must not like you very much." She looked me over more closely. "Are you that Hooker woman? Hell of a name."

I just nodded. It was easier than explaining I'd changed my name back to Winston.

"There was a delivery van back there, behind DiNapoli's, this morning."

"What kind?"

"Just one of them white-paneled van types. And in case you're going to ask, no distinguishing marks, and I have no idea about the license plate. I watch cop shows."

"Okay. Thanks." *What to do next? Go ask Angelo about deliveries, which would make him suspicious, or call the police, which would upset Angelo?* I decided to talk to Angelo first.

As tempting as it might be to walk in through the employee and delivery entrance again, I walked around to the front of DiNapoli's. It gave me a few minutes to think about wording, but all that went out the door when I actually faced Angelo. Because my face crumpled, and tears started to fall.

"Are you okay? How'd it go?" Angelo asked. He led me to a table and handed me a bunch of napkins.

"Fine. Vincenzo said it's nothing to worry about."

"But you're still going to worry."

"Something else happened." My voice caught on the word *happened*. I took a couple of deep breaths and told him about the tire. "Did you have any deliveries this morning?"

"No. And nobody better be running any funny business out of the back of this place. Let me ask a couple of questions, and then we have to call the police."

I followed Angelo to the back. Two dishwashers, Ryan, and Lois were all joking as they worked.

"Anyone have any deliveries made back here this morning?" Angelo looked each one in the eye. I would have wilted under the look.

They all shook their heads no.

"Anyone been in or out that back door that shouldn't have been?"

"A couple of us went out for a smoke," one of the dishwashers said.

"Did you happen to notice a white-paneled van out there?" I asked.

"No. Just that white Suburban," said the dishwasher.

"What's going on?" Lois asked.

"Someone stuck a knife through Sarah's tire," Angelo answered.

"Oh, no," Lois and Ryan said in unison.

The dishwashers shook their heads.

Angelo studied their reactions. "Thanks for your help."

Angelo and I walked outside. "It seems like they were all telling the truth," I said.

"They'd better be if they want to work for me." I showed Angelo the tire. He bent down and looked at the note. "Do you want to come stay with Rosalie and me for a few days? The kids are gone. We have room."

A flood of warmth rushed through me. Tear blurred my vision. "That is so lovely of you. But no. I can't let this jerk get to me."

"Let us know if you change your mind. Safety first."

"The good news is Stella is dating a police officer, so he's there a lot."

"But not all the time." Angelo looked at the tire again. "You'd better call the police. Do you have roadside that will come take care of the tire?"

"No." I pulled out my phone and called the non-emergency number for the EPD. I'd never had to change a tire before. My dad had shown me once, when I was fifteen, but I knew I'd never have the courage to try it on my own.

"After the police are done, I'll help you change the tire."

Pellner shook his head and pointed a finger at me. "I thought Chuck was going to have a stroke when we told him about this."

I shivered in my jacket as the wind picked up. A few snowflakes fell, but they didn't seem serious.

"I wouldn't let him come, because he'd cause a scene and end up in trouble with him." Pellner jerked his head toward the state police officer who had shown up. We watched him place the knife in an evidence bag.

"What's he doing here? This is vandalism, not murder," I said.

"It might have been a murder if Chuck had come along."

"Okay. I get it. CJ's not happy. I'm not, either. It's not like I asked someone to do this."

The statie trotted over with the knife and held up the bag in front of my nose. "Recognize this?"

"Yes."

Pellner's and the statie's eyebrows shot up.

"It was recently in my tire," I said.

Pellner took a step behind the statie and shook his head. I got the message: "Shut up and play nice."

"I'm sorry. It's been a stressful morning," I said.

Pellner moved off and took another look at the tire.

"Other than seeing the knife in your tire, have you seen it before?" the statie asked.

I looked at it. The knife had a black handle, a razor-sharp edge on one side, and steel serrated teeth on the other. I imagined it being plunged into my stomach and twisted. "What's that used for?"

"Hunting," the statie said.

I swallowed hard. "I haven't ever seen it before. Or anything like it."

"Are you okay?" he asked.

I took in a couple of deep breaths and nodded.

He held up the evidence bag with the note in it. "Any chance you recognize the writing?"

I studied the note, trying to focus on the writing instead of the threat. It was neat, tight writing, cursive, not print. I looked up at the officer. "No. I don't recognize it."

The statie conferred with Pellner for a minute and then took off.

"Do you need help with your tire?" Pellner asked me.

"No. Thank you. What did he say to you?"

"Either you deserve an Academy Award or you really don't know anything about who did this."

Ryan came out right after the police left. "I'll put your spare on for you. Angelo could do it, but it will be easier for me."

We chatted as he changed the tire. I tried to watch what he did and wondered if I should up my insurance to include roadside.

"Don't let this shake you, Sarah," Ryan said. "Whoever did this is chicken sh . . . chicken."

"I won't."

"Your teeth are chattering."

"It's cold." I wanted to believe that was what was

causing the chattering, but I didn't think Ryan bought it, and I didn't really, either.

"I'm almost done. Go in and get some coffee."

I started to protest, but Ryan insisted.

"Let me pay you for your time, Ryan."

Ryan waved me away. "Go warm up."

When I got home, after getting my tire replaced, I had a message from the woman who owned the Pez dispensers, asking if I'd sold them and when she'd get her money. I smacked my hand to my forehead. Since they hadn't been part of the crime scene at Juanita's house, I had just brought the box home with me and had stuck it under the eaves. I sent her a quick note asking if she wanted me to repost them or return them. She replied that she'd still like me to sell them.

I crawled into the space under the eaves and noticed a box had been knocked over. I must have done this when I was getting all the stuff out for the February Blues garage sale. The box was full of photo albums. I stuffed them back in but could tell one was missing—before they'd fit perfectly in the box, but now there was space for at least one more. I looked around the space but didn't spot the missing photo album. I thought the missing one was full of fairly recent pictures—ones from the past couple of years.

I grabbed the box of Pez and took it to the couch, intending to look through it. But I couldn't stop thinking about the missing photo album. Where would I have put it? I was too young for memory problems, but darn it, I couldn't remember taking that album, or any of them, out of the box. I sighed loudly. It had to be here somewhere. I should just look for it. It couldn't have gone far.

I searched my living room first. It seemed like the most likely place I'd have left it. Maybe I kicked it under the couch. Nothing. I opened the trunk I used as a coffee table. It was where I kept my stash of vintage tablecloths. There wasn't a photo album tucked inside. I checked the drawers and cupboards in the kitchen. Nope. The bedroom closet, the dresser, and the area under the bed all came up empty. I even checked the clothes hamper in the bathroom, which reminded me I needed to do some wash. The good news was there weren't any dust bunnies, bogeymen, or monsters in my apartment. A prickly feeling crawled up the back of my neck as I realized the album was not misplaced but gone.

Something else was missing, too. My favorite aqua sweater. I had thought I'd left it someplace and had intended to check with Stella, the DiNapolis, and Carol. But I'd never gotten around to it, with my mind on other matters.

The robber. I'd thought he took only things he could sell quickly—my computer, my cash, and my wedding ring. At the time I'd chalked the wedding ring up to the gold having some value. But my aqua sweater had been missing probably since that day, and there was no way a pawn shop would snap that up. I tried to convince myself I'd left the sweater someplace, but I knew better. Whoever had been in here had wanted more than items for a quick sale. They'd wanted my personal things. You couldn't get much more personal than my sweater, photos, and wedding ring.

The robber was my stalker.

Chapter 36

Part of me had known it all along, but I still felt dirty, invaded, exposed. Calling the police about a missing photo album seemed ridiculous. But with all that had been going on, not calling the police seemed stupid. I peeked out my curtains, the ones I now closed as soon as it got dark out. Awesome's car was outside, so I called Stella.

"Could Awesome come up here for a minute?" I asked.

"He's just leaving, but I'll send him up."

I tried to tamp down my nerves by pacing around the apartment as I waited. Finally, there was a knock on my door. When I opened it, Awesome leaned against the jamb, looking very pleased with himself. It didn't take me long to wipe that expression off his face as I told him about the missing photo album and sweater, and my theory that the robber was the guy who'd been stalking me. He nodded while I talked and seemed to be listening intently.

"Did you call it in?"

"No. I'm telling you. It seems silly to file a report over a missing photo album and sweater. It could be nothing. But, on the other hand, saying nothing seemed foolish."

"I think we'd better file a report. This guy's done what? Photographed you, threatened you, slashed your tires, possibly killed for you? I'll drop by the station on my way home. Add this to the list."

I guessed all the fears I'd confided to Stella had been passed on to Awesome. To hear him say it and take it so seriously scared the bejesus out of me.

"Are you going to be okay? Want me to get Stella up here?"

I shrugged, not wanting to admit anything.

Awesome turned to go.

"Wait," I said. "Stella isn't as tough as she looks. Be good to her, or let her be."

He lifted an eyebrow. "Yes, ma'am."

If he were a cowboy, I would have expected him to tip his hat as I left. He seemed nice enough, but I still wasn't sure he was good enough for Stella.

After Awesome left I went back over to the box of Pez, glad to have this task to distract me. I took each dispenser out, shook it, and looked inside. One rattled, and a little thrill went through me. I popped it open, and an old pink Pez candy fell out. *How disappointing.* I didn't know what I'd been hoping to find, but it wasn't an old piece of candy. I grouped the dispensers in small groups, snapped some

photos, and relisted them on the garage sale site.
Before long people started sending me private
messages about the different Pez lots. A couple of
the oldest ones sold right away. I told the buyers I'd
meet them tomorrow at DiNapoli's. No more
strangers coming to my house if I could help it.

I answered questions about the other Pez lots
and ended up selling all but one within an hour
and a half of posting them. Who knew Pez were so
popular? While I was at it, I did a bit of cleanup on
the site. Then I noticed a message from the admin
of the Concord site. At first we'd just talked online,
but as time progressed, we had ended up meeting
for coffee occasionally.

Have you had any problems with threats lately? she
typed.

Yes. More than you want to know about—online
and in real life. Some jerk stuck a knife in my tire.
Why do you ask? Have you been getting them,
too?

No. But I heard there were some problems on
your site from a friend who's on it.

Someone's been allowing fake accounts on my
site. I'm trying to keep up, but a few have snuck
through.

I heard the cops were setting up fake accounts on
sites like ours.

Really? Why?

I have a nephew who's a cop in Lexington. There's rumors about a burglary ring and that the cops in a lot of the towns around here are keeping track of people.

Hmmm, that's interesting. Did he say anything else?

Just that things have quieted down. Let me know if you need any help.

I need lots of help but probably not with anything you can fix.

LOL. Reach out if you need me. And be careful.

Will do.

So my theory about a burglary ring, Juanita, and my site might be valid, after all. My site now had more than three thousand members. I had members who I knew were cops and cops' wives, so there didn't seem to be any reason for them to have fake accounts.

I typed *bump* under my cleaning ad, which made it go to the top of the listings. I'd give it one more try. This time I added the phrase *No job too small.* That sounded more desperate. My best-case scenario was that someone would contact me and ask me to join their burglary ring, would confess to killing Juanita and Margaret, and would apologize for stalking me. In the fantasy playing in my head, they'd reimburse me for the tire and the labor, too. But I gave up daydreaming, and I realized the most likely thing to happen was that someone would hire me, I'd leave them with a nice clean house, and I'd just be one worn-out, tired girl when I was finished.

Thirty minutes later someone sent me a note, wanting to buy the last lot of Pez and asking if I could deliver it to their house tomorrow. Before saying yes, I checked the person's profile. The woman appeared to be real. She lived in Bedford and had elementary-age kids, from the looks of her photos. The woman told me one of her kids was sick and her husband, who was in the coast guard, was out of town. She also wrote that she knew Laura through the Spouses' Club on base. After I verified that with a quick text to Laura, I told the woman I'd drop the Pez lot off in the early afternoon.

A couple of people sent messages asking about my cleaning service, but no one made an actual cleaning appointment. That was disappointing.

On Sunday afternoon, after meeting people at DiNapoli's to sell the Pez, I pulled up to the Bedford woman's house. It was surrounded by woods and backed up to conservancy lands. Isolated. I could see a couple of neighbors' houses off in the distance since the trees were bare. Thankfully, this house didn't have the long driveway Margaret's did, and the house was visible from the road. However, it sat on a cul-de-sac, so there was no traffic passing by. I sat, hands gripping the steering wheel, half tempted to drive off. But if I was going to live in Ellington, I couldn't freak out every time I saw a few trees, because there were lots of trees in this area.

I kept my doors locked, my engine running, and took a very good look around. No one was lurking in the woods, smoking. As a precaution, I grabbed my phone from my purse and held it as I climbed out. I opened the back of the Suburban to grab the Pez. Some of my cleaning supplies had fallen out of the large galvanized metal bucket, so I started shoving them back in.

An arm circled my waist from behind. A hand covered my mouth, choking off my scream.

Chapter 37

I dropped my phone as someone tried to lift me, but all those meals at DiNapoli's had added five pounds, and lifting didn't work. So my attacker began dragging me backward. I lunged for the bucket and just caught it with my fingers. I got a better grip and swung it with every bit of adrenaline-fueled strength I had. A howl of pain behind me told me I'd connected with something. The arm dropped from my waist; and the hand, from my mouth.

Before I could turn to face my attacker, I was shoved violently. My lower abdomen slammed into the tailgate, doubling me over. I lay for a few precious seconds half in, half out of the Suburban. The bristles of the carpet scraped against my face as I gasped for air. I drew my legs in and rolled onto my back, ready to strike out.

I lifted my head, propped myself up on my elbows, but no one was there. My breath came out in short pants from fear or injury. . . . I wasn't sure

which. I scooted farther into the Suburban and
slammed the back end closed. I dug in my pocket
for my keys and locked myself in. I clasped my
knees to my chest and sat there shaking. I needed
my phone, which I could see in the dirt near the
driveway. After triple checking, I darted out, grabbed
the phone, and leaped back in the Suburban. This
time behind the wheel. I leaned on the horn as I
dialed 911. No one came out of the house.

When I got home several hours later, I took a
shower, examined the bruise right below my belly
button, and climbed into bed. Since the crime had
occurred in Bedford, I hadn't known any of the
police officers and hadn't bothered telling them
about my relationship to CJ, Margaret, or Juanita.
All I'd wanted to do was go home. The owner of the
house had been contacted. She was off with her
kids in Florida and swore she hadn't bought any
Pez. The police had decided someone had hacked
her account.

I curled into a ball under my comforter. Why had
someone tried to grab me? Was it my stalker or
someone who thought I was nosing around in the
cleaning-business burglary circle? I might not ever
know. For the very first time since my split with CJ,
I wondered if maybe I should move back to California. There I'd be far away from my stalker, Seth,
and CJ and could untangle my personal life at my
own pace, without feeling pressured by anyone. I

could start a garage sale business out in Pacific Grove and, with the mild climate, could easily run sales all year long.

Next, I pictured selling everything I owned here except for a few personal items. I loved this little apartment, with its bird's-eye view of the town square. I'd adjusted nicely in the past year to the sounds of the church bells chiming and the sirens from the fire station just up the block. *Ugh.* Moving back to Pacific Grove would mean moving back in with my parents, back into a room with a twin bed and posters of New Kids on the Block still decorating the walls. That area was even more expensive than here. There was no way I could afford a place of my own.

Who could be doing this to me? CJ I could rule out immediately. No matter what had happened or was happening between us, I knew deep, deep down he'd never scare or hurt me. Seth didn't seem a likely candidate, either, no matter who said he was too good to be true. He was a decent man, even if he was hanging out with Mike Titone. James—he made me pause; he'd changed, and Stella thought he had a thing for me. I had always accused Stella of being a bad judge of men, but maybe I was, too.

What if it wasn't a man? Who disliked me so much? Frieda? It just didn't seem to add up, although she had definitely had issues with Margaret and Juanita. Hennessy might have resented me, but we'd made our peace. What about Nichole?

She definitely wanted Seth, but was she so disturbed she'd try to scare me out of town?

Those thoughts drove me out of bed. I ate a bowl of cereal. Then I started contacting people to set up spring garage sales. The stalker wasn't going to drive me away.

It was almost five when my phone rang.

"I have some shoes you might be interested in," Hennessy said.

"You do? Louboutins?" My heart beat a little faster. It was ridiculous getting this excited about a pair of designer shoes.

"Yes."

"You must be ready to close. Do you want me to come tomorrow?"

"No. It's fine. You can come by now."

"I'll be over in a few." I hurried into the bathroom, brushed my hair and teeth, swiped on eye shadow, and added a coat of mascara. Hennessy was always so well groomed, and I didn't want to look like a slob when I saw her. I changed into a V-necked sweater and clean jeans. After making sure my socks didn't have holes, I shoved my feet into boots, grabbed my keys, threw on a coat, and headed out.

Fifteen minutes later I stood in front of Hennessy. The floral scent of her store seemed even worse than last time, but she'd done some cleaning and organizing, so the place looked better. "Thanks for staying open for me."

"No problem. Here they are."

Hennessy handed me black pumps. The heels were a little worn, and the backs had a couple of scuff marks, but both things were easily fixable. I flipped them over, and there were those beautiful red soles. I squealed, which wasn't exactly good if I wanted to try to negotiate a better price. But Hennessy had stayed open for me and had held these for me, so I wasn't going to ask for a better price, anyway.

"Try them on." Hennessy pointed to a leopard-print chair that was in the shape of a high-heeled shoe.

I took off my coat and tossed it on the back of the chair. I sat and slipped off my boots. My cameo necklace swung out before settling back against my chest when I sat up. I felt a bit like Cinderella. She could have her glass slippers and her prince. I was going to buy these with my own hard-earned money. I slipped the first one on. It fit like it was made for me. The left one was a little tighter, which almost always happened when I tried on shoes. I stood and took a tentative step. *Perfect.*

"There's a mirror back there, if you want to get a better look."

I passed a section of chairs, a wall of books, and shelves of purses, chanting, "Don't look. Don't look." Even though my left baby toe was a little squished, it wasn't bad enough not to buy the shoes. Sometimes looking good involved a tiny bit of pain, and they'd probably stretch to fit me, anyway. They were leather, after all. I turned my feet this way and that in front of the mirror. I walked away from it, looking over my shoulder so I could catch that glimpse of red. *Vanity, thy name is woman—at least for this moment.*

I sashayed back to Hennessy in my best impression of a runway model. She laughed.

"How much do you want for them?" I was afraid I couldn't afford them even secondhand.

"Fifty."

"*Fifty?* That's not enough."

Hennessy smiled. "You're not a very good negotiator. How do you make any money?"

"Fifty, it is. How can I ever thank you?"

"I guess you'll owe me one."

My stomach dropped.

"I'm kidding. I'm not Margaret."

I handed over the fifty dollars, and Hennessy wrapped each shoe in pink tissue paper. "I'm sorry I don't have the original box or packaging."

"It's fine."

Hennessy started to hand me the bag she'd put the shoes in but stopped halfway and stared at my chest. "Are you Ryan Jones's girlfriend? I thought you were seeing Seth Anderson?"

Living in a small town could be wicked complicated, as Stella would say. "No. Ryan's a nice guy, but we barely know each other. Why would you think that?"

Hennessy pointed at my chest. "That cameo. Ryan bought it from me and said he was going to give it to his girlfriend."

"It must just look similar. Cameos are pretty common."

"No. I'm sure that's the same one. Is it engraved on the back? The one Ryan bought from me had the words *My love* engraved on it."

It felt like all the blood in my body had drained down to my toes. "It must be some kind of mix-up. CJ sent this to me." He had, hadn't he? Ryan wouldn't know I loved cameos.

Hennessy handed me the shoes. "You must be right. My mistake." She said it in a voice filled with doubt, and the crinkles around her eyes showed her concern. Hennessy started to say something else, but three women walked in just then.

"Hi. Okay if we look around? We know you are about to close," the shortest one said.

An unhappy look flashed over Hennessy's face, and she glanced at me. I knew how she felt. Who wanted to stay open when it was closing time? Then she pasted on a smile. "Of course," she said.

On the way out I stopped in front of a case full of jewelry. Maybe Hennessy had lots of cameos and was just confused. I stared down, scanning the contents until my eyes zeroed in on a ring in a box. It was my wedding ring. The deep blue box had MONTEREY JEWELERS written on it in silver. *Don't react, and get out of here*, I yelled at myself.

"Did something catch your eye?" Hennessy called from the register.

"No. Thanks." I waved without turning toward her. If she saw my face, she'd know something was terribly wrong.

Chapter 38

I hustled out to my car and sat in it for a couple of seconds, stunned. How had my ring ended up there? At best, Hennessy was selling stolen goods, but at worst, she was a thief. Or there was a slim possibility that she was innocent and someone was using her. I thought back to the day Juanita and I were attacked as I started the car and gunned it out of there. It hadn't seemed like my attacker was a woman, but I guessed it could have been. Maybe that was the connection between Hennessy and Juanita. Maybe they had been stealing things and selling them. Things tucked in drawers or boxes that might go unnoticed for a while.

There'd been complaints about Juanita, unlocked doors and windows, cigarette smoke. Maybe someone else had been slipping in and stealing things. But that didn't fit at all with what had happened at my house. Juanita hadn't been my cleaning lady and certainly wouldn't have had time to case the place. Or maybe she would have if we hadn't been attacked.

My stomach twisted as I thought about the cameo and Ryan. It was possible that two identical cameos were engraved with the exact same words. Possible. Not probable. How would he know what I liked? *Duh.* I spent a lot of time at DiNapoli's. We talked about everything, and if I wasn't with the DiNapolis, I was there talking to Stella or Carol. Ryan was always around, seemingly in the background, but clearing tables and chatting with patrons, chatting with me. He could have overheard lots of things I'd said. Heck, we'd chatted enough that I might have told him some of those things. He was a member of my garage sale site, so he'd also been able to watch what I bid on. He could have made up fake profiles and sent threats.

Oh, no, and the pictures . . . He could have sent those, too. I thought about the one time I'd been with Seth and hadn't gotten a photo. Maybe Ryan had been working so he hadn't seen Seth coming or going. The thought was chilling. And far-fetched, I hoped. It was one thing to send me anonymous gifts, but to also send threats and rob me? Maybe even attack me? Why would one person do all those things? Why would Ryan?

I pulled into CJ's driveway, startled to find myself here. His car was in the carport. What was I doing here? What if he had a woman over? I put the car in reverse, but the outside light snapped on. CJ stepped out into the carport, arms folded against the cold or me. I wasn't sure which. I slid out of the car and hurried over to him.

"Have you been sending me gifts?"

CJ looked down at me. "It's cold out here. Come inside." He held the door open for me.

I hoped his answer was yes. *Please let his answer be yes.* I entered, turned left in the small foyer, went up two steps into the kitchen. I took a few more steps and turned, almost slamming into CJ's chest. He stepped back.

I unbuttoned my coat and held the cameo up. "Did you send me this? Please say yes." We were so close, I felt heat coming off him.

CJ bent to study the cameo, then met my eyes. "This is the one you had on the other night. I didn't send it to you. Why do you think I did?"

I shut my eyes and put a hand out to steady myself on the counter. CJ pulled me to him. "What's going on?" he asked.

I leaned back so I could watch CJ's face. "I can't believe that I'm going to say this, but I think Ryan Jones is stalking me. Do you know Ryan? He works at DiNapoli's."

"Busboy?"

"And handyman."

"Nice guy."

"Maybe not."

"Tell me what all this is about," CJ said.

"Last fall, not long after I told you and Seth I needed some time, presents started to arrive. One a month. Each one so personal that I figured only you could have sent them."

"What did you get?"

"A box of See's Candies, a DVD of *The African Queen*, a red Coach purse, and this cameo." I pointed at it. "I thought it was your way of telling me you still cared about me." I felt like a fool and tried to step away from CJ, but he held on to me.

"Why do you think Ryan sent these things?"

I explained to him what had happened at Hennessy's store. "Then I thought about it. Ryan's a member of my garage sale site. He could have seen my online argument with Margaret. He could have . . ." I took a deep breath. "Maybe he killed her because of it. He heard me telling the DiNapolis about the attack that involved Juanita and then . . . then killed her, too, out of some very warped idea of love."

"I'll call it in. Have him picked up for questioning." CJ started to move away.

"Wait. There's more."

CJ leaned against the kitchen counter.

"You know someone took pictures of me and sent them?"

"Yes."

"Well, there were also some threats that came through the virtual garage sale site. It would have been easy enough for Ryan to do both things. Setting up a fake account online is simple. Then he'd invite that fake person to join the site, and then he'd create another fake account when I banned the person sending the threats."

"I read the report, but I didn't know it had happened more than once." CJ shook his head.

"It seems like nonsense. I talk to other admins, and they have the same issue. People are crazy." That last statement made me shudder. Was that why Ryan would send me gifts and threats? Was he crazy? "Someone attacked me in Bedford this afternoon. But I'm fine." The bruise on my stomach throbbed as I said it.

"Sarah. You have to stay out of whatever it is that's going on."

"There's something else. My . . . our wedding ring is in a case at Hennessy's shop."

"You're sure it's yours?"

Yours, not ours. "Yes, and it's in a box that has *Monterey Jewelers* written on it."

I took the cameo necklace off and dropped it in my pocket, then walked to the door.

"Wait," he said. "I stayed away, like you asked. I wanted to honor your request and let you figure things out. But it tore me up. I tried dating other women, but it rarely went beyond a date or two. It went beyond a month with a couple, but I regretted it."

I knew what he was trying to tell me. We'd always joked about people sleeping together after a month.

"I know I can't compete with Seth's money or family connections—"

"CJ, if you think those things are important to me, you don't know me at all."

"You didn't let me finish. I was going to say that I can't imagine those things would be important to you. My heart is yours. You are my one and only love. If it's not you, then I'll die a lonely old man."

Oh, no. CJ had laid it all out there, and I needed to say something, but I wasn't ready to. I felt like a young forest creature who had just gotten a whiff of smoke and knew it needed to run but didn't know which way to go.

CJ gave a curt nod. "I'll stop by Hennessy's."

"It's probably too late. The store will be closed."

"I'll try. And then I'll track down Ryan." CJ pulled me into a hug. My head fit perfectly under his chin. "I wish I had thought to send you those presents."

I'd been home an hour when my phone chimed. I reached for it, hoping this wasn't another photo from my stalker. Could it really be Ryan? I really hoped that I was wrong, that I had somehow added it all up but had come up with the wrong answer. I clicked the button on my phone, determined to focus on the sender's user name. It was another photo rimmed with a black heart. This one stayed up longer than the others had. A full five seconds, during which my heart seemed to stop and I didn't take a breath. I memorized as much of the picture as I could, because this picture wasn't of me—it was of CJ, knocked out and tied up somewhere. The floor was bare wood and could be anywhere. In the corner there was something I couldn't quite make out. It was what I focused on. My only hope for finding CJ.

Chapter 39

Then I recognized it, the shoe chair at Hennessy's. The picture flicked off. Why would she take CJ and not me? I'd just been there, but those three women had come into the store as I was leaving. Maybe their presence had saved me. The look that had crossed Hennessy's face wasn't due to the fact that she had to stay open late. They'd screwed up her plan—whatever it was. I should have warned CJ to be careful. But I'd assumed CJ could take care of himself in any situation. My shortsightedness and confidence in my ability to smoke out the bad guy had put him in harm's way. And maybe Hennessy knew what I didn't, that hurting CJ would hurt me far worse than if she had just come after me.

My phone rang, startling me. I answered.

"Don't call the cops. I'll know. I'll send another message to tell you where to meet me."

"Ryan? Is that you?" But the call disconnected. It had sounded just like Ryan. He had to be in on this with Hennessy. The photos, the burglary ring, the stalking. They must have been in it together all along.

My mind raced as fast as my heart. I had one advantage—I knew that CJ was at Hennessy's, or at least that he had been. I needed help, but if they had CJ, they would have his radio and phone and really would know if I called the police. Maybe if I asked the dispatcher not to sound the alarm over the police radio, it would be okay. No. I couldn't count on the dispatcher handling things safely. CJ's life was in danger. If I called Seth, he'd have to call the police. I couldn't risk CJ being hurt.

I had one option. Mike "the Big Cheese" Titone. He and all his friends were always armed. I could tell by the bulges under their jackets or in their pants. I ran into my bedroom and found the card Mike had given me the day he moved in. I started to dial the phone number on it but wondered if somehow my house had been bugged. Ryan knew so much about me. I took my phone into the bathroom, turned on the water, and called Mike.

"I need your help." As I said it, I wondered if I would owe him. Kind of like when the Sopranos did something for someone. It was how the Mob got its hooks in you, as far as I knew. But I didn't really care, because if that was what it took, I'd do it and would worry about the consequences later.

"What's up?" Mike asked.

I quickly explained the situation.

"We're on our way. Where should we meet you?"

"There's a little sandwich shop on East Road, not too far from where I think he's being held."

"Will they be able to see us?"

"No. It's far enough away."

"Okay. We'll be there as fast as we can."

The North End to Ellington was about twenty miles. Since it was Sunday, the traffic should be light, so hopefully, they'd be here in thirty minutes. I changed into all black. I even found an old, ratty black knit cap. It was probably one of CJs. The only thing I had that even approximated a weapon was CJ's baseball bat. I got it out from under my bed and headed out, hoping I wouldn't run into anyone.

No such luck. Stella came in as I hurried out.

"Are you in some kind of new nighttime winter baseball league?" she asked, gesturing at my clothes.

"Yes. I am. And I'm running late."

"We've known each other almost a year. I can tell when you're lying."

I calculated the risk of telling her what was going on. I knew she'd grown pretty close to Officer Awesome, and I couldn't chance her calling him. "I'm sorry. It's a lie. But I can't tell you anything. Don't worry. I'm meeting Mike Titone."

"Oh, that makes me feel a lot better." She studied me with her big green eyes, little lines of worry popping up around them. "I trust you. Good luck with whatever it is you have going on. Let me know if I can help."

"Thanks, Stella. If you pray, say some prayers."

* * *

It took me ten minutes to get to the sandwich shop, which was closed. I hoped no EPD cars came by and decided to stop and see what I was up to. I ran the engine periodically. The next twenty minutes seemed like a lifetime. Finally, two big black SUVs with tinted windows pulled up. I rolled down my window, and Mike rolled down his.

"Let's park around back. Outta sight," he said.

I followed the two SUVs to the back of the sandwich shop. I parked and hopped out of my car, baseball bat in hand. Ski-masked men poured out of both vehicles. They stayed off to the side while I talked to Mike and his brothers. I gave them the address of Hennessy's Heaven. One brother had it up on Google Earth almost the instant I finished talking.

"Tell us about her shop," Mike said.

I gave a brief description.

"Do you know how many entrances it has?" he asked.

"I'm not sure. There's a back room with an office space, a small restroom, and a dressing room. I think I remember a door back there that led outside."

"Does it have a basement?"

I closed my eyes and pictured the shop. "I just don't know."

"A lot of places to hide?"

I swallowed hard. "Yes."

"Looks like it's just woods behind the place. No buildings on either side," Mike's brother said.

Mike nodded. "That's good. Okay, then. Sarah, you wait here. We'll be back with CJ in no time."

"I'm not waiting here. I'll just follow you, so you might as well let me come with you."

"I could lock you in one of my vehicles." Mike studied my face as I stared up at him, tightening my grip on the baseball bat. "Okay, you can come, but you have to stay back. We all have vests and weapons. You have . . . Is that a baseball bat?"

I looked over at the group. The men were checking their handguns, and someone held a shotgun. "I'm sorry I'm not armed. Gun permits are hard to get in Massachusetts and, frankly, I didn't think I'd ever need one."

"It's fine."

"Are you laughing at me?"

"Never," Mike said. And he did look serious.

From behind the building, we set out on foot. The men seemed to move as one and made little noise. I stumbled and tripped in the dark. Mike took my arm to keep me on course. We crossed the back of two buildings and stopped behind the third, which was directly across from Hennessy's. Most of the men put on what looked like night-vision goggles. I didn't want to think about why they had all this gear.

The group split into two. Our group continued along the back of the building; the other ran down its side. One guy in the other group moved like Seth and was almost the same size. I stared as he disappeared around the corner. But Mike's group was moving away from me fast. I hurried to catch up. As we approached the road, Mike stopped our group behind a row of evergreens.

"There's a car parked over on the side of the lot."

"It's Hennessy's," I said. I didn't see CJ's car in her lot.

We crept across the street to the edge of the dimly lit parking lot. Now I was grateful that Hennessy's shop was off the beaten path. If it were on a busy street, someone might spot us and call the police. Mike took his cell phone out of his pocket, clicked on an app, and held the phone up toward Hennessy's building.

I stepped closer and saw the glow of some kind of thermal imaging. "Why do you have that?" I asked.

"Hunting."

I wasn't about to ask what kind of hunting.

"It looks like there's only two people inside," Mike said. He pointed to the screen on his phone. One person stood over near where I thought the cash register sat. I could see another heat signature a few feet away. It looked to be on the floor and wasn't moving.

I pointed to it. "That must be CJ." I hoped he was okay. He was so still.

Mike turned to me. "Stay back." He turned to his guys. "We go in hard and fast."

Two men positioned themselves on either side of the front door, while another picked the lock. I was sure something similar was going on at the back of the store. Mike held up his hand and started a silent count. When he held up his third finger, everyone moved. The guy who picked the lock swung open the door, and the men ran in. I heard shouts of "Clear" and hustled toward the store.

Hennessy came tearing out the front door, looking back, as if hellhounds were chasing her. And since it was Mike's guys, maybe they were.

I swung the bat, catching her in the ribs. I heard a crack that sounded like bones breaking. Hennessy screamed and slumped to the ground. Her head bounced on the asphalt as she landed.

Chapter 40

Mike walked out of the store as his men crossed the street and melted into the dark night.

I ran over to him. "Is CJ okay?"

"Seems to be. Strong pulse, but still out."

I hurried into the store and threw myself down by CJ's side. Someone had stuffed a coat under his head and thrown a blanket over him. I laid a hand on his cheek. His skin was clammy, and his breathing seemed shallow. I leaned in and kissed his forehead and smoothed his hair. "Be all right, CJ." My voice choked. I turned to Mike. "Was anyone else here? A man?" I wondered where Ryan was, what his role in all of this was.

"No one."

"CJ's car is gone. Maybe Ryan moved it."

Mike looked around, like he was making sure we were alone.

"How did she get away?" I asked him, pointing outside toward Hennessy.

"I thought you should join in the fun."

"But what if I'd missed her?"

"We had her. This will help your story."

"What story?"

"The one you're going to tell the cops. Because we were never here."

"I'm going to have to lie? To the cops?"

Mike nodded.

"But Hennessy knows I wasn't alone."

"From the looks of it, you can just tell them she's concussed and rambling."

I drew in a deep breath. "Okay. I'd better call the cops before she comes around."

Mike gave me a small nod as he left.

After I called 911, I flipped on the store lights and looked over CJ again. There was bruising on his cheek and around his left eye. A little blood ran out of his nose. My hands clenched into fists, and the urge to hit someone gripped me. As much as I wanted to stay by CJ's side, I couldn't leave Hennessy out there alone. I couldn't risk her coming to and getting away.

As I exited the store, I heard a moan. I lifted the bat and realized I wouldn't mind whacking Hennessy again. I crept closer to her, bat raised. Another low moan sounded, but it wasn't coming from Hennessy. I held myself still, barely breathing, wondering where the moaning was coming from. My hands grew slick at the thought that I wasn't here alone. I heard another moan, from over by Hennessy's car.

A fourth moan was followed by some thumping. Someone was in Hennessy's trunk.

I dashed over to Hennessy and found her car keys in her coat pocket. I got close to the trunk, clicked it to unlock, and stepped back, bat ready as the trunk popped open. Ryan, curled in a fetal position and blindfolded, moaned again.

He held up a hand, shielding his face. "Please don't hurt me, Hennessy. I'll do whatever it is you want."

"It's okay, Ryan. It's Sarah. The police are on their way." I helped him sit up and took off his blindfold. He had a massive bruise on the side of his head.

"Where is she?" Ryan's voice trembled when he asked the question.

"She's over there. I, uh, knocked her out."

"She's a lunatic. She was fixated on destroying you." His voice caught. "She tried to make it look like I was stalking you."

"I thought it was you. I'm so glad it's not."

"She made me call you tonight. She had a gun pointed at CJ, so I had to call. I'm so sorry."

"It's okay. It's not your fault." I glanced back over to make sure Hennessy wasn't moving.

"She forced me into the trunk at gunpoint. The last thing I remember is her whacking me on the side of the head with her gun. How did you stop her?"

Time to try out my story. It was better to have a run-through with Ryan before the police showed up.

"Grace of God and a bit of luck. I cupped my hands and lowered my voice. I yelled, 'Police. We've got the place surrounded.' She burst out of the store like demons were chasing her."

"Thankfully, it worked." Ryan ran a shaky hand over his head. "Otherwise, we'd all be dead."

Convincing Ryan, who was shaken up, was one thing, but convincing a steely-eyed police officer would be a whole different story. We both turned as sirens screamed toward us and two police cars screeched into the lot.

Pellner and Officer Awesome leaped out of their cars.

"Hennessy's over there." I pointed across the parking lot. "CJ's inside."

"Check on Hennessy," Pellner said to Awesome as he trotted toward the store.

I followed Pellner in, and we both ran over to CJ, who was still out on the floor.

"What happened here?"

I checked CJ's pulse and told Pellner the same story I'd told Ryan. I watched CJ instead of looking at Pellner. "When she came out of the store and realized it was just me there, she ran at me. I swung the bat and whacked her in the ribs. She fell and smacked her head on the ground. It knocked her out."

I glanced up at Pellner. His dimple was deep, and his face serious, but he nodded. He had no reason to believe I'd lie to him, which made me feel even worse.

"Do you think CJ will be okay?" I asked him.

"He'd better be."

The EMTs arrived, and I hopped in the ambulance with CJ, grateful to get away from Pellner and his dimple. I knew more questions would come, especially once Hennessy woke up and started talking. I rehearsed my story over and over on the way to the hospital and as I sat in the emergency room waiting area. The EMTs wheeled Hennessy and Ryan by shortly after we arrived. Ryan gave me a thumbs-up.

Once they moved CJ to a room, I sat by him, holding his hand, as the doctor told me they suspected he'd been drugged. She thought CJ would come around by morning. She was concerned enough about the bruising that she had ordered scans and would let me know when the results were back. His nose was broken.

After the doctor left, I held CJ's hand to my cheek. His long lashes looked dark against his pale skin. He was so very still. "I won't let you die a lonely old man, CJ."

Pellner came in just then, and by the embarrassed look on his face, I knew he'd overheard me. "Hennessy's drugged and babbling. She said a bunch of men burst into the store, and she ran out. She doesn't remember seeing you," he said.

I jerked my head up. "A bunch of men? She must have hit her head harder than I realized."

"Awesome said there's a bunch of footprints in the slush and mud around the back of the store."

"Who knows how long they could have been there? Any footprints in the store?" I hoped not, because explaining that away would be difficult.

"No."

"She must be making it up, then. Trying to look innocent."

"We found a burner cell phone in her coat pocket. It has the pictures you've been getting and the threatening messages on it."

I held CJ's hand a little tighter. "What else did she say?"

"She got so riled up, she almost fainted from the pain of the broken ribs. They sedated her, so we'll have to talk to her later."

"Thanks for letting me know." And by letting me know, I meant telling me what Hennessy had said so I could make sure my story was more convincing. "Have you had a chance to talk to Ryan?"

"He corroborated your story. Said he would have heard if there was a bunch of men running around."

Oh, thank God. Mike and his men had moved so quietly.

"Do you want to go home, and I'll sit with CJ?"

I looked over at CJ's pale face. "No. I'll stay."

"I'm glad you're okay," Pellner said.

I shivered. Pellner looked around and found a blanket for me. I wrapped it around myself. "Could someone bring my car over? It's behind the sandwich shop. Near Hennessy's."

"Why there?"

"I didn't want Hennessy to hear me coming." That, at least, was true. I dug my keys out of my pocket and handed them to Pellner.

"You should have called us when you knew she had CJ."

"I figured she had his radio and phone. I was afraid she'd find out."

Pellner studied me. "I'll have someone leave your keys at the nurses' station."

A movement in the room woke me. I still held CJ's hand. My cheek was pressed into the waffled blanket. I opened my eyes. Seth stood at the end of CJ's bed. I had no idea what time it was.

"How is he?" Seth asked, his voice low and tired. He wore his beautiful wool coat, a tie loosened around his neck, like he'd been working for hours.

I looked over at CJ. His face had a little more color, but he still slept. "He'll be okay." I tried to inject some confidence into my voice.

"And you?"

"I'll be okay, too." My voice choked up as I said it. Seth took a step toward me, but I waved him off.

He studied me and looked back at CJ. Seth turned to go, and I noticed his pants and boots. My eyes widened. The pants were black cargo pants, not the pants that went with his suit. The cuffs were muddied, as were the steel-toed boots he wore, instead of his usual Italian leather wing tips. He *had* been with Mike's men.

"Seth?"

He turned and saw me staring at his pants. He shook his head and pointed at CJ. Then he brought his finger to his lips. I stared at him but nodded.

Seth mouthed, "Thank you," and left.

Chapter 41

By 10:00 a.m. CJ had been awake a couple of hours. He alternated between upset and angry. By the time he'd gotten to Hennessy's store, my wedding ring wasn't in the case. Hennessy had offered him a drink, and he'd accepted to give him a reason to mill about the store. That had allowed Hennessy to drug him, which made CJ angry. Then he was upset because the drink was the last thing he remembered until he woke this morning. He was furious I'd put myself in danger to save him. If only he knew the real story . . . And he was angry because he was still connected to the IV and he wanted to go interrogate Hennessy.

"You look exhausted," CJ said when he finally calmed down. "Why don't you go home and get some rest?"

"Who will take care of you?" The doctor had come in earlier and had told us that the scans didn't show any lasting damage.

"The nurses, the doctors, Pellner." Pellner and

Awesome had looked in a number of times. It had looked like they wanted to talk privately with CJ but didn't have the nerve to kick me out.

Frankly, getting away from the police and all the questions sounded good to me. I had stuck to my story and was almost to the point of believing it myself. I kissed CJ's cheek, retrieved my car keys from the nurses' station, and rode the elevator down to the lobby. Ryan sat there.

"Ryan, how are you doing?"

"A bit of a headache. But I'll be fine." He winced. "Could I borrow your cell phone to call a cab?"

"I'm leaving. I can give you a ride home. Where do you live?"

"In the apartments by the Ellington-Billerica line."

"It's barely out of my way."

He stood but wavered slightly.

"Are you sure you should be leaving?"

"I'll feel a lot better once I get home."

I pulled my Suburban around so he didn't have far to walk. "Do you need anything from the grocery store?"

"Could we just stop and get a couple of things? I just need some milk and stuff to make fluffernutters."

I grinned at him. "My favorite sandwich."

"Mine too. Although I'm a pretty good cook when I have the time."

"I'm a terrible cook."

"I could teach you some easy dishes."

"If I thought it would help, I'd give it a try. But

trust me, I'm hopeless. If you don't mind me asking, what happened with you and Hennessy last night?"

Ryan held his head for a minute. "She called me and said she needed me to look at her furnace. All that was wrong with the furnace was the pilot light was out. I relit it. Like I told you, she pulled the gun on me. Made me make the call. Next thing I remember was waking up in the trunk of the car. Scared to death. If you hadn't been there . . ."

We both sat for a minute, lost in our own thoughts.

Ryan broke the silence. "Something was going on with that cleaning lady, too."

"Frieda Chida?"

"No. The one that was murdered."

"Juanita?"

"Yes. Juanita stopped by the shop a lot. Whenever Juanita showed up, Hennessy would send me on an errand, or they'd go in the office, close the door, and talk. And she brought stuff to her."

"What kind of stuff?" I asked.

"Stuff Hennessy would sell . . . jewelry, cameras, computers."

"Do you think they were stealing things and selling them? I saw my wedding ring for sale at Hennessy's last night. That's why CJ went over there." Did Hennessy kill Juanita for some reason? But why would she kill Margaret? Unless she thought she'd get all of Margaret's stuff for her store.

"Your wedding ring was there?" Ryan's voice rose to almost a shout, and his face was so red, I worried.

"Ryan, this can't be good for you. I'm sorry I brought it up."

"She's not who I thought she was."

"I'm so sorry." I, of all people, understood being betrayed. "You told the police all of this?"

"You bet I did. Even though I didn't want to believe it."

We stopped at a small market. I steadied Ryan when he got out of the car. "Are you sure you don't want me to just run in and get the stuff?"

"I think I'll feel better once I've moved around. I still can't believe Hennessy whacked me with her gun." We both shuddered a bit at the thought of Hennessy.

We walked around the market companionably. "Want some chips?" I asked. "Those always make me feel better."

"Sure. Which are your favorites?"

I pointed at a bag. "Those Cape Cod ones."

Ryan tossed them in the cart. "Hmm, maybe I need some cookies, too. Chocolate chip."

"A man with great taste," I said.

He paid. We left the market and I drove the short distance to his apartment building.

Ryan pointed to his parking spot right in front of his door. He got out and reached for the bags but almost fell back into my Suburban.

"Let me get those, Ryan. I really wonder if I should take you back to the hospital."

"No. Sorry. I'll be fine."

I grabbed the bags and followed him into his apartment. "I'll just unpack this stuff, if you point me to the kitchen. I can make you a quick sandwich. Go lie down."

"Thanks. I'll take you up on that."

I went into the galley kitchen and set all the stuff on the counter. I turned to put the milk in the fridge and noticed it was covered with photographs. Of me.

Chapter 42

I dropped the carton of milk, and its contents flowed out onto the floor. Some of the photos were from my missing photo album, and some must have been printed from my computer, the one that had been stolen. My mind said, *Run*, but my legs weren't on board with that thought. They felt like concrete pilings reaching deep into the earth and anchoring me to stare in horror at the pictures.

"I hope you're going to clean that up," Ryan said. I turned. He stood in the doorway to the kitchen, blocking my exit. "That's what girlfriends do."

"I'm not your girlfriend." My voice came out low and mean. And scared. So very scared.

"Yes you are. I sent you gifts. Things I knew you loved." He moved into the kitchen, hands behind his back, and stood beside me. I tried not to shrink away. Not to show any fear. But my legs, which had felt like concrete, now felt like dust. "You wore the necklace I sent you everywhere. My love."

Ryan had no idea what love was. No idea.

"It wasn't Hennessy? None of it?" And really that made more sense. Ryan would have been the one to overhear me talking to friends or the DiNapolis about things I loved. The thought made me ill.

"I'm the one who knows you, Sarah. Not Hennessy or Seth or CJ." He brought his hands out from behind his back. In one hand was my aqua sweater, but in the other was a hunting knife just like the one that had been stuck in my tire. "See? I even have your favorite sweater, in case you get cold." He put it to his cheek and breathed in. "It smells like you."

I was cold. I was freezing, but no sweater could warm me up. I gestured toward the milk on the floor. "I'll clean this up, Ryan." It would give me precious minutes to figure a way out of here. "You're right that's what I should do for you. And then I'll make you a sandwich so you can rest."

"I'm not tired, Sarah. Not at all." Ryan smiled at me as he put the knife and the sweater on the counter beside him. He moved back and leaned against the counter. He pulled a stun gun out of his pocket and put it next to the knife.

"Why didn't you just ask me out?"

He looked startled at the question. "Because girls want to be pursued. To feel cherished."

I hid my revulsion by looking around the kitchen. It had one doorway and a small window over the sink. If it were an open kitchen, I might have been able to vault over the counter and into another room. *Fat chance.* I wasn't exactly athletic, but at least it would have given me some hope.

"Where are your paper towels?" I asked. Ryan pointed to the counter behind me. I ripped some towels off the roll and scanned the counter for weapons. No knives out on the counter or a rolling pin or anything besides the damn paper towels. I paused in front of the window, hoping someone would notice the fear on my face. The Magda Toilet Cream jar Ryan bought from me at the February Blues Sale sat on the sill. He'd bought it for me.

Ryan yanked me by the hair away from the window. I screamed as loud and as long as I could. He slapped me and pulled down the shade. "What are you doing?"

"I just wanted to look at the view." Which neither of us believed, because the window looked over the parking lot. I held my hand to my cheek. "You don't have to hurt me."

Ryan pointed to the bruise on his temple. "You hurt me yesterday."

That meant Ryan had tried to kidnap me yesterday in Bedford, and I was in worse trouble than I could imagine. He went back over by his stun gun. His casual pose against the counter belied the tension filling the kitchen. I squatted by the milk, making sure to face him, and started to sop it up.

Footsteps pounded from either end of the apartment. Someone else was here. Ryan whipped his head to the left, grabbing the stun gun. I launched myself at his knee and rammed it with my head. He howled in pain as I heard a sickening pop. He grabbed at my hair, but I scrambled out of the way and into the hall. A man in a black ski mask grabbed me and hustled me to the front door. Another ski-masked man slipped into the kitchen. Instead of letting me leave the apartment, the man who had grabbed me trapped me in the corner.

Mike pulled off the ski mask, his eyes blue ice. "The police will be here in minutes. We weren't here."

Another howl came from the kitchen.

"Ryan's being told to go with whatever story you choose to tell the police," Mike said.

"How did you know?" I asked him.

"Hennessy's story didn't add up. We decided to keep an eye out."

I wondered if Seth had anything to do with that. If that was who was in the kitchen. How else would Mike know what Hennessy's story was? "Thank you."

Mike gave a short nod. "Didn't know I was going to end up in the guardian angel business." He waited a few more seconds, blocking my view of the kitchen and hall. Then he moved in even closer and lowered his voice. "You can't ever tell anyone I was here. Last night or now. That's the price of doing business with me. That's what you owe me." Then he chucked me under the chin and went out the back.

I braced myself and peeked in the kitchen. Who-ever had been with him was gone. Ryan sat on the floor. Sweat poured off his face, and his knee was at an odd angle. My stomach twisted.

"All I ever did was love you," he said. "I didn't want anyone to hurt you."

Someone pounded on the front door. "Open up. Police."

I hurried to the door and flung it open. Two officers stood there. I pointed them to the kitchen. "Call an ambulance."

Pellner ran up the walk. "Are you okay?"

I started shaking.

Pellner escorted me to his patrol car and we both climbed in. "What happened after you left the hospital?"

I filled him in briefly.

"You rammed his knee with your head?"

"Yes. I think I dislocated it. Ryan's knee." Or I had just hurt him, and the guy in the kitchen had taken care of the rest.

"I always knew you were hardheaded. Are you okay?"

"My neck's sore. My head aches."

Pellner pulled out of the space and flipped on the lights and sirens. "I'm taking you to the hospital."

"I'll be fine. Just take me home."

"Not this time. Chuck would kill me. When we got the call, Awesome had to physically restrain him to keep Chuck from ripping out his IV and coming over here."

CJ. My eyes filled with tears. At least this way I'd see him faster. Any other time I might have thought it was fun riding in a police car, flying down the streets, watching people pull over or not, as the case may be. While I didn't want to ruin Pellner's concentration, I had questions.

"So is Hennessy innocent?"

"Up to her neck in a stolen goods ring. But according to her, Ryan killed Margaret and Juanita out of some warped love for you. He seemed to go after people he thought had hurt you. She said he had a list."

"Why didn't she report it? Why did she help him?"

"Ryan found out about the burglary ring while he was working over at her store. He was blackmailing her. And she just kept getting in deeper and deeper, trying to save her business and reputation." He slowed at an intersection, made sure it was clear, and floored it again. "She swears she didn't know about the murders or realize what he would do to you or CJ until last night."

"What about Frieda? Was she part of the burglary ring?"

"Not as far as we can tell. She's an angry old woman but not a criminal."

I thought about the gifts, the creepy photos, and all the threats. "I asked Ryan why he didn't just ask me out. He said women wanted to be pursued." I shook my head. "I don't get it. He thought he loved me, but then he'd get very angry, especially if I was out with Seth. Angry enough to send threats and stab my tire. But he never acted like that in front of me. Not once. I thought we were buddies." At least it hadn't been James. I knew something was going on with him, but thankfully, not this.

Pellner glanced over at me. "Don't try to figure it out. His brain works differently than ours. And don't blame yourself."

But how could I not?

I'd been propped up on a hospital bed for a few minutes, sipping a Sprite and waiting for my turn to be scanned and probed. I was low on the totem pole, considering I had no visible injuries or outward signs of distress. I heard a commotion in the hall, loud voices, protests. CJ burst in, toting an IV and followed by a nurse, who was berating him, Awesome, and Pellner.

CJ looked at Pellner, Awesome, and the nurse. "Clear out." He used his commander's voice, the one he'd occasionally used on his troops. It brooked no nonsense. The nurse, after one last protest, left with Pellner and Awesome. CJ eased into the chair by my bed and took my hand. He looked tired but better than he had earlier this morning. A chill settled on me. It was probably stress, but it felt like the same kind of chill I'd felt that day in Jerusha's room at the Wayside Inn. She had had a twisted love story, with her waiting, waiting, waiting for love.

CJ turned to me. "Pellner told me what you said."

I'd told Pellner a lot of things in the past twenty-four hours, a lot of it lies, and I wasn't sure what specific thing CJ was talking about, so I kept quiet.

"He heard you tell me that you wouldn't let me die a lonely old man."

Ah, that. I nodded, wincing only a little when I did.

"Did you mean it?"

Love. It was so complicated. Ryan's version was a warped, sick one. I thought about Jerusha again. How she'd waited for her lover to return, when the right guy might have been there for her the whole time and she just hadn't realized it, so she'd died alone. Maybe that was what she'd been trying to tell me that day in her room. I thought about Seth. He was fun and charming. I liked him. A lot. But I loved CJ. Warmth filled my heart—the chill disappeared.

Then I thought about Mike. Starting a new relationship with CJ meant starting out by lying to CJ. I studied him, his familiar pale blue eyes, the sturdy jaw. I saw past all that to a man who didn't deserve to die alone.

"I did mean it, CJ. Every word."

Garage Sale Tips

Tips for Neighborhood Garage Sales

- Schedule your garage sale near paydays.

- Most people have garage sales on Saturday mornings, but think about other times when there are events in your neighborhood. For example, if there are lots of open houses on a Sunday afternoon, that might be the perfect time to have a yard sale.

- Be prepared for early birds by having your items arranged and looking good before they show up.

- Watch the weather forecast and try to avoid having a garage sale on a rainy or scorching hot day.

- Be friendly, get out there, and talk to the people who stop by, but have at least two helpers to keep an eye on things.

Tips for Online Garage Sale Sites

- Take great pictures, and remember that lots of items look better when shot from an angle.

- Make sure your photos are in focus and use a solid background so the items stands out. Take one picture from farther away and a few close-ups of each item.

- Be honest about the condition of an item. For instance, if something is stained, say so. Also, let people know if the items come from a smoke- or pet-free home.

- Follow the rules of the group you belong to.

- Write a good, brief description of each item. Include the serial number if the item has one, the size if it's an article of clothing, and the age if it's an antique.

- Arrange a safe place to pick items up! Police stations in some towns are now allowing people to use their lobbies as a safe exchange place.

- If you have to go to a stranger's house to pick an item up, don't go alone. And don't be home alone if someone is coming to your house for a pickup.

Grab These Cozy Mysteries from
Kensington Books

Hilarious Mysteries from
Laura Levine

__Death by Pantyhose	978-0-7860-0786-9	$6.99US/$8.49CAN
__Death of a Trophy Wife	978-0-7582-3846-7	$7.99US/$9.99CAN
__Killer Blonde	978-0-7582-3547-3	$6.99US/$8.49CAN
__Killer Cruise	978-0-7582-2046-2	$6.99US/$8.99CAN
__Killing Bridezilla	978-0-7582-2044-8	$6.99US/$8.49CAN
__Last Writes	978-0-7582-7732-9	$7.99US/$8.99CAN
__Pampered to Death	978-0-7582-3848-1	$7.99US/$8.99CAN
__The PMS Murder	978-0-7582-0784-5	$6.99US/$9.99CAN
__Shoes to Die For	978-0-7582-0782-1	$6.99US/$9.99CAN
__This Pen for Hire	978-0-7582-0159-1	$5.99US/$7.99CAN

Available Wherever Books Are Sold!

All available as e-books, too!

Visit our website at **www.kensingtonbooks.com**